SOME ACHIEVE
"GREATNESS,

Frank Swinnerton

G.K.HALL &CO.

 Boston, Massachusetts

1977

MAR 2 8 1977

823
S978s
c.1

Library of Congress Cataloging in Publication Data

Swinnerton, Frank Arthur, 1884-
  Some achieve greatness.

  1. Title.
[PZ3.S9777So6] [PR6037.W85] 823'.9'12
ISBN 0-8161-6452-5   76-51431

Published in Large Print by arrangement with
Doubleday & Company, Inc.

Set in Compugraphic 18 pt English Times

Contents

PART ONE

NEWCOMERS

1
An Unwelcome Name

As Miss Florence Marvell (51, as a modern newspaper would say) walked to market from her cottage in the Berkshire village of Slocumbe, she recognised a figure in the distance. It was that of Mrs Bertha Pledge (49), who lived at the other end of Slocumbe. The day, in late February, was damp and chill; but overnight rain had passed.

'Oh, bother!' lamented Florence, who often, when alone, spoke her thoughts aloud. 'I don't want a long chat. I'm not in the mood.'

This word was one to which her ears were accustomed; and sometimes her 'moods' were very strong indeed. They could have been called 'determinations,' or even 'obsessions'; for under Florence's mild exterior lay an obstinacy, the obstinacy of an artist, which nobody in Slocumbe knew anything about. Today her 'mood' was a wish to be entirely by herself; and Bertha was the enemy of solitude. Bertha, in fact, although in private life a heroine, brimming with kindness to those who appealed to her warm heart, was extraordinarily insensitive to their dispositions and inclinations.

For this reason, instead of impulsively thinking, as the more subtle Florence would have done, 'there's my friend; but she's walking quickly on the other side of the road; and won't want to stop,' she darted recklessly across the traffic-congested High Street, deaf to the screeching of motor-horns, and arrived before her friend, breathless, with the *élan* of a ball-carrying and tail-wagging little dog.

'My . . . dear . . . Florence! Such a . . . . treat! Seeing you! Looking so young and . . . spry! That . . . marvellous erect . . . walk! Terribly enviable . . . to somebody . . . fat and . . . crippled!'

The breathlessness gradually diminished; but the crimson cheeks were alarming, and the manner was Bertha at her worst. Always inclined to shout, so that everybody in Slocumbe knew her affairs and repeated them as 'Mrs Pledge's latest,' she looked this morning, in a hideous purple suit, exactly like a rolled mattress loosely tied around the middle with string, and would have been scorned as a vulgarian by the dainty dames of fashionable London.

The contrast between the two friends, so nearly of an age, was marked. Florence, small, brown-faced, slender, was both composed and compact. She lived alone, apart from certain pets whom she used as models, earning an old maid's income by writing and illustrating books and magazine stories for children, and refusing to think of the inevitable day when editorial taste would change or delicate fingers lose their skill. 'Never meet trouble half-way' was Florence's resolve; 'but, if

5

it comes, don't squeal.' Intelligence and repressed humour gave brilliance to dark grey eyes and firmness to demure lips; but owing to innate modesty she thought herself plain and insignificant, rather like a charity girl of the Victorian age.

Bertha, on the contrary, though an inch taller, lost this physical advantage by a hunching of rounded shoulders and enjoyment of starchy foods. 'I've got a sweet tooth. Adore pastry. And eat it. That's all!' As a person, she was full of fears and regrets, inquisitivenesses, and changes of mind. Chattering from morning to night, addressing disconnected observations to her husband, her dog Pickle, her daily help Mrs Leather, or anybody she met in the street or in a shop, she gave the false impression of being a flibbertigibbet.

She had lived in Slocumbe for twenty years — four times as long as Florence, who was comparatively a newcomer, — liked to think of herself as a sort of Kim, a 'friend of all the world,' and was overwhelmingly genial, except to tramps and the children who stole her apples. To the former she gave a lecture and some food which they immediately threw away; to the latter a lecture and the apples they had stolen. She took no credit for these benefactions, exclaiming:

'I hate the lot of them! Lazy, dirty thieves!'

Ralph Pledge, her husband, prematurely decrepit, needed loving assistance hour by hour. She therefore had no holidays; but watched television, listened to discussion programmes on the radio, and welcomed visits from the Vicar of Slocumbe. There were compensations. As Ralph's pension from sympathetic employers was a good one, and she herself had small investments inherited from her father, a thrifty insurance agent, Bertha was richer than Florence. She also enjoyed another financial advantage; for Florence, with no investments, had the liability of a younger sister, Annabel, a talented actress doomed to small parts and often unemployed.

These three women, Bertha, Florence, and Annabel, being fundamentally innocent, made no complaints of life. All were unaware of their singularity in a world where greed, cunning, and violence grew ever more callous.

Bertha's skittish gaiety made Florence feel as a policeman's horse must do when demonstrators throw fireworks between its legs.

'Thank you Bertha,' she answered. 'If you'd really been fat and crippled you'd have been crushed to death by all the cars you've just defied. As it happens, I feel rather crabbed this morning. This damp chill affects my spirits.'

'Oh, the weather doesn't trouble me at all, unless it's pouring, or snowing. Then I stay indoors; and Ralph has something out of a tin.' Bertha fluttered her eyelashes roguishly, showing her teeth in a happy smile. 'He's very good. Doesn't mind a bit, though I tell him it's no compliment to my cooking. But come snow, come tempest, nothing could quench me today. I'm too full of sensational news. News I know you'll be thrilled to hear. There! Aren't you all agog?'

'I'll try to be. Is it an enormous legacy?'

'How sordid!' The protest was almost a shriek, accompanied by a clucking of laughter at such astonished wit. 'No, this is really wonderful. Something we've all been longing for — the whole of Slocumbe; you, me, everybody. Can you guess?'

'I've no idea.'

'The Manor's been bought! Isn't that magnificent?'

'It is indeed!' Florence did not shout; it was beyond her power to do so. Nevertheless she was delighted. 'Splendid! Do you know anything about the new owner — or owners?'

'Ah, that's something else!' Bertha was teasingly jubilant. 'You'll rejoice! He's a famous man. A giant! Somebody we've seen on TV. At least, I have; but you may not. Very handsome. Very wise. A noble character. Now guess!'

'Good gracious! Impossible!'

'Think of all the public men you most admire!'

' "Admire"?' It was scoffing. 'That narrows the choice very much!'

'Don't pretend to be cynical, Florence.

9

It's out of character. He's a Member of Parliament and a great Advocate. A man who makes Judges tremble and do his bidding!'

Florence's intuitions were quick. This was Fate! She instinctively looked away.

'I don't believe Judges ever tremble. It's their job to make other people do that.'

'You're thinking of the black cap. Horrible! But Judges only make people tremble if they've done something wicked.'

'Something illegal, perhaps; which is quite different.'

'Nonsense! What's lawful is always good. I don't mean little white lies. I tell them all the time, to keep Ralph from getting depressed. He does, you know. I have to jolly him back into good spirits with my prattle. No, I assure you our new Squire does quell Judges. He's like Julius Caesar; a Colossus!'

Heavy-hearted, with intuition confirmed, Florence made no answer.

Luckily, she noticed two rosy-faced little girls who had stopped to hear what was being said in Bertha's loud voice. The children were carrying home a great sack of potatoes in a box on wheels, drawing it by means of shafts made of strips of wood; and they were glad to rest awhile within earshot, hoping to learn something of public interest. Florence, observing their open mouths and pricked ears, warned Bertha with a slight inclination of the head.

'Little pitchers — I can't remember their names — are attending.'

Bertha, immediately alert, dropped her voice to a whisper.

'Awful little Todd brats! A disgrace to the village!' And as the children, discouraged by her evident aversion, trundled their barrow away, she added in a more normal tone: 'What *he'll* do about them, I can't think. Probably have them "taken into care," as the saying is. Of course, he may never notice them. Just drive past in his Rolls — it's sure to be a Rolls — too grand to distinguish such specks of grime.'

'Perhaps he'll be too grand to distinguish us,' suggested Florence, hopefully; 'though we're less grimy.'

'Don't be ridiculous! We're respectable people — you, especially. Distinguished. Besides, he's very kind, they say, in private life. It's only in Court, and in Parliament, that he thunders.'

'Thunders! How awful, Bertha! We don't want a storming tyrant in the village!'

'He won't be that at all. He's a gentleman. Oh, yes, he's going to farm — gaiters, corduroys, tweed cap. And he'll hunt: "Yoicks! Tally-ho!" Hunt and shoot and walk about the village. Just think; in a few weeks we shall be running into him as we've run into each other now. "Hello, Squire; been out rabbiting this morning?" It's a glorious prospect. Don't you feel it?'

'Bloodcurdling,' said Florence.

'And of course, being the Squire, he'll take a paternal interest in us all.'

'He sounds a disastrous character, Bertha. A person to loathe. How have you learnt all these grisly details?'

'Aha! You *are* curious, in spite of your years. It's a way you've got, Florence. I don't mind it, because I know you; but other people think you're satirical. I always tell them you're the kindest person I know.'

'That's very generous. Thank you.'

'It shows in your sweet pictures — just as it does in Beatrix Potter's. By being so quiet you don't do yourself justice. In your place I should wear a long cloak and an enormous feathered hat, and stalk about the village like a witch on holiday. Everybody would stare —'

'And think you abominably eccentric.'

'I should like that. But I haven't got the figure. Nor the face. You have both, in miniature. And a mystical expression, like a saint in some old painting — Raphael, or Correggio.'

'Dreadful!' Florence wrinkled her nose, looking quite unlike a saint.

'Not at all dreadful. True. But I won't tease you any longer. Wait for it! The great man — I wonder you haven't guessed — is . . . none . . . other . . . than Sir Roderick Patterson!'

It was the name Florence had dreaded to hear.

2
Sir Roderick's Wife

Bertha, encouraged by what she took to be the silence of delighted amazement, began to embroider her story. The details had been gathered overnight from her friend Charles Dacre, the estate agent, through whom the purchase had been arranged.

'Apparently Lady Patterson has taken a dislike to the plan where they've been living. Somewhere in Dorset. Immense building operations going on there. What they call "overspill." She's a woman of strong character, Charles says. I should think she could make herself disagreeable to anybody she disapproves of; and the overspills, being quite common, resented that. Of course, she's nicely connected; a cousin or something of the Mattocks, with lots of money and lineage. Charles says she's been the driving force behind Sir Roderick's success. Not his success at the Bar, which is due to his own brains; but his social success.'

'Don't the two things go together?'

'Oh, I think his beginnings were quite humble.'

'He certainly wasn't a barefoot boy. Are they happy together?'

'They must be, with all that fame and money. Just think of the grandeur! It seems ideal. Charles says she sailed about the home, like a valuer, talking about what she was going to do about curtains and things; but it was Sir Roderick who decided to buy. He made up his mind in a flash; nodded, said "all right," and shook hands. A man after Charles's own heart.'

'No doubt,' drily agreed Florence. 'Bang! Bang! Sold! Besides, like Sir Roderick, Charles is a tremendous Tory.'

'Oh, he is. He's sure Sir Roderick will

rally all the Tories in the district. Poor old General Simmons has been rather letting the side down, he thinks, dozing at Committee meetings, and putting everything off. Well, Simmons is really a bit of a fossil, whereas Sir Roderick's not quite sixty.'

'Exactly sixty-one,' corrected Florence.

'Is he? I always forget people's ages. It comes of trying to lessen my own. But Sir Roderick doesn't look his age. He's such a fine, handsome, commanding man. Over six feet; not at all fat; with a rich voice that rings in the ears.'

'You've met him, have you?'

'No such luck. This is what Charles says. Besides, I've seen him on TV. Photographs, too; but in them he's always wearing his barrister's wig — very official. No, not always; there was a wigless one in the *Telegraph* one day last week. I hunted it up this morning, and cut it out. He's got that darling touch of white round the temples that distinguished men often have. I wonder if they use dye? Did you see the picture?'

'I did. I didn't cut it out. I thought he

looked very tired.'

'It was the eyes. As if he's seen too much of the evil in men's breasts. You couldn't wonder if he really is tired. In Court all day; and then, as an M.P., sitting up till all the hours; and having to go to meetings and receptions; and all that sort of thing. Worrying about his cases, and the stupid old Judges; and then interrupted and insulted by those wretched men on the other side. But Charles says he's very strong; not likely to crack up, as some of them do; and sure to rouse us all.'

'If he has time.'

'Oh, great men always make time for everything. They have ordered minds. Marvellous. Not like my higgledy-piggledly muddle. And of course Lady Patterson takes charge of the entertainment, asks all the right people, and sets them talking on their pet subjects. She's very *grande dame,* Charles says; and she'll manage the village like a Queen.'

'Yes.' Florence was dubious. 'Yes, I expect she'll be active.'

'Inject new blood!'

'And, naturally, bring a new broom.'

'Blow away all our cobwebs. Puff! They're gone! I'm desperately keen to meet her. See what makes her tick, as they say. Aren't you? I'm sure you are!'

Florence made no reply. The picture of a grandiose and interfering woman was horrifying to one with limited horizons.

Bertha's thoughts took a short journey. She observed, suddenly:

'A man like that needs a go-ahead wife. Not everybody would suit him. I'm sometimes thankful that my Ralph's not a public man. It must be an artificial life, in one way. I wonder if they ever get a quiet hour to themselves, just hubby and wife, toasting thier toes at the fire, and remembering when they were young, and first in love?'

'I expect they do.' Florence shrank from picturing the idyllic scene.

'Charles speaks of a boy. A clever boy.'

'I should have said there was a girl — soon after they were married.'

'Oh? I didn't know that; but it would make the family perfect. Just like 'Ring-a-ring-a-roses''; ''first a girl and then a boy.'' It's thrilling, isn't it; the ideal marriage. I expect they're all very intelligent, exchanging deep thoughts, and understanding each other in the sort of shorthand very intelligent people use. Of course, I don't mean you're not very intelligent indeed. You are; but somehow you talk so that I can follow all you say. I'm so glad we met this morning. I was going to 'phone; but this is better. You're the first person I've been able to tell. I feel like a Town Crier. ''Oyez! Oyez!'' Charles says I ought to be on the Press — eyes to the keyhole, nose to the ground. He teases me for being a busybody! I don't mind; I admit I'm curious. He couldn't say that of you, dear. An oyster! No, you're not that; but somehow — well, noncommittal. I think it's marvellous you don't get dry and miserable.'

'You must remember that I have the garden, and my pets. They keep me company.'

'Yes; but pets and flowers can't talk and exchange ideas, like us. Have you noticed the crocuses, by the way? And the daffodils, nearly in flower?'

'I have. They're telling me, as the birds are, that Spring's on the way!'

'Like the Pattersons! But the Pattersons are new and splendid birds — or blooms! Better than anything in the garden. Perhaps I ought to say, in my garden, which is a wilderness. I haven't got your green fingers. I wish I had. Oh, there's Mrs Tobin. I must tell her the great news. Goodbye, dear; it's been lovely to see you!'

She darted away, shouting to attract Mrs Tobin's attention.

3
Daffodils

Events, as old writers used to say, moved fast. Bricklayers came from afar to make structural changes in the Manor; and shortly after their work began they were followed by engineers who installed central heating and other modern necessities. Experts whose job it was to restore panelling and renovate the giant fireplaces were busy when painters began to redecorate every one of the enormous rooms. And, finally, upholsterers, garden specialists, and a butler appeared. It was the butler whose known presence brought young women in search of engagements as domestic staff.

21

Florence saw few of the strangers; but Bertha watched them all from various observation posts. She counted the lorries, the workmen's coaches, and the cars of the experts; and she insisted upon hearing from her friend Charles particulars of the work and its cost — 'thousands, Florence, thousands! It would be almost wicked, if it weren't so wonderful!' She even, upon one occasion, caught a glimpse of Lady Patterson herself; but it was so brief as to leave her with no more than a simple ecstatic impression.

'Oh, Florence, you've no idea!' she cried, bursting into Florence's cottage after the event. 'A most striking woman. Majestic gestures — commanding voice — told the foreman what she wanted done as if she was Mrs Siddons. At least, my idea of Mrs Siddons — you know the majestic picture, Florence . . . Not as large as Mrs Siddons, of course; rather thin, in fact; but . . . Did you ever see a photograph of her?'

'No,' answered Florence, who had been brewing coffee for her visitor. 'Neither a photograph nor the woman in person. I was told that as a girl she was beautiful.'

'Were you? How interesting! Who told you?'

'I forget. It was just a description.'

'You were quite right about there being a daughter. She's twenty-five. Charles thinks she's married; but he doesn't know any more. I expect her husband's somebody aristocratic. We shall see after the Pattersons are settled. It won't be long now. We shall have to arrange a sort of welcoming deputation. You'll come, won't you?'

'I shall stay snugly at home,' said Florence. 'And hear all about it from you.'

'Oh, but you must come. We want to show proper attention, and that we aren't uncultured. Mrs. Primrose is quite willing to hand over the Presidency of the Women's Circle. And there's the Musical Society. I don't know if Lady Patterson is musical. Charles has seen a grand piano; but that doesn't necessarily mean that she plays herself. They'll probably invite famous musicians for weekends. Isn't that a lovely thought! Crowds in the grounds by moonlight, listening. Sonatas! Operatic arias! Nothing so wonderful has ever happened to Slocumbe before. I feel like a child when a circus is coming to town. A circus or a fair . . .'

She remembered that she had other calls to make, drank her coffee very quickly, and rose in such haste that she tottered and was only saved from falling by Florence's arm. With one gasped speech of thanks and farewell, she ran down the short path and away.

That afternoon, when brilliant sunshine made open casement windows a pleasure, Florence sat before her drawing-board wall out of sight of passers-by. Propped before her were some rough sketches, made from memory, of two little girls with a makeshift barrow — the 'awful Todd brats.' The children had not been prettified; yet the natural charm of their un-selfconscious bearing amused the artist's eye. She was not displeased with her work.

'In fact, pretty good,' she critically murmured. 'For me.'

The sound of a clear voice made her aware that two women had paused outside the gate, which was less than a dozen yards away. They were evidently attracted by a mass of daffodils between the gate and the window; and the voice she had heard commented again: 'Yes, quite charming!' Another voice, slightly higher in pitch, added: 'And the quaint little house. Like the witch's in *Hansel and Gretel*. I wonder if she eats children? More likely to be a sun-bonneted crone who sells eggs and cultivates her garden. Cottage industries. Unless she's somebody who's been reading *Candide* and taking it to heart.'

Still diverted, but curious, Florence sat upright, to catch a glimpse of the condescending speakers as they passed her low side wall. One of them, she saw, was tall, erect, grey-haired, probably in her late fifties; her companion was young, slim, and as blonde as a film actress.

'Mother and daughter,' she thought aloud. 'Visitors from London. Taking a stroll after lunching at the Three Diamonds.' She resumed her work; and had almost forgotten the strangers when there came, apparently from nowhere, a corrected indentification. 'Not the Diamonds. The Manor. That must have been *she.*'

Restlessness increased. The overheard speeches returned. ' "A sun-bonneted crone who sells eggs and cultivates her garden," ' she whispered. 'More apt than you realise, my girl. In fact, rather a good description. But the mention of *Candide* was a piece of showing off.' Her final comment, made after long silence, was: 'They didn't sound very pleasant. I don't want to meet them. Fortunately, they won't want to meet me, either.'

PART TWO

DISCORDS

4
Troublesome Daughter

Leaving his Chambers in the Inner Temple that Friday evening, Roderick Patterson sat back in his Daimler — not the Rolls of Bertha Pledge's expectation — and observed how cruelly the faces of men and women were blanched in the street lighting. Thus did many appear when sentence had been passed upon them in the Criminal Court, or when they were starving.

He closed his eyes until the strain passed in darker patches of the road. Then he was alert again, filled with preoccupation. He was going, not to the Patterson home in Belgravia, but for his first residential weekend at the Manor, Slocumbe. There he would be able to sit alone in what Evelyn, Lady Patterson, called his 'den,' busy or not with the papers in the briefcase which he held to his side. Blenkinsop, the chauffeur, had made this journey several times already, with Evelyn; and there would be no need for consultation over maps or directions given through the sliding window.

That was good. Nothing was more distracting he thought than uncertainty about one's route; and Roderick knew he could leave all to Blenkinsop. As darkness fell, the outer world would cease to interfere with the meditation to which nine-tenths of his waking time was devoted. He never indulged in reverie. It was said by others that his brain was a calculating machine.

'Roderick's detachment is criminal,' said Treloar, the Editor of *Our Age,* at their common Club. 'Right or wrong, he never deviates. Some might call that a proof of greatness. To me, it shows the mulish obstinacy of a third-rate character.'

Roderick, when this pontifical remark

was repeated to him, as such remarks, and others even less complimentary, always were, kept a straight face. The ability to keep both a straight face and his temper were characteristic. He did not bully, as Bertha ignorantly assumed; he remained calm, even when injustice was being inflicted. 'No imagination,' snorted rhapsodists. 'A cold-hearted brute who thinks only of his own advancement. . . .'

Blenkinsop's broad shoulders were less recognisable now that darkness had fallen; but the road ahead was piercingly illumined, and the grass verges assumed the unearthly green of Nature in theatrical scenery. Roderick again closed his eyes.

Blenkinsop held the car door wide at their journey's end. He was not misled by Roderick's lowered lids, because in Court he had heard apparently sleeping Judges interrupt droning barristers with sudden disconcerting questions, and he believed all lawyers to be perpetually sharp-witted. 'Clever,' he said. 'Foxy. Not him; but most of 'em.' A burly man in his fifties, with round, putty-coloured face,

31

Blenkinsop modelled his demeanour on that of the most imperturbable man he knew.

'Him and me' he told his friends, 'are like them monkeys in the saying — hear everything, see everything, say nothing.'

He did not offer his employer a helping hand; he knew that it would not be accepted. Nor, with the same understanding, did he attempt to take Roderick's briefcase. Touching his peaked cap, he said no more than 'Thank you, sir. Good night, sir,' and watched his master go briskly up the Manor's broad steps and in at the lighted entry.

Then, turning robustly away, he climbed back into his seat and drove the car to an enormous garage, where two other cars were already parked. This done, he went round to the kitchen door. Once in the house, he hung up his cap and uniform jacket, nodded to the cook, and waited to be served with a large pot of tea and his favourite meal of thick meat sandwiches.

Blenkinsop was a great man in the kitchen, almost greater than Symes, the butler; and, as senior members of the domestic staff had all been well trained, he received the attention due to one in the confidence of Sir Roderick.

'A-a-ah!' exclaimed Blenkinsop, setting down his cup, and preparing to bite a sandwich with his huge square teeth, 'I bin looking forward to this all the way home. Made me drive faster than I ought to ha' done. But he never said nothing. Never does.'

While Blenkinsop followed his natural course, Roderick advanced within the house, which still smelled of paint and polish. He did not seek his wife, but went straight upstairs to his own domain. There, packing-cases holding the books which had still to be arranged stood by empty shelving, and his armchair waited before a lighted coal fire. By the window a desk bore nothing but a spotless blotting pad and a neat pile of unopened letters; and it was on this desk that he laid the briefcase which had remained under his hand during the entire homeward journey.

Through one open door to the right of the fireplace he could see a single bed, and through another, to the left, was a white-tiled bathroom. In this way he enjoyed what was in effect a self-contained apartment, as was necessary to a man requiring privacy for urgent professional work. Evelyn alone, upon urgent occasions, ventured to disturb his solitude.

If Roderick had commented upon the arrangement he would have said, briefly, 'mine is an ordered life.' Order had always been his aim. There must be neither untidiness nor unconsidered act. For fifteen years a successful Junior Counsel, he had taken Silk early. Now the world offered greater triumphs in the field of Politics, where foresight promised him a very high place indeed.

Achievement, plan, calculation were all in his mind. Only happiness was absent from it.

His concern at this moment was not with the speech on Public Morals which he would make next week in the House of Commons, nor with a trifling but difficult case over jewels claimed by both a widow and her late husband's mistress. The speech was already written, and he felt no anxiety about it. The case, a bitter one, held only the danger that his client, the mistress, a charming, conceited, over-ingenious woman, would try to pit her wits against Peake, the widow's formidable Counsel.

Roderick had been warning his unreliable client against a display of virtuosity in the witness-box when he received a telephone call from Slocumbe.

'Lady Patterson wishes to speak to you urgently, sir.'

Evelyn's voice followed at once.

I think you should know this, Roderick. That fool is taking divorce proceedings against Sandra.'

Sandra was his daughter; 'that fool' was obviously Trevor Hamburg, Sandra's husband. Although keenly attentive, the beauty facing him could detect no change in Roderick's voice or his expression.

'Indeed? Had you any warning?'

'Certainly not. I'm telling you at the first opportunity.'

'What does she say?'

'Simply contemptuous.'

35

'She'll defend, then?'

'She won't. She says the sooner it's over, the better. I agree. She's entirely done with him.'

'That seems dangerously over-simple.'

'You know what Sandra is.

'Hm. Well, I'm engaged now. You must tell me properly tonight.'

The telephone clicked. That was Evelyn's way of showing disdain for an implied criticism of herself — something always unsufferable to one who is free in criticism of others. Roderick turned again to his client, a Miss Davenant, who was suing for possession of valuable diamonds which her rich lover's wife claimed as heirlooms.

'It is essential that you should stick to the bare facts; not allow yourself to be led into discussion,' he explained, patiently. 'Don't spar with Peake. Look, and be, quick. We shall win the case only if you can persuade the Judge that you are a deeply injured woman of high character. Do you understand?'

Miss Davenant had not understood. Her view was that Roderick always won his cases; and she was determined to fascinate a susceptible Judge and Jury, if there was one, which she had been warned was unlikely; and to outwit not only a greedy widow but the terrible, artful, sneering Peake.

In the car, with his eyes closed, he thought no longer of Miss Davenant. He was considering Evelyn's resentment and Sandra's defiance. The one could be dealt with, as had happend before, by his cool refusal to feed it; the other was more of a problem. How had this situation arisen? Why had he known nothing of its earlier stages? Evelyn might answer 'I didn't know, either.' That would be untrue. She was extremely intelligent. Therefore she must have gathered many hints of disagreement or incompatibility. Or she might say 'I hoped it would blow over,' which meant that she had deliberately kept him in the dark, perhaps at the same time encouraging the break through personal animus. The most likely excuse was 'You were too much occupied with things of greater importance to be bothered.'

Things of greater importance? Surely a daughter's happiness and reputation were very important indeed.

'You know what Sandra is.' He knew that Sandra would tell or conceal whatever the needs of self-justification prompted. She had never confided in him, and would not now confide. A headstrong girl, away for most of the year at a school where hardness was inculcated, and afterwards at Cambridge among other intellectually superior young women, her manner towards him had always been polite, with a touch of condescension. This certainly indicated indifference to his opinion; but whether the indifference was more than refusal to acknowledge his authority he could not say.

His authority? He had always been too busy to exercise it. Both children — Sandra and the boy Saul — were Evelyn's concern. Her influence upon Sandra in childhood had been paramount. Apart from the marriage, when Sandra's self-will overrode everything else, it had seemed to continue through adolescence and young womanhood. The two of them often stopped speaking together when he entered the room; as if he were an untrustworthy servant.

They must have spoken so today, before Evelyn telephoned. Heart to heart? Doubtful. Tears? Unlikely, from either. Evelyn had always opposed the marriage, and, however angry at Trevor's affront to the family, she would be gratified at its collapse. 'The sooner it's over, the better.' In effect, 'I always said he was a worthless nobody, in spite of his money. It was an infatuation. Sandra believed she could mold him into something presentable. She's discovered her mistake, that's all.'

Evelyn would be seeing the affair entirely as that of a woman's right to choose, break, and destroy any and every commitment — or, as she would say, entanglement — she chose. Not her own, admittedly, for whatever her moral views, she had a high sense of duty; but Sandra's, beyond doubt. Freedom was there the cry; modern young women must do as they pleased, whatever the consequences to others. *Whatever the consequences.*

Trevor Hamburg had dined at the Belgravia house as recently as three or four weeks ago. True, he then looked sullen, but no more sullen than usual. A beetle-browed fellow who always suggested a brooding and resentful spirit. He had never been talkative. Could he, when they were alone together for a few minutes at the end of the meal, have tried to speak of quarrels with Sandra? It had not seemed so; but younger men, in company with a senior, often held their tongues for fear of being thought fools — as most of them were.

Would Trevor, smarting and vindictive, reject a paternal intervention? Trevor's father, something of a snorter, would weigh in on the other side. He might even have prompted the threat. An unpleasant character, who shouted at his many employees. Common in grain. Trevor himself was neither a stoic nor an English gentleman of the old school. Graduating from his father's trade as a wholesale manufacturer of windows and piping for new houses, he had made a career of his own in business. No wonder Evelyn sneered at him. And yet he had once infatuated Sandra. That suggested quality, didn't it? Sandra would not have fallen in love with a fool.

In olden days, if a wife wanted her freedom, the husband allowed himself to be divorced. It was not so now, when wives cared less about tarnish. Sandra, apparently, cared nothing at all. That was conceit. Also it indicated superlative arrogance. Was she a snob? Had she, either expressly or by innuendo, taunted Trevor with underbreeding! If so, Trevor would be vengeful. Hell hath no fury like a self-made man's resentment of undervalued distinction.

Roderick had never been so taunted by Evelyn; but on her side there had unquestionably been an inbred sense of aristocracy. The fact that she was thought by her family to have 'married beneath her' was revealed in ways which he had quite early shown to be unacceptable. And, of course, his professional standing had been great enough to check anything more.

Seated in his car or his quiet room, Roderick dwelt long and earnestly upon those aspects of a problem of which the furthest repercussions were still hidden.

42

5
Syd Patterson

Now that the Manor was occupied, Florence could no longer ramble in the deserted and overgrown territories belonging to it: she was forced to use other routes for her early morning exercise. Fortunately, however, Slocumbe was encircled by agreeable lanes, free from traffic, tramps, and — at that time of day — picnickers; and she used these lanes, rejoicing in solitude, listening to the Spring songs of birds, amused by flying clouds in a blue sky, and delighted by occasional glimpses of primroses or cowslip buds under the already burgeoning hedge.

She often lingered, at times standing motionless, to watch a skylark as it rose higher and higher overhead, or a mouse or dilatory hedgehog at her feet, or even a spider or beetle scrambling on some inexplicable journey over obstructive twigs or broken soil. Every natural sight or sound nourished her fancy and confirmed her artistic skill.

Simple and proud, proud to excess, Florence belonged to an old-fashioned type, the members of which will go without food rather than lose independence. Independence, indeed, was in her case almost an obsession. Though modest regarding the talent so highly esteemed by Bertha Pledge, she was saved from pure virtue by this determination to be independent and by a dry sense of fun. It was the sense of fun that gave her drawings of children and animals, which were not at all sentimental, their originality. Because of it she knew both physical comfort and a spiritual contentment denied to the insatiable pursuer of novelty.

About a mile from home, Florence

came, this Sunday morning, to a patch of open ground behind which was a small coppice, made up of trees self-planted over the years. She loved the spot, and knew every one of the trees. Some were very junior oaks, others ash or pine saplings; and among them, as yet bare and prickly, were blackthorn which in a few weeks, even days, would become snowy with bloom. Blackthorn winter! The blossom, enchanting to an artist's eye, would in time be recorded as background for scenes in one or other of her stories; but meanwhile the trafficless silence and the tracery of branches against a stretch of unclouded sky produced a craftsman's impatience.

'I ought to have brought my sketchbook. How stupid I am!'

She had hardly spoken when she instinctively flinched. She was not quite alone. A figure advanced through the copse; the figure of a tall man, heavily bearded, carelessly dressed, with a flowing tie and a wide-brimmed hat. Evidently an artist or would-be picturesque. She was reassured.

Such a man was unlikely to molest her, in spite of the hefty walking-stick which he alternately flourished and dug mightily into the ground. Her best course was to walk straight on, ignoring a strange presence.

The man, however, striding erratically, and twirling the stick like Tom-tit-tot's tail, took notice of a female pedestrian, at first with detached interest, and then with precise observation. His pace slackened. He looked closer still. And, when almost abreast, he gave a great shout.

'Good God! It's Florrie! The last person on earth —'

Now indeed Florence's heart gave a quick throb and seemed to stand still. It was thirty years since anybody had called her 'Florrie.' To her sister Annabel she was always 'Flo.' To others, even Bertha, she was what she had been christened. But this apparent stranger with the exuberant beard and walking-stick, a man obviously ready to thrust himself into any company as a convivial, nay, bibulous comrade, addressed the girl she had once been. Her surprise and discomfort having been simultaneous, she recovered with an effort.

'Hello, Syd! I didn't recognise you behind that tapestry of whiskers.'

'Ah, that's my disguise,' retorted the stranger. 'I baffle the Hanauds and the Holmses with it. But not little Florrie! It's an improvement, don't you think?' He rumpled the beard with long fingers.

'That depends on what you want to hide,' said Florence, coolly.

'Nothing, I assure you. No scars, no discolouration, and certainly not chinlessness. You remember my chin? A good chin. Firm and well-rounded. No, it's simply that I've knocked about a bit in the last — how long is it? — twenty-five years? What? Thirty? Good heavens! Incredible! My fate to knock about. The rolling stone! Now, as you see, I've acquired moss. I've also learned a lot in — you say thirty years; but I can't believe it. Why can't I? Because you're just as you always were; not a grey hair, not a wrinkle in the baby face. The same little prig, I suppose? No wiser?'

'No wiser,' agreed Florence. 'And the

same little prig.'

Syd's body quivered with laughter. The sound of a brief chuckle reached her ears.

'And as saucy!' he declared. 'Well, how are you, darling?'

Florence could with truth have replied: 'And you're the same boisterous, bounding creature who tired everybody with noise and facetiousness; though it's evident that you've been a good deal battered by your rolling and knocking about!' But she had never been one to hit back, nor, as many of her contemporaries did, to mistake rudeness for idiosyncratic wit. Moreover she had always liked this perpetual hobbledehoy. Only when he spread abroad the odour of spirits had she ever shunned him.

Now that the shock of meeting was past she was quite at ease. Nevertheless his eyes, once boyishly clear, resembled boiled gooseberries. Gooseberries in brandy, it might be? The knocking about had included nights of carouse and base company. Poor Syd!

'What are you doing in Slocumbe?'

asked Florence.

'Visiting. Visiting,' he replied, airily.

She understood.

'That was what I supposed.'

'You know everything, then?'

'Practically nothing — in the sense you mean.'

'Are you married?'

'No.'

'I could have told you that. You look like a nun. I don't know why; you weren't nunnish. Prig; but not prude. There's a distinction. Have you seen Rod?'

'No. We haven't met.'

'Does he know you're here?'

'I shouldn't think so. I'm a very obscure resident.'

'Artful creature! Well, I'll tell you why I'm here. I read in the papers about his move; and thought it only brotherly to pay a courtesy call. Not too pleased to see me, I'm afraid. Nor was she. She never was. I knew it. I'm sensitive to atmosphere. Last night it was "What, has that bad penny turned up again? What does he want?" You know? Suspicious. The wrinkled nose; the calculating eye

. . . So I shan't stay. I never stay where I'm not wanted.'

'You simply roll on.'

'Roll on. Also, its seems they're in a spot of trouble. That tiresome little bitch Sandra . . . Do you know her?'

'Not at all.'

'Then I'd better say nothing. No, no; forget that I mentioned her, Florrie. I mustn't lose my reputation for discreetness. Eh?'

'You never had any such reputation, Syd. You'd do well to cultivate it now.'

'Meaning, you don't want to hear anything nasty!'

'Meaning that I prefer to mind my own business.'

'Hm.' He grunted; and looked down at her with great good humour. 'You restrict your business. You always did. It's a primary defect. By the way, I notice you don't press me to visit *you*. Too black a sheep?'

She observed his over-sensitiveness.

'You can come back with me now, if you like.'

'I certainly do like.'

'But, when you get to the Manor, I'd rather you didn't say you've been with me.'

'Why? Are you an *embusquée?*'

'No, I just value my privacy.'

'Grand word! Grand word! What has your privacy brought you?'

'Peace on earth. Goodwill to all men.'

Syd laughed again.

'Hence the nun-like appearance!'

Florence turned, so that he might accompany her.

'Apart from rolling and knocking about,' she said, 'what have you been doing in the last thirty years?'

'You insist on the thirty years. Unbelievable! I suppose you think I've been sponging on Rod, cashing in on his prosperity. I haven't. As a matter of fact I've never had a penny from Rod, Florrie. Never needed it. If I had, he'd have dubbed up. You realise that, don't you? I respect old Rod — within reason. He's an obtuse fool, and as ambitious as Milton's Satan; but he's very straight — if a politician can ever be straight. It's a Patterson characteristic. I'm straight, myself; nobody can say otherwise. Eh?'

'I'm sure you are, Syd.'

'Good girl! Well, then, as you've asked, I'll tell you what I've been doing. I've been overseas most of the time. A little hack journalism — some of it revolutionary; some ordinary ditchwater stuff, — touching up photographs for the Press, scrounging interviews with pompous nobodies, acting as courier, writing a lot of boys' books under pseudonyms, and consorting with good fellows. That's a world you know nothing about, darling; the world of good fellowship. It's taboo to little prigs. Eh? Oh, but it's a world — my world — rich in experience . . . and memories. My God! My God! Yes! Unspeakable memories!'

For some reason the memories were at that moment oppressive. He gave a deep groan, and became silent.

Florence guessed that, for all his brave words, Syd had gone back to a comparison between present rootlessness and former high hopes of something better than worldy success. He had been a brilliant boy, original, defiant, and eloquently eager to change the nature of things; but he had never achieved self-discipline. She could not tell him this; and, through ignorance of the life he had just sketched, she could offer no close and reassuring consolation. But she did, as a gesture of sympathy, take his arm, feeling her hand impetuously pressed to his side.

'You're a dear little thing, Florrie,' he grumbled. 'A prig, yes; but a loyal prig — and a charmer. You could have married Rod, if you'd played your hand well. Why didn't you?'

'The reason seemed good at the time,' said Florence.

'Not so good now? Lady Patterson? Lots of money? Quite satisfied? You look as if you were; but what's behind the façade?' When no reply was made, he roared out the words 'those bloody high principles!' and followed them with a muttered supplement. 'They're not life, you know. Life's not a simple progress to saintliness.'

'Rolling and knocking about,' Florence

reminded him.

'Devil!' cried Syd. 'Complete and utter devil!'

He did not therefore cast her hand aside. The convulsive pressure upon it showed the torment he was suffering as the result of this encounter. In three or four minutes he had traversed a lifetime, as ready now in his self-condemnation as he had formerly been impatient of restraint. She heard him mutter 'Waste! Waste! And what's the point of it all?'

They walked side by side for the rest of the journey back to her cottage. Then, as he refused to enter it, they parted, he sweeping off his big hat in grandiose farewell. The stick was flourished and dug into the roadway as before; but its owner's head was down, and his thoughts evidently continued to be as corrosive as shame.

6
No Farewell

The unexpected arrival of his brother interrupted Roderick's sense of order. As long as Syd remained at a distance, he gave no trouble; but when one supposes a man to be at the other side of the world it is disconcerting to see him by one's fireside, apparently expectant of the Prodigal's fatted calf.

There had hardly been time to raise with Evelyn the question of what was to be done about Sandra's affair when Syd strolled into the Manor, rather muddy after a long walk from the nearest railway station, and as disrespectful as ever to both brother and sister-in-law. He pushed his way into the conclave, not absolutely sober (as Evelyn at once noticed with disgust), just as Sandra, chin high and voice raised, was aggressively resisting her father's questions; and it was Sandra's rebellious withdrawal, followed by Evelyn's cold announcement that she must go and arrange for the visitor's accommodation, which produced a significant dialogue between the brothers.

'I'm *de trop,*' said Syd, cheerfully, with a grimace at the closing door.

'Not so much *de trop* as calamitous,' was Roderick's sedate answer. 'How are you, Syd? I'm always glad to see you, of course; but I was trying to ascertain some facts in a troubled situation.'

'I'll go at once.'

'You'll do nothing of the kind. In fact your being here will give unreason a chance to subside.'

'Very pompous, my boy. Front Bench stuff. I assume the unreason is female. Sandra. My perceptions are as quick as light. What is it Mrs Peachum sings? "I wonder any man alive should ever rear a daughter?" Well, well, that's something

I've avoided.'

Roderick, never as frivolous as Syd, became quizzical.

'One doesn't associate you with caution.'

'Cautious enough to preserve my *panache,* whatever that may be. What is a panache? That old fool Cyrano de Bergerac says he still has it at the end of Rostand's play; but I never understood what he meant. As to myself, I've been a free man. Can you say as much, Rod?'

Roderick's quizzicalness diminished.

'I lead a full life.'

Syd's comparison of their fortunes held affront and defensiveness. He was his brother's junior by five years; but he looked, today, ten years older than Roderick, whose fine physique and the authority gathered by distinguished public life gave him the advantage. Syd, though expressing contempt for all authority, knew this. The fraternal relation might justify every candour; but the candour must be his own. Roderick, ever self-controlled, did not retort. Thinking only that Syd, besides lacking good manners, had worn badly, he observed the studied patience which he used in Court against a strident witness.

Syd was not so to be quelled.

'Yes,' he persisted. 'You're a conspicuous man, Rod. You fraternize with all the Nobs. They kow-tow to you. You like it. All the same, wouldn't you be better off — spiritually better off — without the trappings? Eh? Don't look at me so snootily!'

'I should never do that, Syd. We've both done what suits us best.'

'I meant "happier," Rod.'

'I knew you meant "happier." It's a question of temperament. I never cared for your way of life or your sort of crony.'

'And never disguised the fact. I doubt if you ever cared for *me.*'

'On the contrary, I'm very fond of you. We're fond of each other.'

'That's true.' Syd had a quick wish to be reasonable. 'I sometimes wonder if I should have been different if you'd been different.'

"How different?"

'Less high-minded.' Syd was so reflective that his words were almost inaudible. Roderick pressed an advantage.

'My dear Syd, I never pretended to superiority. We're both exceptional men. I've always admired you very much; and I don't think you ought to blame me because you've followed your natural bent. You underrate yourself. If you lived to make a bid for success, you could bring it off, even now. You're not too old. You have great gifts. I'm sure you could startle the world.'

Syd was too much convinced of grievance to tolerate his brother's kind intention.

'You look on me as a failure, then?'

Roderick's affectionate smile was misconstrued. It deeply wounded Syd's hyper-sensitiveness.

So, when the clang of a dinner-gong forced the brothers to separate, did Evelyn's disapproving observation of the amount he drank at, and after, the meal. During the night, therefore, he boiled at his treatment; and, rising very early, he stormed out of doors, feeling suffocated by the atmosphere within.

'Blasted woman!' he fumed. 'The whole place stinks of decorum — and varnish! God! How I detest them all, including that supercilious chit Sandra! Not good enough for them! Bad character! Discreditable! And so — look down noses, watch the harmless glass, withdraw from contamination! . . . . Pah!'

It was when his lungs were full of the countryside's sweet breath that he met Florence. With her, at least, he could freely engage in rodomontade. She wouldn't look down her nose or sneer, or shrug in distaste. She, though a wretched Puritan, appreciated him as he was. She was as satisfying as the morning breeze!

His good humour restored, he coughed several times, like a horse, and resolved to quit the Manor at once.

'I'll be off. Back to civilisation. They'll be delighted. Well, thank God I was never a toady or a climber! The world's my oyster; and Florrie's a little pet!'

Stirred by this thought and his overnight resentment, he took the opportunity, when they were out of Evelyn's hearing, to deliver to his brother what he hoped would be a sharp reminder of past humiliation. It was very malicious.

'By the way, Rod . . . I went for an early ramble before our aristocratically late breakfast. You should do that, sometimes. Explore the district, meet the unspoiled natives of England at close quarters. They'd aerate you; recharge your arteries. Florrie Marvell's one of them. Did you know she lived here? I met her. It was a treat. She's as adorable as ever.'

Conscience reminded him that he had been asked not to mention Florence at the Manor; but he blustered conscience aside. 'Shut up! Shut up! I didn't promise. No promise at all. Not asked; not given. And the fellow *ought to know!*'

Syd had no reward for the deliberate indiscretion. Roderick, well used to heckling, remained impassive. He might not have heard the words. Smiling, he said:

'Goodbye, Syd. Come and see us again — whenever you feel inclined. And do try to keep in touch. Even an occasional picture postcard would be better than nothing.'

Exasperated at one more failure, Syd ignored his brother's hand, striding down the long avenue, flourishing his stick, and talking loudly to the gods, while his heart seethed with rage and shame for his treachery to Florence.

7
Roderick Alone

Evelyn felt relief as, from her place by the open door, she observed the abrupt departure of an unwelcome guest. They had endured for thirteen or fourteen hours the presence in her new home of an untamed, quarrelsome, insatiably thirsty brute; and when that ear-racking voice no longer jarred upon her sensibilities the quiet was exquisite. Gracious to the last, but incapable of pretending a warm affection which she had never felt, she turned to re-enter the house, stiffening both her arms in a gesture of thankfulness.

'What an infliction!' she thought. 'He'll go back to his pubs and smoking dens as ungrateful as ever. I hope I wasn't too obviously inhospitable. No. He's too thick-skinned to think me more than "Unclubbable." But he makes me shudder. It's like having a wildly demented child in the house. Ah, child —'

This word stung Evelyn. It reminded her that she had to face a disagreeable conversation with Roderick; and it was with a heavy sigh that she braced herself for battle. She did not fear her husband. His courtesy never failed, and he would neither shout nor indulge in any of Syd's convulsive movements. He believed she understood him very well — much better than he understood her. All the same, she was too proud to rely upon any of the devices by which a less scrupulous woman might have eluded his forensic skills. Hence the sigh.

Sandra was still upstairs. Owing to dislike of her uncle's outspokenness, she had gone to bed immediately after dinner and had not come down to breakfast. Nor had she troubled to speed Syd's departure. The high-handedness with which, until his arrival, she had tried to meet every inquiry was gone. In the night she had wept in anger and contempt for Trevor. Now she was exhausted. Her bitterness had increased.

Thus no member of the Patterson family was at ease this morning.

Once in the house again, Roderick took Evelyn's arm.

'The same old Syd,' he said.

'Only further down the hill,' was her cold answer. 'Did he want money?'

'He's never done that. His pride is too strong. He'll rant; but he won't beg. If I offered help, he'd throw it back in my face. No, don't underrate him. He's noisy, quarrelsome, spiteful, if you like; but he's no sponger. Look, Evelyn. I suggest that you should tell me, between ourselves, all you know about this business of Sandra's.'

It was the way in which he usually began his examination or cross-examination of a witness — urbane, but with an indication that either sternness or menace lay in wait. He knew that Evelyn, being naturally positive and a taker of the lead in conversation, would be irritated by such an approach. What he did not know was that his unconsciously legal manner always aroused her feminist prejudices. It was the Feminian which distorted her manner from that moment.

'I can't stand Roderick when he's being a Queen's Counsel!' was her reaction. ' "I want you to tell me, in your own words, what happened when you went to the chemist's to buy the arsenic." That's all very well in Court; but at home it's insufferable. This is going to be very difficult indeed. I mustn't lose my temper!' Aloud, she said in a tone of extreme dryness: 'I told you what I knew, on the telephone.'

'Tell me again. When you rang, I was talking to a very tiresome woman.'

'To you, all women are tiresome, Sandra at the moment the most tiresome of the lot. The only thing I can tell you is that Trevor is suing for divorce.'

'Yes, I remember that. But how has this come about? How long has it been brewing?'

'I don't know.'

'You must surely have seen rudimentary signs of friction? Arguments, frowns, impatiences?'

'I haven't live with them, Roderick.'

'No daughterly communications?'

'Nothing.'

This was so obviously untrue that Roderick, feeling Evelyn to be doing herself less than justice, remained silent. At last he said:

'Is there a co-respondent?'

'She says he names three.'

'So many? Is he mad?'

'Insensate, apparently. Everybody he can think of.'

'He won't succeed, then.'

'She won't defend. She's too furious. She wants it all over at once.'

Roderick shook his head.

'Months before the case comes on. She'll change her mind before then. We must see that they're reconciled.'

'Quite impossible. Quite.'

'The consequences would be very serious indeed; not only to Sandra.'

'She won't consider that.'

'I think you should invite her

to consider it.'

Evelyn brushed aside an intolerable reproach to herself as a mother.

'Too late. In any case, you exaggerate the consequences. The whole thing — whenever it comes on — will be forgotten in a week. Trevor's will be the name mentioned in Court: and Trevor's a social nobody.'

'Unfortunately we're not exactly social nobodies. Surely you see that such a case would be a feast for sub-editors?'

'Sandra's a modern girl. She can't be expected to abide by antediluvian rules. They're what you're thinking of, aren't they?'

'Yes, if by rules you mean morals and social responsibility.'

'Quite Victorian, Roderick.'

'English, my dear Evelyn. Victoria was an embodiment of the national spirit. I've seen Jurymen's faces when they thought morality was being flouted. What about the co-respondents?'

Evelyn threw forward rigid arms, as she had done when thinking of Syd.

'She says he might have cited half-a-dozen.'

'She's not a whore, is she?'

Evelyn was further exasperated.

'Of course she only says it in the first mood of outrage.'

'One would have been enough if he merely wanted to get rid of her. It looks as though he meant mischief; to destroy her. His father dislikes us, and would like to see us humiliated. Is Trevor claiming damages from any — or all — of the co-respondents? Are they, in their own interests, proposing to defend?'

'I don't know. I don't know who they are.'

Roderick hid gathering impatience.

'Well, we must find out. I must see her Solicitor, whoever he is; and talk to Sandra alone.'

'She'll tell you, as she's told me, that it's her affair — not yours.'

Roderick looked gravely at Evelyn. He saw himself confronted by two women in a conspiracy of defiance. If the case actually came on, mud would be slung. She herself would not escape it.

Alone again after Evelyn's withdrawal

in hostility, he turned across the study to its great window, from which he surveyed a still only partially reclaimed garden. Trees stretched their bare branches at intervals until open grassland took their place. All active life seemed dormant. No birds sang, and no breeze stirred. Angers suppressed during almost thirty years of married life swarmed like bees in the next few minutes of thought.

'My work called for incessant concentration. She knew that; supported me in it. I hardly saw the children. They were her responsibility. But she didn't see them, either. Parental love wasn't in her programme. Nor in mine, I agree. This is the result. Sandra blindly self-indulgent — and making a fool of herself; Saul — well, what the devil is Saul doing? I never see him. He never writes. A moody boy who — like Syd before him — hated school; but, unlike Syd, hated sports, made no friends, never hinted at any ambition. I simply do not know him. He continues to take my money — that goes without saying; it's the modern spirit; — but otherwise he might be dead. . . .'

This was all the attention Roderick now had time to give to family matters. He had many legal papers to read before nightfall, and there was one political theme to which he must attend. The opposition had been making a concerted attack on his colleague Sam Wrekin, who in Roderick's view was the ablest of them all. The Opposition hated Sam, not for any evil that was in him, but because his manner in the House appeared to them to be supercilious. Sam was a chivalrous aristocrat and a scholar; but his opponents portrayed him as a parasite who treated them as *canaillo*.

They accordingly bellowed all through any speech he made, laughed loudly if, being a thoughtful man, he hesitated, mocked his fastidious gestures, and did their utmost to decry him out of doors. The whole thing was an outrageous injustice to Sam; and they all knew it. Roderick meant to castigate the offenders in his next speech. He proposed to do this in his most deadly manner.

The speech was prepared in outline. Effective phrases were already in his mind. He would make notes of them. Sandra,

Evelyn, and the uncommunicative Saul must be pigeonholed. He was a politician for the next hour.

As the hour ended, Roderick remembered Syd. Syd, besides minor splenetic ridicule, had tried to pass responsibility for his own ill-success in life to a cold-hearted older brother who had engrossed their mother's regard and the public suffrage. There was certainly truth in what he believed about Mother; but Syd had been born unmanageable. Some essential co-ordinating link was wanting in him. He had never worked for his exams, saying, because they demanded application, that they were a useless bore. So he had failed them. Truancy, preference for the company of other wild boys who exploited Syd's ingenuities for their own ends, and desperate efforts to establish leadership over them, had ended in expulsion from school. Always unstable he then talked about his 'genius,' and expected all follies to be pardoned because of it. They were not pardoned. Mother, the perfect Roman matron, had no use for 'genius.' Syd became a bitter disappointment to her.

'I, on the contrary, was what's called "the industrious apprentice." Syd could not understand, and couldn't forgive, my sense of responsibility — to Mother, among other people. He took the line that a lovable scapegrace is always the hero. So he is, in romantic fiction. Syd read too many romances. They went to his head. For him no boy who passed his exams could be lovable. I passed my exams.'

Continuing in this vein, Roderick interpreted Syd's attacks as signs of envy. He had compared the Manor's air of solidity with his own homelessness. The grapes at once became sour. Poor Syd!

But there was another aspect. Syd had wanted for some personal reason to inflict pain. He had wanted to see an immaculate brother rattled by his taunts. Well, that wasn't so good. When the taunts had produced no apparent wound, he had flung off in anger.

'Silly fellow. Silly fellow. We're really fond of each other, and we ought to be close friends. I thought I'd met him more than halfway. Evidently not. Where's the fault? Is it in me?'

Recalling their conversations, and Syd's refusal to shake hands as they parted, Roderick again approached the window. And in doing this, by some trick of light or quirk of fancy, he seemed to catch a glimpse, in front of a tall old cypress hedge, of a young girl. She was bareheaded, small, and very slight, and she wore a cotton frock which made her look fairylike. He stared; the figure was gone; he knew it had never been there.

And yet how vivid the impression had been! It was of somebody, hardly thought of for many years, who had been called to mind by one of Syd's taunts. Somebody quick-witted, exceptionally candid, and as sure of her own rightness as a dedicated novice. Still adorable, Syd had said; and as young as ever. That was obviously impossible; a detail in Syd's malice. Nevertheless on a casual meeting, that might have seemed true. The girl had been a very rare girl indeed, brimming with fun, and as nearly selfless as human nature could allow. There was no question about that. Florrie Marvell; extraordinarily ready to sacrifice herself for others — for one other.

'Yes, yes, yes; that may be.' The impatient words were spoken aloud, as if addressed the cypress hedge. 'That may be. But as obstinate as a Hindu woman contemplating *suttee!*'

Phrases she had used, buried in the interval under millions of others, read, heard, and spoken by himself, crowded suddenly into Roderick's memory. Experiencing anew his sensations when they were first uttered, he heard them, broken by laughter or emotion, as if they came from another world. It was the world of his youth, of early dreams, when the future was uncertain and hope coloured with assurance. An odd world, it now seemed; almost unrecognizable.

With renewed impatience, he turned from the window to survey the noble room, with its bookshelves, piled books, and rich carpet. Pride filled his heart.

'Splendid!' he murmured. 'Splendid!'

Equally splendid were three brilliant pictures by living artists which Evelyn had bought and given him. They hung upon walls papered in a warm brown; and their richness of colour was such as to delight his pride. Room, pictures, and books were the distinguished possessions of a distinguished man.

Roderick had been nourished all his life by rewards, by the gratitude of clients whose causes he had successfully pleaded, the applause of audiences in great halls which his voice filled with musical eloquence, the admiration — sometimes reluctant — of other men, and by material prosperity.

And what of the man himself? He coolly assessed his own character.

'Fairly able. Thorough. Orderly. Considerable integrity. Because I've never touted or flunkeyed, I think I'm respected. The determination to succeed came from Mother. She fulfilled her own ambition through me. Curious, because she wasn't a big woman, either physically or intellectually. Spirit rather than soul. No great talent; the one object she cherished was my success. . . .

'She died triumphant. Very emotional at the end; holding my hands. "So proud of you, my darling boy. So proud!" Tears on her cheeks. Very affecting. I don't think I can have been quite dry-eyed, myself. I can't remember that. . . .

'I'm glad I did what she wanted. I suppose I, too, had some grounds for pride. I certainly have nothing to regret. Nothing . . .'

There was a long pause. It ended with a curious exclamation.

'To Hell with Florrie Marvell!'

PART THREE

FLORENCE GOES TO LONDON

8
Lunch with Mr Leadbitter

Publishers, or their Art Editors, or, too often, only their very junior reception clerks, are used to the sight of picturesquely untidy young men and women who carry large portfolios under their arms. These unfortunates have come, hoping to show specimens of their work to potential enthusiasts, and even more extravagantly hoping to receive on the spot passports to fame and fortune.

Florence no longer lived in days of hope and disappointment. Never picturesquely untidy, she had quickly become the inconspicuous figure seen in the village of Slocumbe. When she visited London she carried, instead of a portfolio, nothing but a small packet of commissioned work to Mr Leadbitter, the Art Editor at Gimblett's, her publishers; and by Mr Leadbitter she was received with the warmth reserved for two or three of his favourites. Florence liked Mr Leadbitter very much, and greatly enjoyed his abrupt praises and equally abrupt silent nods. All expressed approval. Every artist needs approval. It is too often withheld.

This morning Mr Leadbitter was superlatively kind. After paying close attention to the new drawings, he gathered them together with the precision of a crack card-player.

'Splendid!' His voice, curiously high and sharp, made Florence think of a pin being stabbed through a sheet of parchment. 'Splendid, Miss Marvell. I don't know how you manage always to be at the top of your form.'

'I'm industrious,' said Florence, demure, but lighthearted.

'Of course you are. Otherwise they wouldn't look so spontaneous. You're punctual, too. Most businesslike.'

'Thank you. I sometimes feel that professionalism is nowadays considered rather discreditable.'

'These amateurs!' Mr Leadbitter showed his contempt for the non-professional by slapping a long-fingered white hand upon his desk. 'Can't draw; so they pretend they're Picassos and don't want to. However, they soon starve; unless, if they're female, they marry and get lost among the nappies and teething powders.'

'I should hate to starve,' observed Florence. 'It's demoralizing.'

Mr Leadbitter gave her one of his sharp looks.

'You do look after yourself? Enough to eat?'

'Yes, thank you; to both questions.'

'Took a young artist out to lunch the other day. Quite good; but a skeleton. Wouldn't eat this; couldn't eat that. All she wanted was Tio Pépé and spinach, grapefruit, unsweetened black coffee. Said abstinence produced high thinking. I told her an early grave ended all that. No good. So I mentioned that men didn't care for brides who rattled. It struck her. She had steak pudding and Burgundy; and went away singing. Quite dizzy, she said.'

'I don't wonder, Mr Leadbitter. She wasn't used to Burgundy.'

'Yes, she did rather lap it up. Her work will improve — in fact it's already improved. More body. By the way, care to lunch with me today?'

'I'm not sure about Burgundy at lunch. Otherwise I should love it. Thank you. What time? I'm calling on my sister this morning.'

'Bring her, too. Yes, do. Meadows's. One o'clock O.K.?'

'O.K. I'm sure Annabel will jump at the prospect of a square meal. She's — unwillingly — one of the starvelings.'

'We'll fatten her up. I saw her the other night in a dud new show. It's off, already; but she was excellent. Like you, in a way.'

'Far better than I am. For one thing, she's five years younger.'

'Her face is the same shape. What's it called? Pear?'

'Sagging cheeks and a top-knot? A dreadful picture!'

'Stalkless, and upside down, of course.'

Having, with no change of expression corrected his smile, Mr Leadbitter fell back into sleuth-like gravity.

This was at eleven o'clock; and by half-past eleven she was in Annabel's *pied-à-terre* over a shop on the way to Hammersmith. Annabel, who slept late, even when she had not been acting the night before, was still in a dressing-gown.

'I know I look a sight, darling; but you're always charitable.'

'And you, glamorous.'

'This dressing-gown's quite attractive, isn't it? I've got the sort of figure to go with it.'

The sisters, as Mr Leadbitter had remarked, were much alike. Annabel was fairly tall, and as a more restless life had sharpened her profile she looked, off the stage, older than Florence. She also had a louder voice and a more striking enunciation. She referred to the latest failure as something normal.

'Poor Bunty Smithers is terribly upset. Her part was quite stupid; and the last act appalling.'

'All that hard work wasted,' lamented Florence. 'I saw a bad notice.'

'All notices were bad, darling. As usual, the so-called critics were beastly to Bunty. They know she despises them; and that's something the conceited wretches can't forgive. Sitting there in their free stalls, sharpening their rusty daggers. Because they hate Bunty, they mostly commended *me,* which I suppose did me no harm, except with Bunty, who won't employ me again. Of course, she's a bitch to work with. She drove poor Harry Buckton, the leading man, to tears. I spent half of my time dabbing his makeup with cotton wool while he sobbed on my shoulder. Any way, I'm out of another job. You'll just have to have bread and cheese today, unless you've got the price of a meal.'

'I can do better,' boasted Florence. 'I can take you to lunch with a Publisher's Art Editor. He expressly invited you.'

'What an angel! Is he your lover?'

'He sees me as a harmless drudge.'

'Eating his heart out for you, poor dear. How lucky I've got something to wear! It was the first thing I did when I drew my salary. You're looking very smart, yourself.'

'One should always look smart when visiting a Publisher. It makes him feel one's a credit to him.'

'I know. All men are alike. They wear a woman companion like a mayoral chain. Unfortunately I've never had what you could call a wardrobe. Funds don't permit; and I'm not handy, as you are, with a sewing-machine. I suppose you made that suit yourself? Clever girl! In the Profession clothes are watched by every spiteful eye back stage. If you're quiet, you're dowdy; and if you glitter, you're being kept. That's where pictorial artists have an advantage, Flo. Their rivals are all trying to hide inky fingers and paint-splashed bras.'

'I have no rivals. Mr Leadbitter says I'm unique.'

'Oh, Flo, he *must* be in love with you!'

'You'll see for yourself. One o'clock, at Meadows's.'

'Meadows's! Gracious, he's rich! But Publishers always are, aren't they?'

'They say not. They used to tell me,

when I began, that publishing was dead, too poor to pay more than five or ten shillings a drawing.'

'How on earth do they expect you to live, then?'

'On air. On air.'

'That's what I do, mostly. But you do get paid, don't you? I mean, five or ten shillings?'

'They don't mention money, now; just sent little cheques.'

'And an occasional lunch to salve their consciences, if they've got them. In the theatre there are no consciences. Beginners always starve. And I'm a chronic beginner. But I shall feed well this day; and Mr Leadbitter — it ought to be Goldbeater, or Maecenas — will pay like a trump. I suppose there's no danger that he'll want us to go Dutch?'

'No money will pass. He has an account at Meadows's.'

'Oh, Flo! Do marry him!'

Florence had no thought of marrying Mr Leadbitter, who, she knew, was fifteen years younger than herself, and had a wife who answered all his hopes. Fortunately,

Annabel never expected to be taken seriously.

Mr Leadbitter, as host, was much less hawklike than he was in the Gimblett office. He greeted Annabel as an old friend.

'You don't know me,' he announced, when they were seated; 'but I've been your steadfast admirer ever since I began going to the theatre. You were the ideal *ingenue.*'

Annabel, having sipped her sherry, was in bliss.

'Heaven! Your nurse must have been a prodigal!'

'I formed my own taste, which is fastidious. I found your leading lady the other night intolerable. In fact, I only went to see you.' Having bowed over his own glass, Mr Leadbitter cast an eye upon Florence. '*She's* very good, too,' he assured Annabel, proceeding then to address Florence herself. 'We're all enchanted with your new drawings, Miss Marvell. I'm to tell you so, from Mr Gimblett. He'd like more and more of them. But also he longs for you to do something really ambitious.'

'What, frescoes?' demanded Annabel. 'Like the Sistine Chapel? You'd have to go up ladders, Flo!'

'No frescoes.' Mr Leadbitter was determined. 'Perhaps something in oils? No, I said that wouldn't appeal to you. What about illustrating a new edition of *The Little Flowers of Francis of Assisi?* Or *The Pilgrim's Progress?*'

'I think I'll stick to my cat and children.' Florence was equally determined. 'They're more my size.'

Annabel interposed, with marvellian truthfulness:

'She won't risk a tumble, Mr Leadbitter. It's a fundamental defect.'

'A grave one.' Mr Leadbitter became a wild bird again. 'Whatever she did would be A.1. Like Jane Austen, refusing to write a novel about the House of Coburg.'

'Nobody would want to read a novel about the House of Coburg.'

'And Jane Austen knew what she could, and couldn't, do,' added Florence, defiantly. 'She was a wise woman.'

'Take no notice, Mr Leadbitter. I can give you the entire explanation of this false modesty. Her father used to say "Don't get big ideas about yourself, Florence. These little sketches, very well as an amusement, won't get you a living. Stick to shorthand-typing." Well, he stuck to book-keeping, and died a nonentity. He was frightened of talent. So he ruined her character.'

'Bosh!' cried Florence.

Mr Leadbitter turned to Annabel.

'Did your father head you off the stage? He didn't succeed, apparently.'

'He couldn't have headed me off anything. But in any case he died before I was sixteen. I never told him I meant to act. I was artful. I played the part of a simple 'gairl'' who always got her sums right by a method he'd never learned. He checked and rechecked them — in vain. He was completely bamboozled. That's why I don't share Florence's humility. I'm ready to play all the big parts.'

'Yet you don't.'

'Very ungallant of you, Mr Leadbitter. I'm not allowed to. When I drop a hint about Cleopatra or Lady Teazle — I should be the ideal Lady Teazle — I admit Tragedy's not my love — the agents and producers say "Not this afternoon, darling; there's a small part going in some wretched farce. How about it?" I grind my teeth. I smile like the Mona Lisa. But, as I haven't got my *claque,* or rich manufacturer from the North to back me, I take the small part in the farce, which is always a flop. This is a hard world for actresses.'

'It's a hard world for us all,' agreed Mr Leadbitter, with solemnity. 'Otherwise I should be painting those frescoes myself.'

Afterwards, Annabel, greatly cheered by her lunch and company, said frankly to her sister:

'At any rate, old Michael Angelo Leadbitter doesn't repine, as I do.'

'You don't repine much,' answered Florence. 'You're resilient.'

'Well, *that's* true. *That's* true.' The compliment made Annabel feel indomitable. 'I'm like the man in the poem: "One who ever marched breastforward; never doubted clouds would break." You remember?'

'I remember.'

'I liked Michael Angelo. It's clear that he thinks well of you.'

'That's because he's not my sister.'

'I wondered how you'd like my little exposition. Not much, I gather. But he did; he can put work in your way; money in your pocket. That's all-important to us girls. I'm now absolutely on the rocks.'

'I'm very sorry. Come and stay with me for a while.'

'Oh, no; too boring. Old Bertha Pledge, and the Granny next door, stuffy! Besides, the bright lights are necessary to me. I haven't any resources in myself, as you have. Has it ever struck you, Flo, that you're really very enviable? I mean, in a small way.'

'I live with the thought. By the way, I met Syd Patterson the other morning.'

'My first love! How was he?'

'Noisy and jocular as ever; but he hasn't worn well, physically.'

'Hm.' Annabel was suddenly grave. 'I always felt that in my bones. I thought

"Yes, my boy; charming; but you're a dodger." What he needed was the guiding hand of — not so much a good woman as a strong-minded woman. You wouldn't have done, though he had a crush on you. Nor should I. Would you call me a good woman, Flo?'

'Off and on, yes.'

'Like you. Odd that we've neither of us married. Selfishness; fastidiousness; lack of opportunity? I never wanted to be an old maid. Nor did you. Yet look at us! Never mind; we had a good lunch today. I think I will come down and stay with you soon. You make me feel I'm a better woman than I thought.'

9
Last Minute Traveller

For Florence, the day had already been full of incident. The work she had taken to Mr Leadbitter had been approved. Necessary money would accrue. She had also, as usual, been diverted and stimulated by Annabel's chatter, with its undercurrents of sadness and unrealized hopes. Mr Leadbitter's rueful admission that he had once aspired to something loftier than Art Editorship had suggested further comparison of her own modest success with the dreams of others. And she had been reminded of her father.

Annabel's arraignment of him was only half-true. That poor little man, so anxious for the future subsistence of his beloved daughters, had indeed discouraged her from artistic ambitions; but she had the insight to interpret his warnings more charitably than Annabel had done. Thinking now of the atmosphere of a motherless home, through which the breadwinner had spread his own painful humility — and futility, — she returned to childhood, to girlhood, with warmer love for a virtuously unimaginative man. It was not, in his case, that any high hopes had been disappointed; he had simply, as a boy, accepted hard-working servitude as his lot; and he saw no prospect of anything but servitude for Annabel and herself.

Had she inherited his timidity? The fear that she had done so — aided by Annabel's charge — was depressing. It had its effect upon her actions that day and in subsequent hours of indecision.

Dusk was falling when she reached Paddington Station; and she sought an empty compartment in which to relish again the day's happiness, but not its doubts. If she could travel alone, she could count her blessings and be content for the remainder of the day. A lovely prospect!

The prospect was not to be fulfilled. Just as the train began to move, the sound of running footsteps was accompanied by raucous shouts of 'Stand away there! Stand away!' The door of the compartment was wrenched open. A panting young man flung himself within. As a porter slammed the door from the platform he stumbled against Florence, gasped an apology, and collapsed in the further corner of the opposite seat.

Her reverie destroyed, she did no more than glance quickly at the interloper, who seemed to be a boy, hatless, and oddly dressed in a lavender-coloured shirt, green corduroy trousers, and a jacket that looked as if it had been made of shark's skin.

That was all her glance revealed. The train jolted over points in the semi-darkness; and only when they were again under a clear sky did she see that her companion, no longer panting, was sitting upright and looking surreptitiously at her. He immediately averted his gaze, perhaps as much disappointed as herself at the company of a stranger.

How long must they be uncomfortably alone? As he sat still, and neither whistled nor produced some dreadful musical instrument, Florence strove to recapture the mood of solitude. In vain. It was of her father that she thought. Thomas Marvell, small and over-worried, must have known despair. He had done little, all his life, as Annabel said, but add up columns of figures; but he added those columns so devotedly that he was valued even by skinflint employers. His great troubles were poverty and the early loss of his wife, who had drowned before his eyes while swimming. They led to morbid concern for the welfare of two bewildering daughters.

He feared these daughters would marry scoundrels or drunkards, or, worse, become destitute spinsters. His nagging advice to Florence arose from inability to appreciate the charm and fun of her drawings. 'Be practical!' he urged. 'These little drawings are pretty enough, and clever, in their way; but they won't earn you a living. And I shan't always be here to look after you. It may be sooner than you think!'

'Shan't be here; shan't be here,' echoed the train wheels, settling to a steady rhythm. 'Shan't be here; shan't be here!' Florence closed her eyes in sudden exhaustion.

'I say!' cried a desperate voice. 'Excuse me! But would you very much mind if I spoke to you?'

She looked attentively at the boy for the first time. And although too mature to betray emotion by cry or movement she knew that her cheeks burned and that her heartbeat quickened. Just so had a young girl once responded to the sensation of falling in love. This — unmistakably — she had no doubt of it — was Roderick's son.

The shock was so great that she could not answer immediately; but, just in time, before silence could grow bleak, she heard a muffled voice, unrecognizable as her own say:

'Of course you may do so.'

He gave a long sigh of relief.

'You really don't mind? I know it's cheek; but I'm in such a terrible mess that I'm afraid I shall go mad if I don't tell somebody about it. I mean somebody kind, as I'm sure you are.'

The face she saw was ravaged by fear. Never had she experienced so strongly the impulse of compassion.

'Yes, I understand. Do tell me.'

In reply, the boy moved quickly along the seat, until he directly faced her; and still closer regard was possible. The resemblance to Roderick was extraordinary. But Roderick's mouth had never drooped so sensitively at the corners. Nor, although their eyes were of the same grey, had her companion's silver glint of concentrated mental activity which had made Roderick's magnetic. He was a less resolute character than his father, more imaginative, more tender, more easily driven to vehemence.

Nevertheless, almost magically, his despair had become less abject. His mouth straightened into something akin to

Roderick's attractive smile. He showed trust, and sweetness of nature. Florence leaned eagerly forward.

10
Florence Saves a Life

The train was moving smoothly through the north-western suburbs. Every now and then a gleam from the declining sun caught the carriage window and startlingly flushed the boy who struggled for words of explanation. He was unaware of the fact as he stammered an admission of his difficulty.

'I . . . don't . . . don't really know where to begin. I'm afraid of . . .'

Florence, too, had experienced that paralysing doubt; and had conquered it.

'Don't hurry. Sometimes, I know, the right words won't come. They do come, in the end, though, if you're sure they'll be understood. I suggest you begin by telling me your Christian name. Would that help? It would help me.'

'Oh, my Christian . . . It's Saul.'

'Thank you. I shall think of you as Saul. My name is Florence Marvell. You can feel straightaway that we're acquainted; but of course only as much acquainted as you need for our — talk.'

The name, because her drawings were made for children, meant nothing to an adolescent whose childhood was farther away than it would be in later life; but her mention of it, with the promise that she would not force inquisitiveness or any claim upon him, was effective. Words rushed to his lips.

'It's awfully kind of you. I do appreciate it. As if we were friends. Some people freeze me. I just shut up, and feel idiotic. I knew you wouldn't do that. It's something in your face. I can't explain. My only fear is that, having understood, you'll . . . think less of me; despise me. But I don't think you will.'

Florence, warm towards him, smiled.

'No, I couldn't do that.' She did

not tell him why.

With a tremendous effort, he embarked upon his story.

'Well, then, it's this. Some time ago — four or five months — I met a man — an older man — not old; middle-aged; perhaps fifty. We sat next to each other at a concert. They'd been playing something tremendous; it might have been Beethoven — no, I think it was Berlioz; his Fantastic Symphony. . . . We talked about it — awfully enthusiastically. Left the hall together. Had supper at a restaurant. It was wonderful for me. He seemed familiar with all music, with all the books I liked, and all the painters. You know; Chekhov; Pizarro; and especially Berlioz. I felt we'd known each other for years.'

He groaned, choked, flushed.

'I realize now that he must have been laughing at me all the time — my callowness — silliness. I was garrulous, thinking what an impression of good taste I was making; thinking myself clever. He encouraged me to do that. It was easy. If you're lonely, you get to think how much better you are than the people who don't appreciate you. Other fellows are interested in politics, games, girls, betting, drinking. I'm not. At school I was always treated as a softy. Perhaps I am one? That's one of the humiliations — I mean, the after-discoveries.'

'You had no friend at all at school?' asked Florence. 'That's unusual, isn't it?'

'I know. It's quite true. I've never had one. I wasn't good at football, and I thought cricket was a bore. I expect it was my fault. But when you're packed off to school, and find yourself a sort of odd man out —'

Florence, instinctively recognizing self-pity, which she detested, checked him.

'Not as extraordinary as you suppose. We're all odd men out.'

His attention was caught.

'You?' It was incredulous. 'You don't look —'

'Oh, yes. But I was lucky. I had — still have — a younger, and very affectionate, sister.'

The sensitive face flushed again.

'My sister's older. She never had any use for me. Nobody's ever really taken any interest in me — until this man —'

'Ah! The man! He's the one you want to tell me about.'

Saul shuddered. She heard his teeth chatter. He had been recalled from momentary forgetfulness of the more urgent dilemma.

'Yes, the man,' he muttered; following the words with an exclamation — 'I must hurry; or you'll be getting out. Or sick to death of me!'

'I shan't be,' said Florence. 'Have no fear.' Indeed, her loving imagination of the lad's torment almost led her to add: 'Our destination is the same; and if necessary you shall finish the story in my cottage — however long it takes.'

His response was a flush of gratitude.

'Oh, that's wonderful! I feel . . . But the man . . . We got awfully friendly. Chiefly, we talked about music; and went to several concerts together — he getting the tickets so that we could sit together as we'd done the first time. He seemed to share my preferences — for Berlioz, as I said, and older composers such as Vivaldi and Monteverdi. Those are the ones I really love, people with faith; they do me good. Then, one time, he asked me to his flat near Marble Arch, a beautiful place full of pictures, a grand piano, and foreign books that I'd never heard of before. He'd read them all — a linguist. We talked the whole evening; and he gave me a lot of advice . . .

'I thought it was wise advice; but I remember now that he was slipping in questions all the time — what did I want to be? To do? Naturally, I blurted out — all sorts of things. Things I hadn't been able to tell anybody before. Things about Father and Mother — I didn't say who they were — I thought it would make him appreciate me as an anonymous individual. But I found he already knew who my father and mother were. I ought to have seen that from the first. He hadn't been deceived by my — call them subterfuges — they were concealments of the fact that Father was a well-known man, as he is . . .

'That's one of my troubles — my discouragements. I think all sons of well-known men . . . However, that's not what I want to tell you about. I only mention it because he sprang a surprise on me by showing he'd been enjoying my simplicity in pretending to be a sort of orphan. It was galling . . .

'After that, we got on to the subject of independence. Wouldn't I like to be independent of Father; of family ties? I said it was my desperate ambition. He said he'd recognized it quite early in our friendship; and the first thing to have, to secure it, was money. Without money, nobody could be independent. He wasn't a rich man himself; but he knew exactly how I felt, and exactly what to do — to enable me to get money.'

The narrative was again checked by a stiffening of the limbs and a trembling of the sensitive lips. This last, for Florence, was the most painful of all signs; for although Roderick's lips had not trembled in weakness they had been equally sensitive in forming the eloquent phrases which she loved to hear. She saw the boy's eyes close as he struggled to concentrate his thoughts. Just so had the young

Roderick's eyes closed with the same object. Had Saul been at her side she would have pressed his hand in consolation as she had pressed the hand of his father in delight.

Neither perceived that the train was now running through open country, with meadows speckled here and there by single buildings unidentifiable in the darkness and by lights both stationary and in motion. For both, the world had narrowed to a small railway compartment.

'Get money. That was essential. He called it "playing the market," meaning to buy shares that would appreciate in value. He was to advise; I was to buy. When I said I hadn't any money to spend in the first place, he laughed. It was the easiest thing possible, he said, to get that. Didn't I want to be independent? Of course I said I did. Well, we would raise the money. All I had to do was to sign a few papers that he would guarantee. He was my friend, wasn't he? . . .

'I thought he was my friend. By that time I was completely besotted. I'd have signed anything. D'you see what I mean?'

'I guess,' said Florence, full of concern.

Suddenly she was alarmed by an hysterical outburst.

'Oh, God! Oh, God! I can't bear it!'

It was evident that in this surge of excitement he was ready to tear open the carriage door and fling himself into the unknown.

'Saul! Stay where you are!' she cried, starting up, throwing herself to his side, and seizing his hand.

As if awakening to consciousness that another person was now involved in his suffering, the boy turned a wild gaze to herself, staring quickly, but by degrees growing calmer. But in this calm Florence read another danger, the capacity for deliberate, as opposed to impulsive, self-destruction.

'You mustn't think of it!' she screamed. 'It's evil!'

He had heard, and understood.

'I've frightened you,' he said in a different tone. 'I didn't mean to do that. I've no right. I'm sorry. I was just . . .

thinking. Thinking aloud, I suppose. As you must have guessed — I've made it plain — the fellow was a scoundrel.' Desperation returned. He snatched away his imprisoned hand, laying it upon hers a moment later. 'You're so kind. And he . . . Oh, my God! The humiliation of it! Grotesque! What I'm telling you is what I know *now*. It was different then. . . .'

Words came at great speed as he understood the intensity of her sympathy. He half-smiled, with almost doglike trust.

'I had to sign papers — printed forms — all sorts of things. He practically guided my hand! At every turn we had to have more money. More. More. I see he was in a sort of fever. Gambler's fever. He kept saying "It's quite all right. Quite all right. I know what I'm doing." Money must be borrowed. All very simple. No delay. No complication. Everything would be achieved in a week — in a fortnight — three weeks at most. And he had good friends; friends in the business. They would understand. They would help. That was what they were there to do. You see? He introduced me to them. Jolly, hand-rubbing men . . .

'They understood all right. They were his friends. All Christian names. I never heard the others. I wasn't a minor, was I? No, he knew I'd had my twenty-first birthday several weeks ago. Splendid! Splendid! So we made marvellous plans. They grew finer and more ambitious. And of course I felt absolutely on top of the world; I even — for the first time in my life — had considerable sums of money in my pocket: he took care of that. It was all a part of the . . . I felt wonderfully rich — and independent; — thinking I was showing everybody that I knew my way about. . . .

'Then, a week ago, he was arrested. The police came to see me. Quiet men. Not in uniform. Not threatening or hostile. But asking terrible questions. My castle came tumbling down. They told me they'd been watching him for months, waiting for the inevitable slip. What I was involved in was only one of his adventures. I wasn't being charged with anything *yet;* but must expect a lot more questioning. Any passport? No, no passport. Right. They knew who my father was. I said, "Oh, for God's sake don't go to him!" They said, "For the present, no," and just looked at me, expressionless. They said they were sorry; but evidently they thought I knew more than I pretended. Couldn't imagine I was such a fool as I'd been. The shock, the uncertainty, the feeling that I couldn't convince them, or escape —'

Once more, overwhelmed by his sensations, he was forced to stop. Florence heard a single gasping sob. She looked in agitation at the carriage doorhandle, in case his hand should stretch convulsively towards it.

Both, struggling, would be thrown to the line, Death, lacerated and terrible, would follow. The imagination made her feel sick.

Seconds passed; fear receded; quick thought was again possible to her. Roderick: how could he have allowed this to happen? He was humane; he was a man of honour; his sense of responsibility was tremendous . . . And — like a vicious flame — came thought of Roderick's wife.

How could this boy's mother have ignored such potential tragedy? Surely she must have seen it? Saul should have told his story to her, and not to a stranger. Whatever sort of a mother could she be? A heartless demon?

Memory returned of the tall woman who had coolly praised her daffodils. The praise had been bestowed while a son was being driven to madness by realization of a trusted friend's perfidy. However poised and self-assured her public manner might be, one must assume that she loved Saul, the child of her body, and was capable of suffering with him. And yet . . . And yet . . .

Helplessness was an emotion unfamiliar to Florence. It now oppressed her almost to despair. She watched Saul's trembling lips, the jerking hands, the return of wildness to his expression; and she was shaken by more than fear for the moment. Other, older, self-accusing thoughts attacked her. Unversed in all but the intimations of love and the delight of laughing invention, she was roused to excitement never before known.

Saul, however, after that collapse, seemed to recover. His eyes no longer sought the dangerous doorhandle. Though his face remained white, he must have been strengthened by the relief of having told his story.

'You see?' he asked. "All this has been working in my mind for a week. I haven't been able to sleep. And the worst of it was that I had nobody to tell. Not a soul who would understand. Then, when I looked at you, so quiet, so — oh, I don't know — somehow — kind — kind — I couldn't resist the temptation. I know I oughtn't to have done it; but when one's at the end of everything, ashamed and afraid, one thinks only of one's self. You wouldn't know that. You've never been ashamed or afraid . . . And you've listened so patiently. If you hadn't, I can't imagine what I should have done. Probably thrown myself on the line. Ended everything.'

'Never do that!' cried Florence, so fiercely that the boy was visibly shocked by her unexpected change of manner. He flushed like a schoolgirl, staring at her as he might have done at a Prosecuting Counsel. 'No fear, no humiliation, could justify such cowardice. It would be base. Do you understand? A wretched cruelty to those who love you.'

He was contemptuous.

'Who are they?' he demanded.

'You say you're of age. You have fifty years to live, splendid, exquisite years —'

'Splendid? Good God! If I'm sent to prison?'

'Even if you were —'

'You can't understand what public disgrace means to somebody like me!'

'I understand very well. I also understand what shame it would bring to your father. Have you never thought of him?

'In his ivory tower!'

'In his great position. After a lifetime of noble integrity.' She again ignored a cry of protest, continuing: 'What you must do — you're going home now, I suppose?'

'I don't know where I shall go.' He became hysterical. 'I tell you I don't know what to do.'

'Then I'll tell you. Go home now. Go straight to your father. Tell him everything you've told me — exactly as you've told it to me. He'll know at once how to help —'

'Hoh!' The boy again flushed deeply. 'He'd simply say: "You've brought this on yourself. Now get out of it yourself." '

'He will say nothing of the kind, Saul. And you know it.'

Their bitter glances met; and while Florence, under an air of restraint, was hot with the struggle to recover calm, Saul's pallor returned. He looked quickly away, muttering almost inaudible words. . . .

'You don't know my Father.'

These words were more than she could bear in silence. In a voice strained with suppressed agony, she savagely answered:

'I know him, evidently, better than you do!'

'Have you ever seen him?'

'More than seen.' She was trembling as violently as Saul had done earlier.

'But . . . but . . . you can't possibly understand his character.'

'None better — except your mother.'

'Oh God! My mother! You don't know *her,* either. *She* wouldn't help.'

He rocked to and fro, in an agony of resistance; and at sight of that resistance, falling suddenly in love with him, Florence lost all wisdom, all self-control.

'Listen!' she cried, urgently. 'I know your father's mind, his heart. I know he can and will help you, as nobody else could do. I know. I know. If I hadn't been an obstinate fool, I might have *been* your mother!'

She pressed back, eyes closed and heart beating as if it would burst. She was appalled at her folly in betraying, to a stranger, however beloved he might be, not only herself, but Roderick.

11
Good Advice

Saul at first appeared to be paralyzed by this extraordinary declaration. His mouth fell open. Amazement, incredulousness, belief, and again amazement were all evident to her outflowing tenderness. His head jerked with each impulse. His fists clenched. On partial recovery from shock he spoke in passionate longing.

'You? Oh, God, how I wish you had been!'

He saw her for the first time, not as a stranger who had listened with sympathy to his abject confession, but as one very dear. Doubt of his father's understanding still confused him; the words to express a new relation could be no more than stammered.

'I . . . I . . . don't know what to say; how to tell you —'

Florence, with an effort, recovered.

'I ought not to have said that. It was very wrong. I did it only because you *must* do what's right. You don't understand your father. I do; and I know that because of his love for you —'

'No love! No love!'

'Love. It couldn't be otherwise. . . . He's the one person in the world who can help you. Absolutely trustworthy. He'll tell you just what to do.'

She heard a faint despairing murmur.

'I haven't the guts.'

'You have the guts to do anything you make up your mind to. You wouldn't be his son if it were otherwise.'

Silence. At last.

'I daren't.'

She became impatient, peremptory.

'You dare. You must. If you don't, I shall go to him myself.'

The boy was astounded. He tried again

to say 'I can't'; but the words were not spoken.

'That will be much worse. It will be repugnant to me, and it will put you in a bad light. You see that, don't you?'

She heard him mutter: 'Yes, I do. As a coward!' and understood the struggle taking place within him. Aloud, he stammered: 'I . . . I shouldn't . . . know how to begin.'

'Begin "Father" — or whatever you call him — "I'm in great need of advice and help." That will be enough.'

'He'll shut me up.'

'He'll remember that he wasn't always as experienced as he is now.'

'You mean, he was never as weak.'

'I didn't say that. I said he didn't always know what he knows now.'

'Is that why you're not my mother? Oh, it's incredible! You suggest you were a jilt. That's impossible.'

'No, I wasn't a jilt. I was a young girl, very much in love; but obstinate. He was an ambitious man; everything that was honourable in all his actions; but equally obstinate. Saul, do get this right, and go to him *at once.*'

She spoke firmly, looking straight into the boy's eyes with a mother's readiness to sacrifice her own happiness on his account. They were still face to face, and silent, when the light of a station platform flashed into the compartment. A single voice was shouting. They had reached their destination; and she knew in that moment that she had won the battle.

The train stopped without a jerk. All was smooth, composed as if there had been no combat. Allowing Saul to spring down first and offer a helping hand, she jumped to the platform, walked with him past a grave-faced ticket-collector, and out into the semi-darkness of the station yard. Her last words as Saul gripped and retained her hand were:

'Goodbye for the present, Saul. Think of me as your affectionate friend.'

'I do. Indeed I do.' She had withdrawn her hand, and he touched her elbow. 'I wish we hadn't to part.'

'We'll soon meet again. I live in the village, and am easily found. Then you'll be much happier and I shall be glad to see you happier. Meanwhile, don't tell your father it was I who advised you to come to him. He hates busybodies. So do I. Go of your own accord. I shall be thinking of you.'

'As if you were my mother!'

Florence stepped into the hired car from Slocumbe which stood waiting for her. She did not invite Saul to share it. She was thankful to be rid of an emotional boy who had made her heart ache and set her nerves on edge; and during the homeward journey she sat almost stupefied in the darkness. Only in familiar surroundings, when she had been ardently welcomed by William, her cat, did self-control lapse reaction. The day had been too exciting. She was convulsed by a single great sob.

PART FOUR

ADVERSE TIDE

12
Father and Son

The human mind, at first simple, gathers such complicated associations as the years pass that it becomes overcrowded. This is the reason why elderly men and women cannot immediately remember names or catch the meaning of what is said to them. They feel shame at decaying powers, when they should really be proud of mental opulence.

Roderick Patterson knew his superiority to other men in retentiveness of facts. He had at command a great mass of information. Unlike some barristers, he studied his briefs thoroughly before going into Court; and once there he never faltered. Nor did he forget any detail about his clients, past or present. His memory was like an index. In normal affairs he could talk with equanimity to Cabinet Ministers, Journalists, or Dons; to Blenkinsop, to his Political Agent Morton and his Clerk Hichens, to his wife, Evelyn, or the Chairman of any Committe or meeting he attended. He was never at a loss. What he lacked was imaginative insight into natures different from his own.

This fact explained the barrier between himself and Saul. Saul was impulsive, sensitive, inarticulate; and he thought at twice the speed possible to Roderick. But he had no judgment. Defensive before one whom he had always feared as a tall, unwelcoming stranger, and embarrassed by consciousness of his own intellectual inferiority to that man, he was wretched in his father's presence. They had no point of contact. If he had known of his Uncle Sydney's attitude to the same man, he would have found a helpful clue to his own feeling; but Syd's jaunty teasing of a sensitive child had long ere this been fatal.

'I *hate* Uncle!' was Saul's repressed cry. 'He despises me because I'm not as rough as he is. I'm not. I don't want to be. He stinks of whisky!'

Roderick, conning a brief, was surprised to hear heavy breathing. He put a finger on the brief, to mark the point he had reached in a statement of claim, and looked up. Saul, bent upon noiselessness, was shutting the study door behind him. Father and son were alone together, cut off by this action from the rest of the world.

As only the desk lamp was alight, Roderick could not at first see the boy's pallor; but he still heard the heavy breathing which seemed to contain the echo of a smothered sob. Any interruption of a train of thought was tiresome; so he frowned.

Immediately afterwards he dismissed the frown.

There must be a reason for this particular interruption; and he was never deliberately cruel. The brief was set aside; not pushed away in impatience nor with an air of boredom; but almost smilingly. . . . Roderick knew that witnesses in Court were sometimes made dumb by fear. He was skilled in the art of giving them confidence. 'Let me see if I can help you' was a phrase he often used. In this instance he substituted a more direct inquiry.

'Hullo, Saul. What brings you here? Come and sit nearer. Let me look at you.'

Saul's expression was one of desperate resolve. He tiptoed across the room and sat awkwardly, like a schoolboy visiting his headmaster for punishment. As Florence had done in the railway carriage, Roderick observed the signs in one glance — unsteady lips, averted eyes, clenched fists, rigidity of body. Evidently this was something very important indeed.

'Are you all right?' Roderick could not guess that his tone was, to Saul, astonishingly kind. Coming immediately after Florence's assurances, it brought tears to the boy's eyes; and Roderick, seeing the tears, was moved. Poor kid! 'Don't be afraid. Tell me the trouble.'

Saul had dreaded cold impatience or peremptoriness such as barristers affect in handling refractory witnesses. This kindness was a revelation: and he did not guess that, as yet, Roderick's sympathy, though not assumed, was that of a professional advocate. Roderick's legal manners were excellent. In consultation or conference they indicated reserves of strength; in Court, standing quite still, without distracting gesture, he used his beautiful voice and great variety of intonation to encourage trust and responsiveness.

The effect upon Saul was instant. His fear diminished. Sustained, furthermore, by the determination Florence had inspired, he stammered less than he had done in telling his story to her, feeling that she was at his side like a good angel. His thought was: '*She* understood, She told me *he* would understand: I mustn't let her down. I won't let her down!'

Roderick, always prepared for glibness, suspected two or three times in the early stages of narrative that he was hearing something previously rehearsed with a mentor; but Saul's occasionally frantic candour, revealed by hoarseness, caught his interest and conviction. He listened carefully.

The story ended. There was an exchange of steady glances. They were father and son, calm on the one side, trembling but thankful on the other. A few questions followed.

'What is the man's name? Did you never address him? He told you to call him "Dan": no surname at any time? What did the others, the money-lenders, call him? All Christian names? I see. Did you notice where their offices were? He was always conducting you, and talking — I suppose deliberately, to prevent note-taking. I should like to examine the documents you signed. They would have to be produced if any claim were made against you. Have you any idea of the total involved? None? Hundreds? Thousands? The man has been arrested for fraud: had you no suspicion that fraud was intended? What, exactly, did the Police say when they called on you? That was everything, was it?'

No moral judgment was expressed. Saul

was not denounced as a fool. As if in the hands of a medical specialist, he was quietly persuaded to amplify the details; and his explanations, although at times elucidated by supplementary questions, were received without comment. Finally, Roderick was satisfied that no part of the story had been rehearsed.

'Have you told anybody else about this?'

Saul caught his breath. He looked imploringly at his father.

'I should . . . I told a lady what trouble I was in. A lady I met on the train.'

'Somebody you knew?'

'No. A stranger. I was — well, I was worked up. Father, I promised I wouldn't mention her name. I must keep my promise.'

Roderick, half-amused and half-curious, replied courteously.

'Of course. You knew her name, did you?'

'Yes, she told me. She didn't tell me what to say. Only that I must come to you at once; that you would understand. She didn't want to come into it because she said you hated busybodies — as she did.'

'Hm. An outspoken lady, evidently. Outspoken and sagacious — a rare combination.' But Roderick noted that mention of the lady was reviving latent hysteria in Saul. 'We needn't bother about her name. At this stage it's not important. I shan't press you!' Although noting the fact that the mysterious unknown claimed a characteristic in common, he continued smoothly: 'Yes, you did well to come. These things should always be brought into the open as soon as possible. You'll certainly feel happier — less alone. Well, now, we shall have to have another talk — tomorrow or the day after. Meanwhile, I'll consider what you've told me. Probably consult Munster, the best solicitor I know, who will find out all he can about "Dan" and his friends, and advise on the best course to follow. I know him to be both competent and discreet. You'd like me to consult him, would you?'

'Thankful' was the only word Saul could utter.

'Good. Now get off to bed. Have a

good night's rest, if you can. I imagine you haven't been sleeping too well. I've got to work late on something altogether different.' He touched the brief before him, and smiled. 'But I shan't forget you — or the kind friend who said I hated busybodies — as she does.'

Saul could not remember that his father had ever before offered a cordial handshake; and after his own wild grab at fingers which were cool and firm he stumbled confusedly from the room.

'Oh, thank God! Thank God! He was decent, wonderful! She was right! My *Mother!*'

13
Husband and Wife

Alone once more, Roderick found that he could not resume the consideration of his brief. That, concerned with a problem of Company Law in which he was to appear for the Defence, needed precise attention; and it must wait for ten minutes or so. What was the time? Eleven o'clock? Well, the work had to be done. . . .

He passed in quick review the facts that his daughter and then his son were in dilemmas of their own creation, that his wife was in one of her more intractable moods, that his much-loved brother was going down hill, that several of his clients, under cross-examination, would probably say the very things they ought not to say, that his choleric Prime Minister, like other P.M.s, was a self-centred and evasive character with gleams of genius, that half-a-dozen men on his own side of the House, as well as many in Opposition, would be glad to see the impeccable Roderick Patterson discomfited, that after the weekend he had to plead a trivial case which might be wrecked by the perversity of his client and that Florrie Marvell, unfortunately, lived close at hand.

Florrie's nearness gave rise to a small train of relevant thought. She would be bound to travel from London, as Saul had done, by train. She and Saul could well have ridden together in the same compartment. She had long ago expressed disdain of 'busybodies.' These were all interesting links. Furthermore, the mysterious 'lady' had told Saul not to mention her name; but she had been able to persuade the boy to come at once to his father.

That showed will and — call it witchery. No ordinary woman would have bothered to rescue a frightened lad whom she was seeing for the first time. This one had intoxicated Saul with her wisdom. Obviously she could be none other than pig-headed Florrie Marvell, with her ridiculous sense of duty and her passion for self-sacrifice. How absurd! How characteristic!

But note the effect on Saul. He regarded his 'lady' almost as a celestial being, devoted to his salvation. How had Florrie managed to suggest that? What had prompted her? What, in her immaculate scorn of human weakness, did she think of Saul's abysmal folly?

'I can't answer such questions,' said Roderick. 'I can only put them.'

A man of different temperament would have resented these interferences with his professional business. He did not resent them. He was familiar with Evelyn's moods, unshockable by any instance of personal frailty, well acquainted with many types of avarice and unscrupulous chicane. If not imaginative, he had learned by sixty years of experience.

Though he had once been greatly

irritated by Florrie's perversity, he still saw her as one who insisted upon doing what she thought was right for others, even if it involved unhappiness for herself. He had found this cold-blooded; and he had made his conclusion clear to Florrie herself. She had been obstinate. Very well. But her insistence on right behaviour had impressed Saul as superhuman, as saintly.

Roderick did not love interference. Its application to himself, or a member of his family, seemed an impertinence. None the less, Florrie's kindness to his boy moved him more than Evelyn's moods or the follies of the two children. It came nearer to his heart.

Damn Florrie! He had been made to think of her after thirty years of near-forgetfulness. He recalled the first time they had been together in a seaside theatre, to a performance of *The Mikado;* and as he lived again that delicious evening, contrasting Florrie with Evelyn, and smiling grimly as he did so, he found himself humming a little tune from the Opera:

'If that is so,
    Sing derry down derry!
It's evident, very,
    Our tastes are one.
Away we'll go,
    And merrily marry,
    Nor tardily tarry
    Till day is done!'

Simple pleasures! Evelyn had no use for Gilbert and Sullivan. Her musical taste was for Bach, and, in Opera, the *Ring*. Well? On his part some tasteful endurances of the *Ring,* which he found and endless bore, had enabled him to consider many a legal argument. He preferred Rossini to either Bach or Wagner. But he did not say this to Evelyn. Nor did she comment on his closed eyes during *Siegfried*. She was an intelligent woman.

Florrie and Evelyn had never met. They were now bound to meet as neighbours, however unequal their positions in the world. Of course, any intimacy between them was improbable. Both would be unsympathetic, Evelyn as a great lady, and

Florrie as one to whom greatness in ladies was a pomposity. The advantage of experience would be with Evelyn; but Florrie, owing to prior knowledge of himself, would have the situation well in hand.

Conflict between them was as undesirable as it was unlikely. If it came, Evelyn would resent and misunderstand his association with a social and intellectual inferior. Brought up in the *monde,* she would at once assume that Florrie was, or had been, his mistress. She would not be ostentatiously rude; she would be gallingly distant. And Florrie, ungalled, would in return show no rudeness to Evelyn, because Florrie was never rude to anybody.

Both remarkable women. Both charming, sincere, and of decided character; the one simple, the other complex. Florrie's simplicity had first attracted him to her. She was like a child in spontaneity; and her laughter at others was always free from spitefulness. She was a pet. Evelyn also was free from spitefulness; but the lack arose from pride.

She had no fun. Humour, yes, of a restricted kind; a strong sense of loyalty; a shrewd awareness of her own limitations; but even in the matter of sex full of secrecy. Florrie? Florrie was an unsolved enigma. He did not understand the springs of her nature.

Still speculating about that nature, Roderick began to hum the song about merry marriage from *The Mikado*.

Evelyn had never heard him sing or hum. She knew that, when speaking in public, he used an effective variety of tone; but if she had been asked whether her husband was 'musical' she would have replied: 'He listens *attentively* to Bach; but I think he appreciates the mathematical element in music rather than its fundamental quality. No, on the whole *not* musical. The legal mind, you know.'

While making this distinction, she would have smiled indulgently. When she smiled at all, she was always indulgent. More often, she was grave. The eldest of three beautiful sisters, she had been forced by her mother's sudden collapse in health to take the lead in household affairs; and on their father's re-marriage to a goodhumored vulgarian the three sisters, silently rebellious, determined to escape from home as soon as they could do so.

The younger ones continued rebellious; but Evelyn, falling in love with Roderick, found a new purpose in life. This handsome young soldier was not only charming and good to look upon; he had brains and eloquence. Her father expressed a rather quizzical admiration for him. Her aunt, worldly wise, murmured in Evelyn's ear: 'With the proper wife, that young man might become Prime Minister.' To a heart already radiant, such words were a positive injunction. Aided by her aunt and other hostesses, who made so much of Roderick that he enjoyed a hero's welcome everywhere, Evelyn did not fail. She had beauty, wealth, and social position. She was indeed the proper wife for a potential leader of men.

Roderick had gratified her by becoming very distinguished indeed. Evelyn worked with proud energy to that end, entertaining the great who could be useful in his career, and tolerating their vanities and their wives even when she detested either or both. Repressed and always hidden sensuality was stirred by his manliness; and she continued to love her chosen husband without regrets. Her reward for effort and self-control was an absolute freedom from sexual humiliation.

Being easily bored, she did not much care for reading. Great poetry called for too much effort, and verse was trivial. Novels, if she was told they were first class, were skimmed for conversation's sake; otherwise they seemed a waste of time. 'Life's too short for imitations of the real thing,' she said; 'and it's the real thing that excites me.' The real thing could only be enjoyed at second hand if it chanced to be the biography of a notable woman.

She enjoyed listening to classical music, which at its best soothed and stimulated. She also relished pictures, and saw with remarkable acumen whatever promise young artists showed before they were generally acclaimed. The artists were quietly included in her larger parties; and, although rarely grateful, often owed to her their first steps to fame.

Her chief pleasure, however, lay in public life. Though her success here was less conspicuous than Roderick's, it had its satisfactions. Women's Societies rejoiced in securing her patronage; Bazaars were as familiar to her as Supermarkets are to humbler shoppers, and in opening them she spoke charmingly. Her smaller London parties, in which she mingled celebrities in the Arts with legal and political men of note, were almost always successful. Tact and resource inspired their composition; while, being tall, still slim, and naturally dignified, she was an august hostess.

Asked whether she was happy, she would shrug her shoulders, responding: 'Who is, in this noisy, unspiritual world? I should have preferred to live in France before the Revolution, when my dear Madame de Sévigné was at her best.' She thus dismissed happiness and current manners with authoritative detachment. 'One can't discuss such things as if they were positives.'

'Very *ancien régime,*' said Evelyn's detractors. 'All the same, she'd miss her creature comforts, such as plumbing, baths, and cars. Nor would she have enjoyed riding in a tumbril.'

This sort of thing is easily said; and Evelyn was no sybarite. She was neither greedy nor censorious. She enjoyed the company of her own sex, and had never seen a man she preferred to Roderick. 'Roderick was always my destined partner. I knew it at our first meeting. As a result, our marriage has been a success. We both lead full and independent lives, as wife and husband should do.'

Her statements were all true, and she was convinced of their accuracy; but the truth was not in them. At the moment she was fiercely at war with Roderick, and for almost the first time, with life itself. Life had taken an unpleasant turn. Evelyn hated unpleasant turns. Because under the composed manner, which some mistook for overweening arrogance, she was an emotional woman, they gave her headaches severe enough to be called attacks of *migraine*. Her temples throbbing, therefore, and with a sensation of nausea, she rested this day in her bedroom with every curtain drawn.

She was not evading the conflict with Roderick which she knew to be inevitable; she was really ill. A complete removal from one house and district to others as yet unexplored had drained her strength. Sandra's behaviour, which she had defended, was something full of menace to peace, to social prestige, and to the future. Roderick's warnings had been unwelcome because she recognized their truth.

Sydney's restlessness and rudeness to herself, both long familiar, would normally have been borne with indifference; but in present circumstances they were an outrage. And Saul's unexpected arrival home, shivering and starting at every sound, moodily looking at her as if in horror, produced further disquiet. Added to Roderick's obvious distaste for Sandra's conduct, and his silent charge that she was responsible for it, seemed like punishments for sins which she was not conscious of having committed.

'I'm too busy, too tired, too unwell to be persecuted in this way. The children are both idiotic, full of themselves, like all modern juveniles. They want freedom to do as they please; and when they run into difficulties they come home — to have them cleared up. Ridiculous! Completely irresponsible! If one could knock their heads together —'

The word 'heads' heightened the pain in her own head. It became so acute that she groaned. Ghastly! She had never known such crushing agony. Lying in the darkness, busy with anger and helplessness, she longed for oblivion.

14
The Snapshot

Oblivion had come, for Evelyn, in drug-induced and consequently heavy sleep. She awoke, still hot-lidded and leaden-hearted, to find Roderick in her bedroom, overcoated as if he proposed to leave the house at once. He had come quietly into the room, wanting to communicate with her, but reluctant to disturb a sick sleeper.

Checking a moan with proud stoicism, Evelyn drowsily asked what had happened. Roderick came nearer.

'I have to go to London at once,' he said hurriedly. 'I didn't want to rouse you; but Morton has just phoned. The P.M.'s had a stroke. They're keeping it quiet; but Morton thinks I should be at hand. So I've called Blenkinsop, who's having his breakfast; and we shall be off in about two minutes.'

Her mind confused by illness, Evelyn could not at first understand what she had been told. When Roderick repeated his explanation she struggled to seem as practical as she usually was.

'A stroke? Yes, I heard you say that. But if he's ill you can't do anything, can you? You're not a doctor.'

'Only be there if I'm wanted.'

'Why "wanted"? It's not as if you were in the Cabinet.'

'In some circumstances, I might be.'

'Oh, I see. Yes, the Cabinet. He may die, I suppose. He's rather old; that fat neck. Would there have to be a General Election?'

'I hope not. If there were, we should probably be out.'

'Wretched creatures!' She meant, not only the Opposition, but the vast body of ignorant electors who, because they could put crosses against names on a ballot paper, had the power to bring down one ramshackle Government in favour of another, still more ramshackle. With a

150

further effort, she demanded: 'Are you really likely to get anything?'

'Very doubtful: they'll probably call in Temple, who'll be afraid to make any changes.'

'Why Temple? He's no good.'

'In an emergency, a nonentity is the inevitable choice. He'll hold the reins while the others get busy with their jockeying. The real fight will come if the old man does die.'

'You'd rather have Sam Wrekin, I know.'

'Sam has no chance. He's too straight, and too proud to stoop to the sort of thing that would go on.'

'So are you.'

'I'm not in the Cabinet, as you said. Sam is. He'll never get a vote. If things are serious, Plowman will win hands down. He's a master of all the arts, and if he's in, there will be nothing for me.'

'Detestable man! Dishonest pusher. And she's as bad as he is.'

'Nevertheless, he's the ablest of a poor lot. And with her help he's collected quite a retinue of expectant friends.'

'You mean paltry toadies. Not one of them thinks of the country.'

Evelyn's head was full once more of darting pains. She could hardly restrain a moan of distress. In this agony she recurred to something personal.

'I wanted to ask you: What is the matter with Saul?'

'Callowness. A confidence trickster. While I'm in town I'll see Munster.'

Who was Munster? Why had he to be "seen"? Roderick was too cryptic to be understood. Evelyn moved convulsively.

'But what am *I* to do?'

'Get better. Nothing else. Now I must go. I'll keep in touch.'

He bent over, and kissed her lips. Evelyn, already distraught, was moved to clasp his head fiercely in her arms, so that their cheeks were pressed together. It was a rare betrayal of possessive love, of desperate reliance upon his strength. A moment later, comforted yet comfortless, she was alone with yet another problem to agitate a tortured mind.

Within two hours, having tried and failed to eat the breakfast which Rhoda, her maid, who rustled as she walked, had brought on a tray, Evelyn rose and took her bath. The hot water soothed her, and by degrees the sight of many iridescent soap bubbles captured her interest. She watched them as a child might have done, being led thereafter to take pleasure in the whiteness of her arms and body. Here was no sign of illness or decay! By the time she was dressed, reassurance had come again. Her head no longer ached.

'I'm better! I'm well! As Roderick commanded! The obedient wife!' As a wife, she remembered their parting kiss, which reminded her of former passionate embraces. 'I'm a wife first of all! I don't want to see either child. Both dislikable, tiresome, selfish, unloving. Saul has always been half-savage, like some oaf from the slums! He'll be on his way to the Devil, like Sydney, unless he pulls himself together. Wretched boy!'

Casting aside the unpleasant subject, and craving fresh air, she decided to walk.

But the grounds were too rough for thin-soled shoes, and Slocumbe was not a place for the sophisticated diversions she preferred. Glittering sunshine suggested the mass of daffodils seen the other day in that cottage garden. They would now be in full bloom, solacing in their purity. She would stroll that way, confirm her expectation, and make closer acquaintance with a delicious aspect of this interesting, and as yet unfamiliar, village.

So while Roderick, who had been surprised at an unexpected resurgence of his wife's passion, was arriving in London, bent upon learning at first hand how the Prime Minister's stroke had affected Party Leaders and his own prospects, Evelyn walked alone down the Manor's gravelled drive, along a broad country lane, and, by way of Slocumbe's one shopping street, towards the admired garden at the villiage's farther end.

Yes, as she had imagined them, the daffodils were a blaze of gold. They were visible from a distance, so beautiful beyond the little gate that she drew a quick breath of pleasure. Furthermore, behind the daffodils was the little dwelling compared by Sandra to the witch's cottage in *Hansel and Gretel*. It was very small, containing perhaps only four rooms with lattice windows. Quite unpretentious, though she doubted if its occupant was the old crone of Sandra's fancy. An old crone would not have halted the decay of crumbling walls, and would have grown vegetables, rather than daffodils, in the garden. Ah, but this garden extended round the cottage. Evelyn felt that one must make some inquiry about the mysterious person who lived there.

She had not reached the end of her quest when she saw the front door of the cottage open and two people appear from within. To her astonishment one of these people was Saul; the other, no crone, but a small, slim woman whom she at first took to be a girl. Saul — a girl — what did that mean? Evelyn instinctively drew aside, into the gateway of a larger house, less for the sake of concealment than from a wish not to be thought prying.

She was, however, partially concealed,

and her curiosity was so great that she looked long at the pair. They were talking ernestly, and Saul was looking down into the girl's face. No, she was evidently not a girl; her expression was that of one who had conquered all the immaturities of girlhood. How old? In her forties, perhaps, in spite of the youthful carriage of her head and the slim shoulders.

'Dangerously attractive to a boy,' Evelyn decided. And as she looked with new suspicion she was aware of something familiar in the women's face. Had they met at some party in London? No, she felt sure they had never spoken together. Only the face was in some way known to her. How could that be?

The two were parting at the gate. Quite idyllic against the old cottage and the daffodils! Would they kiss? No, the woman held out her hand, which Saul took in both of his own as he spoke eager words of farewell. Then, raising his hat, he moved quickly away in his mother's direction. The woman, smiling, stood by the gate for a moment before shutting it and returning to the cottage; while Saul, with a look of radiance imcomprehensible to Evelyn, walked away like on entranced.

'Saul!' cried Evelyn, sharply, as he was about to pass her.

Saul stopped. Radiance disappeared.

'Mother?'

'I'm taking a walk. I've just caught sight of you.' There was almost self-excuse in Evelyn's tone; but she immediately recovered, and became imperious. 'Do you know the person who lives in that cottage? Who is she?'

Radiance, if diminished, returned to Saul's eyes.

'She's my friend. My true friend.'

'But you've never been here before. Where did you meet her?'

'On the train.' Saul was far away, in a dreamland of memory. As Evelyn began to walk homeward he fell into step beside her. 'She's wonderful! Wonderful!' The word was raptly, not extravagantly, pronounced. It came as an unwelcome shock to his mother.

'Yes; but who is she?'

'She's an artist. She was at work. I saw some of her pictures.'

'An artist, eh? That explains the daffodils. But I still don't understand how you came to know her. What is her name?'

'I forget. Oh, it's Marvell, I think. I don't know. Yes, it's Marvell. She speaks of her work as if it were nothing; but it's perfectly delicious.'

'Like her daffodils. She evidently has taste. But you seem extraordinarily enthusiastic. What made you go and see her?'

'I felt I had to. She was so kind. So understanding.'

Evelyn's head was aching again. An artist. 'Wonderful . . . so kind . . . understanding.' Was the woman — or girl — a trickster, ready to take advantage of a simpleton? But surely she could not hope to find in Saul, who had no money, a buyer for some wretched daub?

'How was she kind to you?'

'She let me talk to her. Tell her things. She advised me what to do.' Saul's arms rose in impatience at his mother's questioning — exactly, although she did not know it, as Evelyn's would have done in like circumstances. 'Oh, I can't explain.'

Evelyn instantly added the words 'to you.' As earlier sickness returned, she pressed her lips together and quickened her step. Haughtily angered by the feverish praise of another woman, a stranger, she was in no state to listen further.

The rest of the homeward journey was made in silence, on Saul's part dreamy, on Evelyn's quelling.

While walking, she returned again and again to her glimpse of the slender woman at the gate, so young-looking, so quietly smiling, and with the carriage of good breeding. The sense that she had seen that tranquil face before made her sharply envious. Saul, it was plain, would say nothing helpful about his 'friend.' Probably he was ignorant of everything about her. They had fallen into conversation in a railway carriage; the woman had listened to some sort of rant; and Saul, in gratitude, had become infatuated.

So much was evident; but there was more in the relation than that. There must be a warm feeling upon both sides. Evelyn had seen the parting. Saul's fervent respect, even love, had been unquestionable. Only kindness had been given in return. The woman must be one of those sentimentalists who suffer fools gladly.

What was the name? Marvell? An artist: wasn't she in some way associated with little coloured drawings of animals? Quite inconsiderable. Such a person might well describe herself as an artist; but of course she would have no standing among real artists. They would laugh at her pretensions. Perhaps she didn't draw animals at all.

'I must make inquiries,' was Evelyn's conclusion. 'She may be — the cottage and the daffodils, suggest that — quite interesting, in a small way. I wonder why I feel I've seen her before?'

She continued to search for the occasion; and suddenly memory came with such force that she stopped abruptly, disturbing Saul's dream. Though her head was still racked, she ignored pain in the excitement of her discovery. She had never once seen this woman in the flesh. What she had seen was a photograph, an enlarged snapshot; and Miss, or Mrs, Marvell had been standing in that photograph much as she had done a few minutes ago when Saul held her hand, stammering a farewell. Slim shoulders erect, her hair slightly ruffled by a breeze, and a smile — more mischievous than it had been today — lighting a face that one would call extremely pretty rather than beautiful. Yes, evidently this was the same person.

Evelyn's conviction did not relieve her head of its increasing pain. It added to her discomfort. For the photograph she remembered was amongst some old and apparently treasured papers of Roderick's which she had sorted and arranged, quite lately, before the removal from Dorset to Slocumbe. At sight of it she had felt a peculiar stab of interest. Why?

The girl must evidently have been somebody known to Roderick; somebody whose likeness, for some reason, he had preserved; but somebody of whom she had

161

never heard. Why was that? Evelyn had met a number of Roderick's early friends, most of whom she had dropped because they did not 'belong.' But this girl had never appeared. She must have been — the words were used without animus — deliberately suppressed. She was not a sister; Roderick had only the tiresome brother, Sydney. A mistress? It was possible, although Roderick was no Lovelace. He had given no sign of disloyalty during their married life. Why, then, keep the photograph?

Pride had forbidden any direct question. The snapshot was returned without comment to the old leather portfolio in which it had been found. Before that, however, Evelyn had closely examined every feature of the smiling face, until it became familiar for ever. 'I should know that girl anywhere,' she told herself. 'Anywhere; and in any dress.'

The prophecy was true. Having watched Saul's farewell to the woman at the gate, and heard his outburst of enthusiasm for her, Evelyn experienced new doubts. Did Roderick know she was in Slocumbe? Had he kept secretly in touch with her for all these years? Why had everything suddenly become unbearable?

Migraine returned. The pain was so head-rending that Evelyn caught at Saul's arm for support in overwhelming dizziness; and the sense that he flinched distastefully from the contact increased her agony.

15
Politics

Roderick's Agent, Tom Morton, was waiting for him in the lofty drawing-room of the Patterson London home. He jumped up from an armchair to greet his employer; very short, thin, grey-haired, and evidently preoccupied with great matters. There was no handshake; their relations, though not formal, were marked on both sides by a kind of familiar distance.

Morton prided himself so deeply on discreetness that his remarks, usually spoken as if between clenched teeth, were too brief for outsiders to follow. He seldom pronounced a name, but jerked out 'he' or 'she' after a hum which seemed to come from the back of his throat, and whenever possible he omitted a definite article. *'Him . . . other day . . . No good, sir. Nothing there.'*

This morning he could not say 'the Prime Minister'; but made a little noise, accompanied by a significant glance or shrug, to indicate an invisible person who might have been in an adjoining room. His lips did not open. *'He,'* with special emphasis, was in Morton's view somebody godlike. Political journalists, bent upon catching every hint, would have guessed that he meant the Prime Minister; but they always called Morton 'Mute,' sometimes 'Pretentious Mute,' and sometimes 'Dumbo.'

Unknown to Morton, this discretion was unfortunate for Roderick. Roderick's air of intense concentration also harmed him with those who prefer geniality, false or calculated, to reserve. No affectionate little paragraphs about his idiosyncracies appeared in the press; caricaturists could not seize upon nose, chin, or clothes for their purposes. Handsome austerity, however effective in Court or drawing-room, is useless as material for those who must distort in order to amuse. Therefore, a minimum of caricatures: when one appeared people said, unless the figure bore a written name: 'Who's that, then?' When told, they were full of admiration for the man.

Roderick himself was quite as ignorant as Morton of his lack of news value. He rested upon his acknowledged integrity; and, as barrister and House of Commons man, on his natural but unimpassioned eloquence. For the rest, he was far too proud to scheme or flatter, and while aware that he had enemies he underestimated them. Amused by Morton's conspiratorial nods and shrugs, he likened them to the performances of Grimuad, the servant of Athos in *The Three Musketeers*. 'But of course I have no Porthos, and no Aramis,' he thought. 'Above all, no D'Artagnan. In the modern world one runs in packs or fights alone. I fight alone.'

Morton, standing below a fine portrait

of Disraeli as an old man, with something, he hoped, of Disraeli's masklike expression, was at his most characteristic.

'Mmm,' he hummed, like an actor who communicates to the audience what his fellow actors are supposed not to hear. 'Improved. *He's* active.'

Roderick thus learned that the Prime Minister was reported to have rallied, and that his own political arch-enemy, Plowman, had already taken steps to exploit the situation. Plowman never missed a chance of self-advancement. He cultivated, not only newspaper commentators, but their editors and proprietors. Having a big, lop-sided nose, wide mouth, and a blue chin, together with such adjuncts as would suggest that he was a man of the people, he was a boon to the caricaturists, who never tired of guying him. At Party Conferences he could be grave, sonorous, or a demagogue, so that when he sat down the audience always stood up. However much Party Members might scoff in private at his efforts, most of them believed him to be the man likely to win Elections.

Roderick did not admire Plowman. He thought him over-aggressive and over-confident, with far too much bluster and a far from excellent vocabulary of *clichés*. Nevertheless, acknowledging Morton's tactful indignation of danger, he nodded.

'Is the P.M.'s speech affected?'

Morton's shoulders moved. On hearing the first whisper, 'a stroke,' he had summoned Roderick to town. Later, he had learned of Plowman's efficient descent upon the bedside. This was all.

'Not told. Normal.'

'It doesn't necessarily follow. Is Plowman still there?'

'Office. Seen the doctors. Phoning half hourly.'

'His jackals are with him, I suppose?'

A nod. Roderick considered the situation. He then added:

'Have you consulted Wrekin?'

'He phoned. Wants you to go to the Pyramid, if you can.'

The Pyramid Club, in St. James's Street, being non-political and very select, would be a safe place at this early hour for private talk. A meeting there would be excellent.

'At once?' Another nod. 'Right, I'll go. Did he comment?'

'No. They say, keep mum. "A slight chill." Bulletin later.'

'This is for the Press, is it?'

'Or if people start phoning.'

The conversation would have ended there; but Morton had other unpleasant tidings.

'Mm,' he said; and an unaccustomed flush spread to his neck. 'Mm.' He was seriously embarrassed.

Roderick waited. The struggle in Morton's mind grew even more powerful.

'What do you want to tell me?' This was the coaxing tone which often produced essential admissions from a fright-paralysed witness.

'Hardly know. Not "want." Er, no relation . . . mm . . . to *him*. Arlingborough. Tedder 'phoned. Last night. Trouble there.'

Roderick's attention, otherwise occupied with the occasion of his summons to town, was caught. It was as Member for

169

Arlingborough that he sat in Parliament. The place had grown rapidly in the past ten years; and it was from the neighbourhood of Arlingborough that the Pattersons, owing to Evelyn's disgust with her surroundings, had lately moved to Slocumbe.

'They don't like our leaving? Very understandable. You know why we did it. That immense urban sprawl and invasion. My wife, being unwell, at last found it intolerable.'

'Quite. Tedder thought it might be . . . mm . . . *wise*' — the word was significantly emphasised — 'for you to be there . . . a lot. He's nervous. The women. Lady Patterson . . . mm . . . upset them. Newcomers . . . very egalitarian.'

Roderick smiled. He could imagine Tedder, that bluff ex-farmer, exploding over the telephone: 'Tell him . . . Tell him . . .'

'And so Tedder thinks I ought to woo the women?'

'This . . . mm . . . young Labour fellow. Active. Good-looking. Glib.

Egalitarian stuff. "We Workers." That sort of thing.'

'And our majority might slide. Is that it?'

'Inferiority complex. Lady Patterson . . . a few home truths. Very sound. All the *ladies* impressed. But easily garbled. Distorted. Very mischievous. Result, resentment; common people not good enough for her ladyship.'

'When, in fact, they were rather too much for her. The new estate was right on our doorstep. Children screaming in our gardens —'

'Quite. Need of privacy. Quiet. Not understood.'

'You think we ought to have put up with it? Didn't flatter them enough?'

'Oh, I'm . . . er . . . only Tedder's mouthpiece.'

'You give the revised version, Morton.'

No smile rewarded this jest. Morton supplied further details.

'He says — his words — "an ignorant lot." his Labour man panders. Calls them "comrades." Tedder says he'll soon run up Hammer and Sickle.'

'The modern equivalent of the skull and crossbones. But you also say he's charming.'

'In *their* way. Beer and darts with the men. Tea with the women. Remembers the children's names.'

'Evidently dangerous. I don't wonder Tedder's on edge. I'll go down. Tell him to suggest a few dates for me to speak.

'Thank you.' This really was all that Morton would bring himself to say. He was temperamentally incapable of speaking his mind, or Tedder's mind, on Lady Patterson's home truths and the manner of their delivery. Roderick understood this, and more.

During the journey to London he had considered, not the querulousness of his constituents, but matters of higher concern. Since, as Evelyn reminded him, he was not in the Cabinet, he could not expect to be summoned to any select conclaves; but his position in the Party was such that one or other of the great legal posts had been within sight. He had counted upon the probability that, in what is called a Cabinet re-shuffle, his ambition would be fulfilled. Superior ability had earned him general respect; tangible reward seemed likely.

Now the position was changed. If the Prime Minister's stroke was merely the result of overwork, and he recovered with days or weeks, news of it could be smothered, as many major facts in politics, including the true reasons for policy changes, were smothered. A brief absence from public life of its central figure would allow of manoeuvre among contestants for the prizes, and, in the end, inevitable bargains and compromises. But Plowman, by seizing his advantage, by being on the spot and rushing in like the devil he was, had secured first place in the scramble. Most of his colleagues were out of London for the weekend. Not Plowman. As Home Secretary, and as a man of tremendous drive, he had singular advantages. He would use them without scruple.

Had Plowman been forewarned?

With eyes and spies everywhere, in the persons of sharp-witted and cynical Party

Members, shoulder-rubbing newspaper controllers, whispering journalists, secretaries, even members of the domestic staff in all sorts of homes, he might well have received the essential tip a week or a month earlier. Any one of his cronies could have noticed a shake, a flush, a stumble, or the unconscious movement of a great man's hand to his heart; noticed and interpreted, as gamblers interpret the falterings of their opponents. Within five minutes news would be conveyed to Plowman. Action, already planned, would be automatic.

'A determined man doesn't delay,' thought Roderick. 'A calculating man is never taken by surprise. I ought not to have been taken by surprise, as I am. I have no spies, no toadies, and no schemes. Just over-confidence in my own merit.'

A dreadful memory assailed him. It was of the same sprite — or obstinate girl — whom he had seen overnight against the yew hedge; but this time he did not see her. He heard her voice. 'I'm sure you'll succeed, Rod — as you need to do. I'm just afraid —' 'What do you mean, "afraid"?'

'Don't be angry. Well, contemptuous then. I can't tell you. I don't know. Darling, I think you have all the gifts.' In a lower tone, which he had been meant not to hear: '*Almost* all the gifts. Except . . .'

Damn Florrie! Why remember her devastating doubt? Evelyn had never felt the smallest doubt. Or had she, with greater discretion, breathed no word of it?

Rumination continued: 'I'm not seen as a distributor of favours. Plowman is. A nod here, a pressed elbow there; and expectation rises. Robert Walpole's "All these men have their price." I have never pressed an elbow, or offered an elbow to be pressed by Plowman. He'll keep me out.'

In this mood he joined Sam Wrekin at the Pyramid Club. Sam's political future must also be in jeopardy, for he, of all those in the present Cabinet, would be looked upon by Plowman as a non-supporter and therefore a liability. What would Sam have to say about their fates?

'Too damned philosophic for practical issues,' thought Roderick.

Sam, tall, thin, white-haired, and

elegant, like some Duke of Victorian fiction, already knew what had happened and was happening. Indeed, as the Prime Minister's close friend and long-time colleague, he must have been among the first to be told of the stroke; and he had had time to assess every probability. Personally, he could not suffer; having an ample income, and a satisfying record of past achievements in office, he was ready to leave public life for good.

This morning, at a first glance, as he lay back in one of the Club's armchairs with his knees crossed high before him, Sam appeared inanimate. His face was as yellow as old ivory, and the long head was covered with sparse white hair. Just so, within ten years, would he look in his coffin, emaciated but resigned. At sight of Roderick he sprang youthfully to his feet. There was no sign of the melancholy reflectiveness which opponents mistake for scorn.

'Dear Roderick!' He warmly extended both hands. His eyes were frank and clear as ever; his clasp as cool and firm. There was no falsity. He really was delighted to see one whom he liked and admired. 'I thought myself doomed to an hour of sadness; and you restore me to hope. How extraordinarily fortunate that you're in town!'

And yet, in this great cordiality, there was a second message for Roderick. Sam, besides expressing affection, was conveying sympathy. Having read the auguries, he had seen in them no prospect of fulfilled ambition. He knew Plowman. He knew how Parties react, as mobs do, to a Dictator with an army behind him. Plowman's army was his caucus.

The two men sat together in comparable intimacy of thought.

'What do you know, Sam?' Roderick looked sideways at the distinguished face. In the same undertone Sam communicated his knowledge.

'Charles has rallied wonderfully. A few days, and he'll be out of bed. But he's been warned. The doctors are unanimous. Shut down; go slow; or there'll be a second; and, if that's disregarded, a third. The third will be fatal.'

'He listens, does he?'

'Growing like a mastiff; but, to my ears, fatalistically. Oh, yes; he knows he's finished.'

'Will he resign?'

'Yes. Not this week. Perhaps not next.'

'The outgoing P.M. always recommends a successor, doesn't he? Must it be Plowman?'

'Inevitably, Roderick. Plowman has all the guns. He's clever, aggressive, and the right age — fifty-three or -four. Charles admires all those . . . attributes. Also, Plowman should be the universal choice. That's the news from the Constituencies. They say "we want a strong man." It's a delusion; but I see no alternative.'

'Why not yourself?'

'Too old; and supposed to live in the clouds.'

'Charles know you don't do that.'

'I think so. But he's a politician. He prides himself on understanding the People.'

Roderick considered.

'Does it mean the end for you?'

'Within three months.'

'In spite of your prestige?'

'Because of it, Roderick. Plowman will reward his henchmen. He actively dislikes me as a man.'

'And me, of course; not that I've ever been "in." '

'In or out, you're one of our best. I know Charles meant you to be the next Attorney General. We discussed it. But as a man of integrity you're a reproach to our rather unprincipled colleague.'

There was no comfort in this for Roderick. Yet he could still think of his friend.

'I'm very sorry on your account, Sam.'

'Oh, I shall have my books. I'm planning great things there.'

'And the country?'

'The country will survive. It's survived all the mismanagement of the last two hundred years. I'm a great believer in the country. I think it will outlast many Plowmans.'

'In the mean time,' reflected Roderick, without speaking the words, 'Plowman will be appearing everywhere, in halls, on television — to prove that he's the man of Destiny — while I am bidden to show myself in Arlingborough in a desperate effort to retain the seat. A meaningful contrast!' Aloud, he ruefully said: 'We're told a country gets the Government it deserves. What price decadence?'

'Or reaction! We shall have to see.' Sam leaned forward and patted his colleague's knee. 'I'm disappointed on your account, old boy. You don't need me to tell you that.'

These words meant simply: 'Bid farewell to your dreams of high office. By the time Plowman goes, if he survives the next General Election, you'll be too old to get anything from his successor.'

Too old! Too old! That was the devastating implication for Roderick. He had never challenged Plowman. Now it was too late to do so.

Nobody would have guessed from his expression that he was seeing himself for the first time as a failure in life. Nor did he show the humiliation he felt at Sam's philosophically ready acceptance of the failure. Nevertheless it brought back in a rush of emotion Florrie's words of thirty years ago: *almost* all the gifts.' What gifts had she seen to be missing? 'Almost . . . almost . . . almost': it was like the Raven's word of doom. And Florrie had foreseen this very moment, the little Devil! How? Why?

Back in the past, with its laughing sweetness, its sudden vehement exasperation, its conflict of desires, and its never-admitted secret relief at Florrie's disappearance from his life, Roderick relived his youth. Evelyn, as a young woman with so much to offer, had played but a contributory part in the most vivid episode of his whole career. But it was Evelyn who would suffer the great mortification in the ruin of their common dream. Poor Evelyn!

16
The Law

The Royal Courts of Justice stand at that point in London still known as Temple Bar; and they are built in a curious style described as Monastic Gothic. To a modern functional architect, who loves the featureless rectangle, this style appears fussy, since it is highly decorated; but the Courts have their own character, and when besieged by grey-wigged, black-gowned barristers they provide one of the sights of the town. They are also a peepshow for all who love to watch men and women at odds over their possessions and privileges.

Roderick, like his fellow-lawyers,

believed in the British Legal System. He had his reservations about its performance, because he knew that, like their lay brothers, Judges vary in quality. Some are pedants, some brutish, and some interfering. Not one, in his experience, was venal; and most were fantastically scrupulous. He was displeased, today, when upon arrival at the Courts he was greeted by Leonard, his Clerk, with the breathless words:

'We're on in Court Five, sir. Within half-an-hour. McAndrew.'

This was one more blow in a morning of blows.

'Why McAndrew?'

'Thelwell's ill.'

Very bad. Very bad. Thelwell was a Judge whom Roderick respected. They were not friends; but they had not been rivals, either. McAndrew was a different character, a bachelor, prickly, sure that all women were rakes, and, through sensitiveness to Roderick's calm, as nearly a personal enemy as one-sided dislike would allow. He always sat uncomfortably sideways, perhaps because of sore bones, perhaps through deafness; and an incessant smile played upon his lips. It was not a smile of amusement or benevolence, but one of sarcasm. Like Pooh-Bah, he had been born sneering.

'Hm.' Roderick, striding past Leonard to the Robing Room, there met his opponent in the case, Theodore Peake, towards whom his feelings were altogether different. Peake was a quick, ruddy man, whose weekends, as long as daylight lasted, were spent on the golf course near his home at Aylesbury, and whose fund of ribald stories about Judges was inexhaustible. McAndrew was one of Peake's favourite butts, always presented with excellent mimicry as an example of the primitive grotesque.

'We'll lead him up the garden, shall we?' suggested Peake. 'Get his mind working. When I see him I always think of Cassius, skinny, itching palm, and all. No vices, except meanness. He doesn't drink, does he?'

'I've seen him down a glass of medical port,' answered Roderick, gravely.

'I bet it turned sour on his stomach and

made him headstrong. Upset inside. Upset on appeal. Oh, well, I'll see you in Court. Happy hunting!'

As Peake withdrew in uttering this taunt, Roderick foresaw that his day would continue to be disagreeable. Peake was evidently anticipating with malicious pleasure the demolition of a ludicrously self-confident Plaintiff, about whose character he had privy information. Roderick had only his own judgment, as a result of which he would have preferred to keep his client out of the box altogether. Her testimony, however, was essential; and she insisted upon giving it. All his tact would be needed.

The Court was not a large one; and it was well-filled, as a Court always was when Peake or Roderick was to appear. Although this case was essentially a trivial one, arising from the rivalry of two inconspicuous women, every Junior able to attend was jostling his fellows in the seats crowded with such small legal fry. To the traditional camaraderie of the Profession they added eagerness to learn.

The contrast was between Dignity and Mischief. Peake's eyes were never shut. He looked over his shoulders, up to the high ceiling, and at the Judge, beaming always with derision at pomposity and the evasion of witnesses. Roderick, with his commanding height, was Dignity personified. He could survey and assess the scene without moving his eyes or his head. He kept absolutely still, used no gesture, and relied upon courtesy and persuasiveness to do everything necessary. Experienced Juniors considered him a model; but they enjoyed Peake better as a creature of quips and sudden revelations.

All stood when the meagre Judge entered; and, being a man of greater kindness than Peake, Roderick admitted that McAndrew had a sufficient air of authority for his job. Heavy eyelids drooped over steel-grey eyes; the thin lips had not yet assumed the sarcastic grimace which they would wear when witnesses stammered or over-elaborate Counsel bored. A cold glance round the Court took methodical note of both Plaintiff and Defendant, Miss Davenant and Mrs

Montague, who sat at a distance from one another, eyes averted in mutual detestation, and of the jerkily bowing Peake, but, almost ostentatiously, not of Roderick, who was the best worth looking at of them all.

What did McAndrew feel when he saw Peake? Roderick guessed that he knew all about the mimicry and ribaldry; but today he was bearing himself as a Judge should do, and was a masked official. This emphasized his failure to recognize Roderick. Roderick himself thought it strange that animosity should exist when he could not remember that they had ever been opposed in Counsel; but Peake would have given the airy explanation: 'Sense of inferiority, dear boy. Something you never felt!'

And so the case began, McAndrew perched high, and the empty witness box upon a comparable level. When Miss Davenant went into that box she and the Judge would be near enough to each other to exchange whispered comments which nobody else could hear. They would not do so, for reasons quite plain to both Peake and Roderick.

The two Counsels had briefly met their Clients before the Judge's entry; and for his part Roderick had been appalled by Miss Davenant's appearance. Instead of dressing quietly and — with whatever guile — assuming the air of a refined woman reluctantly claiming what was her own, she had come prepared to dazzle. A flamboyant peacock blue dress, a feathered hat, and a carriage suggestive of vulgar assurance drew the eye, certainly; but the effect was deplorable.

McAndrew, with his general suspicion of the sex, was bound to think her a common tart. He would thus begin with a fatal misconception of her character. No doubt her physical attractiveness had seduced and gratified the dead man's taste; but Roderick believed that she had genuinely sought to ease the life of a difficult creature whose marriage had become intolerable. A jury might have brought humanitarian insight to bear upon one who had defensively bedizened herself; McAndrew could do no such thing.

Disappointed of a jury, Miss Davenant had hoped to disconcert Peake. Her hope was unrewarded. Also, as Roderick and all other Barristers could have told her, there came from the back of the Court, affecting untutored spectators, attendants, listening Juniors, and at last even Advocates and Judge, the extraordinary moral verdict of the crowd. It was adverse.

In his opening speech, Roderick outlined the stages of Miss Davenant's acquaintance with the dead man, from their meeting at a moment when he was ill, to discovery of his morbid irascibility, his domestic unhappiness, and his need of the sympathy which only a tactful and affectionate woman could supply. In this opening McAndrew, whose sarcastic smile had already gathered, was boldly challenged. He was warned by implication not to let his prejudice against a whole sex run amok, and entreated to dismiss the unfavourable impression made by Miss Davenant's dress and bearing. Although he did not use any such words, he was saying: 'Please don't jump to the conclusion that this young woman is what she looks — a mere gold-digger. She is a person of heart. Though her taste, as you see, is for shoddy, she realized that the dead man was desperately in need of love. The fact that he was rich, and she relatively poor, is material only in so far as it accounts for her acceptance of his presents.'

Continuing, he explained that Miss Davenant had sacrificed a promising career, not on the stage, but in what are called Public Relations, for the sake of this association. Mr Montague had promised that they should be married as soon as he was free. In the meantime he had made her a number of presents, including jewellery worth a considerable sum.

A note from Mr Montague, accompanying this valuable jewellery, would be produced. It ran: 'My own darling. These sparklers do not equal your eyes in brilliance. They are offered to one who is the Koh-i-Nor of my life.' Another note, showing Mr Montague's determination, read: 'When I have ridden myself of the Hag, and we can be married, you shall have everything I can wrest from a settlement made when I was *non compos mentis.*'

Roderick continued:

'Owing to Mr Montague's sudden death and intestacy, Miss Davenant finds herself deprived, not only of a prospective husband, but of the jewellery given to her in warm affection. The jewellery — let there be no mistake about that — had actually been in her possession. It was hers. But she had personally urged Mr Montague to return it for safe custody to the bank's strong room. He did this, along with other valuables, which included letters from Miss Davenant which have been returned to her. The jewels have not been returned; and the wife's representatives claim that they were never given to Miss Davenant at all.'

So far, the opening. Roderick's quiet and persuasive examination of the Plaintiff followed. Miss Davenant testified to the facts, and as the questions were put in such a way that 'yes' and 'no' were in

191

almost every instance the appropriate answers she was kept strictly to the point. Even so, Roderick had difficulty in repressing her emotional explosiveness. She swelled; she bubbled; she was eager to display histrionic skill proper, not to this case, or this Court, but to the old Adelphi melodrama. 'You may kill me; but you cannot take my Victoria Cross!' Having been a dozen times checked, she needed soothing. She was soothed; she was quieted; she became almost dignified. But Roderick knew that Peake would rouse her again, and that his task of re-examination after Peake had used all his mischievous destructiveness would be terribly difficult.

Peake, gravely derisive, rose to his feet.

17
Judgment

All the Juniors were alert, anticipating fun. Roderick almost heard the indrawing of breath behind him, and the cracking of relaxed muscles which preceded a silence proper to the Opera House or in the Concert Hall. How these boys relished Peake!

Cross-examination began.

'You were very much attached to Mr Montague?'

Answer was given with spirit, and a triumphant smile, as if Miss Davenant, shaking off the trammels of her own unappreciative Counsel, greeted an opponent worthy of her foil.

'Yes, I was. Ardently attached. I understood him, you see.'

'You saw him as a Paladin?'

'I saw him as an unhappy man, very sick, and in need of a love he was not getting elsewhere.'

'That was what you gave him, was it? No consideration at all of pecuniary advantage to yourself?'

Still half-smiling, and now fully confident, Miss Davenant ridiculed Peake's long words.

'If that means I was after his money, you're quite wrong. I was making a good living at my work. I loved that work. My prospects were excellent.'

'But you *are* suing for valuable jewellery?'

'I'm suing for jewellery given to me by Mr Montague, wrongfully kept back after his death. Quite wrongfully.'

'That, of course, is for the learned Judge to decide, Miss Davenant.'

'I presume the learned Judge will see that I'm an injured woman, Mr Peake. A deeply injured woman.'

Peake, knowing McAndrew's opinion of

194

women, was not discountenanced.

'Most of that jewellery consisted of diamonds, didn't it?'

'Yes. His note to me expressly says so.'

'Did you know the diamonds were heirlooms, and therefore inalienable?'

'I know they were given to *me.*'

'I suggest you were allowed to wear them on one occasion?'

'Certainly not. Charles gave them to me. He said, "If anything should happen to prevent our marriage, these will assure your future." '

'What did he think might happen to prevent your marriage?'

'What do you suppose? He'd been ill. He thought he might die. So might you, or anybody else.'

'He thought his wife would survive him?'

'He was always afraid our happiness couldn't last. He'd had twenty years of the other thing.'

'You seriously suggest that his marriage had been unhappy?'

'I do. He'd been tormented by a nagging wife.'

'And, if he died, his wife, whether nagging or not, would, quite rightly, inherit all his property, including the family jewels?'

'It wouldn't be right for her to appropriate my diamonds.'

'Heirlooms?'

'I don't know anything about heirlooms. These diamonds aren't the Crown Jewels, are they?'

'But they've been in the Montague family for generations?'

'That's what you're now pretending, Mr Peake. Nothing of the kind was ever said before. I only know what really happened.'

'Did it really happen? Let me take you back a little. How often, in fact, did you wear those diamonds?'

'Several times. I didn't count them. I was fond of the stones.'

'They were precious to you?'

'They still are.'

'Were they ever actually in your possession?'

'Of course.'

'I suggest that they were only shown to

you. You were allowed to put them on; and they were immediately replaced in their cases and returned to the bank.'

'Absolutely untrue.'

'If the bank manager testifies, as he is ready to do, that they left the bank only once, for a single day, will you challenge his truthfulness?'

'I should certainly deny his accuracy.'

'Did Mr Montague, in his lifetime, pay the rent of your flat, give you money and minor pieces of jewellery from time to time, but make no promise whatever of future support?'

'The diamonds were to assure my future.'

'Heirlooms?'

'You keep on talking about heirlooms. To me, they're diamonds.'

'To be sold?'

'If I wanted, yes.'

'Had you had other lovers, before Mr Montague?'

'As Miss Davenant stiffened under the unexpected attack, Roderick intervened.

'I suggest, my Lord, that the question, besides being highly objectionable, is irrelevant.'

Peake retorted:

'On the witness's credibility, my Lord.'

McAndrew's smile broadened.

'Go on, Mr Peake. The question seems to me highly relevant.'

Roderick's 'Devil,' Foster, whispered: 'I went into all this with her. Seduced at eighteen; says no other man.' But Peake, apparently, had better information, how gathered they could not know.

'Another lover, Miss Davenant? A little trouble about jewellery?'

Miss Davenant was white. She was greatly agitated.

'I don't see what anything that happened long ago has to do with this case,' she cried, in a loud voice.

'Not such a very long time?' queried Peake. 'Shall we say three years? Another unhappy man? You have a large heart, haven't you?'

McAndrew's smile broadened until it spread right across his face.

Roderick, penetrating to the heart of McAndrew's enjoyment, was much troubled by this turn. He sensed that thumbs were being turned down all through the Court. And he remembered the advice he had given Miss Davenant: 'Don't spar with Peake. Stick to the truth. Look, and be, quiet. We shall win the case only if you can persuade the Judge that you are a deeply injured woman of high character.'

Her expression had struck him as rebellious; but she had said she understood. He had earnestly pressed her to say if there was anything they might have to counter. She had insisted that there was nothing. 'I've told Mr Foster all I know, Sir Roderick. Absolutely all.' Now it seemed that, as far from telling 'all,' she had hidden from both Foster and himself another episode relating to a 'gift.' Very bad. Very bad. It was already unfortunate that they were appearing before McAndrew; but Peake's mysteriously obtained knowledge was calamitous.

McAndrew was looking sideways at the witness. A jewel-fancier himself, he was assessing the value of the stones she wore today; and was waiting for Peake to ask whether these were what her previous claim had produced. The malice in that sidelong glance was overwhelming. If Miss Davenant saw it as Roderick did, she would lose all assurance.

Peake was putting his questions with an air of omniscience. That was part of his technique. He and McAndrew, at the moment, were like two wine-bibbers raising convivial glasses; and Miss Davenant was obviously disconcerted. If she broke down, she would be finished. Of course, the claim that all the Montague jewels were heirlooms was preposterous. Foster had already worked on that aspect, ascertaining that some of them, at least, had been bought by Montague within the past ten years. The bank manager must be pressed closely on the number of times they had been taken from his strong room. And there must be complete repudiation of Peake's innuendo that Miss Davenant had been involved in any similar action. Why the devil hadn't the woman told him about the other lover?

Re-examination would have been easy if

there had been a jury to win over; but since McAndrew alone was to be persuaded a different note must be struck. The first essential was to destroy Peake's representation of Miss Davenant as an avaricious woman of loose morals.

'My learned friend described you as having a large heart. Would it be accurate to say that you are a generally kind person? Warm-hearted, not only to jewel-giving lovers, but to all who are unhappy, female as well as male? Your own purse always open? Your spare time and energy devoted to good causes, young orphans rather than middle-aged valetudinarians? This lover, of whom Mr Peake made so much, did he, by any chance, give you the jewels you are wearing today?'

The jewels she was wearing were so clearly of lesser value that McAndrew put a hand to cover the smiling lips.

'No,' said the witness. 'There were no jewels.'

'My Lord!' Peake was on his feet, very animated. 'My instructions —'

'There were no jewels!' shouted Miss Davenant. 'I bought these myself!'

Roderick imagined McAndrew muttering 'I don't doubt it' to his veiling hand. He took advantage of that retort to carry Miss Davenant directly into the main question. She was not an expert; she valued the Montague diamonds, not because of their monetary worth, but because they had been given to her by a man she loved. It was she who had urged Mr Montague to replace them in the bank's strong room for safety. Mr Montague's death had been quite unexpected — a tragedy for her and for all who knew him. Marriage was to take place as soon as he could get a divorce from an unloved and unloving wife. . . .

She had been willing to be cited as co-respondent so as to hasten divorce proceedings and enable Mrs Montague to retain the bulk of her husband's estate. She had used no arts to attract Mr Montague. He was not an old man; certainly not a senile Sugar Daddy. His expectation of life was good. They had looked forward to years of happy married life. So far was it from being true that she made a habit of seducing rich men, the former lover introduced into the case by Mr Peake was a poor author of great reputation but small sales. His family had sued her for the return of the author's letters in case she published them, which she had never thought of doing. It was another instance of a vindictive wife —

Here Roderick stopped her — in time to prevent rising excitement from reviving the bad impression she had previously made. That, he said, was the Plaintiff's case. She was an injured woman, a person of honour and good faith, who had no enemies, who had lost Mr Montague's care and who wanted no more than the jewels which were her property.

The widow followed.

The widow was an entirely different kind of woman from her opponent; and she showed herself possessed of greater powers of calculation. Small, outwardly hesitant, but in reality as tough as leather, she was a model of restraint. A black costume without adornment suggested mourning, and emphasized her lack of flesh; and the pinched mouth and insignificant nose made Roderick assess her as a shrew. In an excellently clear voice she spoke with a preciseness outside Miss Davenant's capacity. Everybody in Court felt she would give nothing away, and that, woman for woman, she had an advantage in resoluteness over Miss Davenant. Both were obstinate to excess.

Contrasting the rivals, Roderick concluded that the late Mr Montague had found his wife's silences particularly galling, and the tartness of her tight-lipped comments an affront to his more generous disposition. Looking round for appreciation, he had found Miss Davenant, whose physical attractiveness made Mrs Montague seem a bag of bones, and whose very vulgarity was a relief to his starved senses. Gratitude to her, and aversion to his wife, had dictated the gift of the diamonds. They meant nothing to Mrs Montague; but to Miss Davenant they were both a delight and an insurance against poverty.

This, therefore, was the line he followed in cross-examination. Mrs Montague did not value the jewels. Had she ever worn them? She was otherwise well-provided-for? A rich woman, in fact? She had never met Miss Davenant? No personal hostility to her? If she retained the diamonds, she would simply leave them in the bank's strong room, for some remote connection of her husband's to inherit? Was not her sole motive in resisting the claim that of a woman determined to prevent another woman benefiting from her husband's generosity? But if it were proved that some of the stones could not have been in the Montague family for generations? Had not Mr Montague a passion for buying diamonds? She was unaware of such a passion? He had never bought jewels for her? Was that because she did not care for them? Never wore jewels?

Mrs Montague had a composed answer to every question. McAndrew was delighted with her, as he had been, for different reasons, with Miss Davenant. Miss Davenant was a natural harlot, out for all she could get; Mrs Montague typified malignant possessiveness, of a man and his property. There was not a pin to choose between them. McAndrew had escaped all huntresses, luscious or skeletonized. He congratulated himself on his bachelor freedom.

In looking at Peake he remembered that Peake derided him; that was objectionable, but could be shrugged off. In looking at Roderick he was conscious of an underlying inferiority. Roderick might be a noble character as was claimed by his admirers; but he was arrogant with pride, and he despised men morally or physically smaller than himself. To Peake, the loss of a case would be all in the day's fun. To Roderick, it would be a deeply wounding humiliation.

McAndrew decided that Roderick must lose the case.

18
The Storm

Blenkinsop's back was an extraordinarily reassuring expanse. Having once been seen beyond the glass panel, it became as fixed as a wall or a black chimney pot, and as restful as one's favourite armchair. Blenkinsop was strong, unimaginative, and competent. When he drove a car, passengers never thought of watching for dogs on the road, nor dangerous turnings, nor the reckless drivers of other cars. They left everything to Blenkinsop.

Roderick, as a rule, did this. Tonight, returning to Slocumbe after two other conferences in his Chambers, he was in an unaccustomed mood of irritability, and considered the relief it would be to snatch the wheel from Blenkinsop's hands and thrust that bulk aside as one more obstruction.

During the weekend he had been confronted with the problems of his son and daughter. He had been snarlingly reproached by his brother, Syd, and seen his wife, Evelyn, in states of unreason and illness. Today he had been told that his life's political ambition would never be fulfilled, and that his very seat in Parliament was in jeopardy. And he had lost a case.

McAndrew's insulting decision, though it galled, could have been anticipated; and, coming from such a man, would have been negligible but for its consequences. The domestic troubles could be dealt with or shrugged off. What rankled, what indeed made all the other problems lose their triviality and become threatening, was Sam Wrekin's assumption that his friend Roderick Patterson, however skilful, was a second-rate man who must submit with good grace to effacement. This was an outrage. Blenkinsop's back offered no comfort; like a pall, it suggested oblivion.

Closing his eyes, as he always did when concentrating, Roderick turned to what he regarded as the least important question to arise that day — the case he had lost. What was Miss Davenant doing at this moment? She had rushed from the Court as soon as McAndrew had delivered judgment. There had been no farewell, no word of reproach or resentment; only blind agitation. She was now probably telling herself that Mrs Montague was a fiendish liar, the Judge a fool who took bribes, and her Counsel a pompous duffer who had let her down. No realization that she had contributed to disaster by complete misconception of the part she was to play. That ridiculous costume, the cheap jewellery; over-confidence in her power to outsmart Peake, had done great harm. And of course Peake had sprung a calculated surprise upon her.

'Did I in fact let her down? Miss some essential point? I don't think so; but it's a possibility. Was I subconsciously weakened by the memory of Sam's manner? I'm not used to losing cases. I'm not used to humiliations. McAndrew knows that. So does Plowman. I now see both of them as my enemies. . . .'

The perception of enmity in another is very bitter. It produced in Roderick emotions of contempt and burning anger; but the anger cooled almost at once. Its residue was, first, pain, and then refusal to consider retaliation or acceptance of defeat. Stoicism regained its power. Thought continued.

For Miss Davenant an appeal was not only possible but practical. McAndrew, cynically assuming the role of Solomon, had advised the parties, and their representatives, to settle things among themselves. Knowing nothing of women, whom he despised, he thought this a possibility. But Peake, encountering Roderick afterwards, had revealed deeper understanding. 'Our friend,' he whispered, 'is still in the Kindergarten stage. As well ask two tom cats to shake paws and be friends. What?'

That had been the crowning absurdity. McAndrew had also been wrong otherwise. He had too readily accepted the bank manager's obviously misleading dates, and had disregarded the argument that Montague himself had bought at least some of the jewels on purpose to give them to his mistress. Probably the receipts, which were not available, had been destroyed by Mrs Montague, that small-souled embodiment of avarice. McAndrew's view that all women were untruthful had told, for some reason, against Miss Davenant, when it should have been clear that, for all her mishaviour, she believed what she was saying. He had described her as 'a most unsatisfactory witness,' meaning, of course, that she had a most unsatisfactory Counsel.

Mrs Montague on the contrary, coached to the last syllable by Peake, and very tough indeed, had been unshakable. Her obstinacy was as great as that of any witness Roderick had ever met.

'Peake, with his extraordinary gift for innuendo, could have demolished her. I wasn't clever enough — or offensive enough — to do it. Too kid-gloved. Those hard eyes showed how well she had been primed about me. I can hear and see Peake drilling her. And she was out to win, not to impress. My poor deluded woman played into their hands. McAndrew saw her as a lascivious huntress of men, covetous of possessions, and mad about diamonds; when she's in reality a warm-hearted creature who had heard all about Mrs Montague's sins from a man who, as an aphrodisiac, exaggerated his sufferings and played on her good-nature.'

In due course, when the first fury of defeat had subsided, Miss Davenant would see her Solicitor, the excellent Bright, who drove four-in-hand as a diversion and stood no nonsense from female clients. Bright, who in Court today had done no more than jerk up his chin as a comment on the proceedings, would give her a lecture on deportment, and sound advice as to an Appeal; afterwards telephoning in his husky little voice to Foster. Foster would devil again, with improved chances of making Miss Davenant come clean; and with Bright and Foster working together, and the Appeal resting upon legal argument, without witnesses, McAndrew's judgment would probably be reversed.

'Please God it will!' thought Roderick, impiously.

Having cynically assessed McAndrew's attitude to women, which had been illuminated by today's case, he turned naturally to the problem of two women in his own household. Both were outside the range of McAndrew's comprehension. (Had McAndrew, by the way, in sexually ingenuous youth, received cruelty from some sophisticated maiden, or maidens? It was an interesting possibility.) Evelyn's principles were high; sometimes a little rarified, but never less than scrupulous. Sandra? He could not tell. She was of another generation, coloured by the assumptions of the modern world, which Roderick disliked.

But three co-respondents! If they were being cited, as was alleged, Trevor must be determined to brand his wife as a harlot. That argued vindictiveness. On the other hand, it might indicate a desperation of jealousy arising from still consuming love. If this were so, Trevor might already be regretting his own extravagance; but supposing the proceedings were not stopped, the scandal would be appalling. Why couldn't Evelyn grasp that?

Of course she grasped it, or would do so when anger subsided; but with the aristocrat's indifference to public opinion she supposed that Trevor would make himself a laughingstock and leave Sandra unspotted. No; that was altogether too simple. Yet one couldn't go to Trevor as a suppliant. Sandra, being high-mettled, certainly would not do so. Death would be preferred. Was there no possible intermediary? What really went on in the minds and bosoms of obstinate young females? And of their middle-aged mothers? How apply reason to their incalculable performances?

'Something I don't know,' thought Roderick. 'Look at those two women today. Mrs Montague digging in her toes because Miss Davenant was another woman; Miss Davenant wild to get the better of a shrew. What did Peake suggest? A lost fight? Well, there it is; something else I don't understand.

Saul's affair, though murky, was different in kind. No women were involved. Therefore it could be handled, by threat or by bargain. He had meant to consult old Munster, the Solicitor who had given him his earliest briefs; but the summons from Morton, his disastrous chat with Sam, the enforced attendance in Court, and the two subsequent conferences had left no time for that. Munster must be seen tomorrow; though it would be difficult to squeeze the consultation into an already crowded programme.

'Damn! It's the lack of time! The lack of time!'

Roderick's days, and even, with attendance at the Manor, his nights, were so full that only a cool head enabled him to keep up with the demands made upon him. Well, he must keep that head cool. Should he take Saul with him? Could the boy, highly strung, and liable to hysteria, stand up to relentless questioning?

Just then, perhaps because of an abrupt change in the car's speed, he opened his eyes. Blenkinsop's back was still before him; but there was a difference. The darkness beyond him was silvered as if with lacquer: Ah! there was the lightning! It streaked down the sky just ahead; and the thunder followed immediately. Crash! The car seemed to jump with the force of it. Silence followed. The headlights showed rain sheeting down like a giant waterfall.

However, leave it to Blenkinsop. He was there in front, like a rock, his screen-wipers working, his eyes and hands, no doubt, as steady as ever. But it was lucky that they were well on their way home. The road was quiet, with an ample grass verge on either side, and for the next mile it must run very nearly straight. Good! In another twenty minutes, at most, they would be indoors, out of the storm, and amid dry comfort.

Thank God for that placid creature, Blenkinsop! He never lost his temper, never hesitated, never criticized. 'Very good, sir' was his stock reply. True, one did not pose him with unexpected questions about legal, ethical, or political affairs. Indeed, his politics were unknown. They were probably sound Tory politics; but that did not matter. He was one's chauffeur. Taking his ethical standard for granted, one gave him instructions. The 'very good, sir' implied neither approval nor enthusiasm: it was the good servant's unquestioning obedience. What did Blenkinsop think about anything on earth or in outer space? For example, of his employer?

Hitherto grim, Roderick relaxed into smiling indulgence. 'What would be your verdict on me, Blenkinsop? I know McAndrew's is spiteful; Sam's, once the suave courtesy is penetrated, is that I'm not out of the top drawer — a fatal defect in any Tory administration; Evelyn's is that I'm a conventional bore to be propped up as a man of mark; and Florrie Marvell's, once she had consulted her tea leaves, was that I should inevitably end in frustration. But what would yours be,

Blenkinsop? Tell me, as man to man!'

He had reached this point of rueful jocularity when, without warning, the car gave a great plunge into what appeared to be an abyss. Water slopped upon its roof like a tidal wave. The headlights went out. All Roderick could perceive was that he was surrounded by rushing water, while, apart from the whirring of rain above his head no sound at all was audible. The darkness was intense; and in that darkness Blenkinsop had been obliterated.

A moment passed. Roderick strained his eyes in search of Blenkinsop, guessing that the sliding window between them had been opened.

'You all right, sir?' asked a hoarse voice.

'Except that I can't see you. What is it? A waterspout?'

'Cloudburst, I should think. Road dips here; and there's a stream somewhere. I'll get down and have a look.'

'Shall I do that?'

'You stay where you are, sir. No sense us both getting wet.'

There was something less than normal respect in Blenkinsop's tone. He was like a ship's captain rebuking a passenger who had clambered to the bridge in an emergency. Roderick sat back, thinking: 'Put in my place!' He saw a faint speck of light in front of him; while Blenkinsop's silhouette became monstrous. Evidently a torch had been switched on. The click of a door latch was followed by a movement to and fro of the tiny light.

A short pause enabled Roderick's eyesight to adjust itself to what was apparently a seascape. Blenkinsop's face, like the moon obscured by cloud, showed dimly at the door. Blenkinsop's voice, subdued by pessimism, croaked:

'Water's over the axles. Distributor's flooded. Can't move. We're stuck.'

'What happens now, then? Do we wade?'

'You'd spoil them clothes.'

'I have others at home.'

Blenkinsop was not amused.

'There's a call box half a mile up the road. I'll go and 'phone — if I can get in.'

'Let me do it!' Roderick's hand was extended for the torch.

'Stay where you are, sir!' It was peremptory. The ship's captain had become an Army sergeant. 'I'll leave you 'ere, 'phone home, tell Fox to bring the Rover as far as it's safe, and some rubber boots for you. Stay there! I shan't be ten minutes.'

Before any reply could be made, there was a heavy splashing as of strong legs forcing a way through deep water. The flicker of light disappeared. All was darkness.

'Yes,' muttered Roderick to himself. 'I'm to stay here. But what if another car comes up behind, and bumps into me?'

He did not fear this possibility because any vehicle would be stopped by the swirling tide before it reached him; but he was discomposed. No doubt the ten minutes would pass. Blenkinsop would return. Fox would bring the Rover and the boots, and stop at a safe distance. Then, presumably, they would all three push this heavier car onto the grass verge, to be left there until daylight and a subsidence of the flood made retrieval possible. Could they manage it? Fox was nothing like Blenkinsop; he was a frail boy with arms like matchsticks.

'I must help. Blenkinsop will try to stop me. "You stay there!" Impudence! We shall see who's master! I'll threaten to sack him!'

This jocular assertion was followed by another thought.

'As he knows, I should never dare to do that; too indispensable. That's the sort of person to be, in the modern world. A cog's but a cog that must be there. I never asked his opinion of me. He made it clear. His verdict: "Useless in an emergency." '

At first this unserious conclusion seemed comic enough; but amusement was dismissed altogether by the discovery that, as he sat alone, hearing the swish and whirr of running water and the continuing rattle of falling rain, icy water was spreading about his feet.

'Good God! This won't do!'

He drew up his feet, and sat cross-legged, holding the loaded brief-case against his breast.

'How much longer? Blenkinsop said ten minutes. To him, ten minutes is like an Irish mile. I'm in no state to swim. In any event, I couldn't see where I was going. Could I climb on the roof? I doubt it. Damnation!'

The sound of rushing water continued. The stream was endless.

Twenty minutes. More than twenty. The floor of the car was awash. What had happened to Blenkinsop? Had he tripped, fallen, been swept away? Poor brave man, vulnerable in the end, as all were. But headstrong. Over-estimating his own strength. He had insisted upon going alone, leaving his master in safety, he thought, like a pampered dog. That was the good servant in him. He was a splendid fellow. But what if his courage led him to death?

Roderick stared into the blackness, trying to catch the returning flicker of that small torch. Where was the call box? Blenkinsop had said half a mile; but in this torrent who could find it? They should have gone together, linked like mountain climbers. Was Evelyn anxious? She always kept a cool head. Not quite always.

Yes, Evelyn. She was supposed to be cold. That wasn't true. She was probably, like the earth, burning within; but, through pride, determined to behave as the spectator of other people's passions. A repressed Sadism in women of her temperament. Sadism? Masochism, rather. These generalizations! He was thinking nonsense, to distract his mind. Very silly. Stupid . . .

Increasing cold led to numbness in his hands and feet; and in an effort to suppress concern for Blenkinsop's safety he began to reassemble memories of the disturbing weekend and the depressing day, now ending in physical danger. Sam's acceptance of another man's ruined hopes showed underlying callousness. Public life did that, hardening not arteries but hearts. One could always bear the sorrows of others. By comparison, Tedder's fear that his boss's Parliamentary seat might be in danger was generous. But the possibility was grim. If the seat went, his life as an

223

M.P. would end. He wouldn't stand again. He would be stranded, like every other deposed man of influence; and soon forgotten.

Stranded, yes. The word had been suggested by the black swell of water surrounding him, and by his feeling of isolation from the world. If this isolation were confirmed, half his ambition would be destroyed. He had long been full of plans for the simplification of British Law. Though belonging to the so-called Conservative Party, he was no reactionary, but first of all a humanist who wanted to see every person in the land happy and free. Why else desire power?

'At least I'm not a hypocrite,' he muttered. 'I want power because all public men want power. It's called "fulfilling one's self." I don't snivel about "the lads on the shop floor" because I need their votes; but I do want to feel that I've justified my election by producing benefits.'

The names and persons of a dozen, a score, any number of men whose aims were less noble flew across his mind. All were base; some had sold themselves to private interests, and some, he suspected, to worldwide political gangs. Such men had always vilified him. Base themselves, they supposed him to be comparably base, and had delivered attacks by misrepresentation or innuendo. A few, such as McAndrew, were hostile on personal grounds.

Why? Why had McAndrew, in dismissing Miss Davenant's claim, chosen to be insulting to her and scathing to her Counsel? The object, naturally, was to humiliate both, to ensure shame which they could not retort upon a Judge. The case, among many cases, had been trivial. Defeat in it could have no lasting effect upon his reputation. But it was defeat. It had been inflicted with the object of showing contempt. Was not contempt a sign of envy?

The same might be said of Plowman's hostility to Sam and himself. That was the sow's ear challenging a couple of silk purses. Plowman was coarse; refinement was anathema to him. The stupid always despised subtlety.

Here Roderick's head was shaken.

'That's too smug,' he warned himself. 'It smacks too much of present-day self-righteous Liberalism. I must beware of it, however damp and disgruntled.'

His mind turned slightly aside from the Law and Politics to contemplation of Syd, whose resentment was sharpened by preoccupation with his own lack of worldly success. Probably Syd, in the night, when bravado deserted him, lamented the waste his old bright talent. He would put the blame on his stars, or adverse circumstances, contrasting his own lot with that of a prosperously self-complacent brother. He would never arraign his own love of drink and the applause of inferiors: 'Poor chap!'

'He says I started him off on the wrong road. I certainly don't admit that. I've never spoken harshly or discouragingly. Never wished him ill. If he'd let me, I'd have introduced him to my own friends. He wouldn't have that. He regarded it as discreditable to have me for a brother. I expect his pot-companions sneered at me as somebody "respectable. . . ."'

226

'Yes; but he goes back to a time long before that — to Mother, and me as the school prizewinner and good boy of the family. It's true; Mother took pride in me, and I did win prizes. She was ambitious for me. He was rude to her. But what if I'd tried to help him, sought him out as a companion, when we were children? Not in my character. I've never sought anybody. I've always been too proud for that kind of thing, too . . . what? Uneffusive? Stiff? Cold? It might be. I do, in some sense, see his point of view. . . .'

Physical discomfort was sending chill to Roderick's heart. He knew that if he once relaxed his determination to fight what was in effect a child's loneliness in the dark, his teeth would begin to chatter, not from fear, but from bodily weakness. How humiliating that would be! Was he not Roderick Patterson, known far and wide for his resolute sense of duty?

At this moment, unluckily, he remembered the words he had been meant not to hear thirty years earlier. Florrie!

That fatal creature! The words came into his ears like a long-hidden sentence of death. '*Almost* great'; '*almost* all the gifts.' They were being fulfilled.

She might have said 'almost happy.' 'Man never is, but always to be, blest.' What was happiness? A mirage? And now the mirage — damn this wretched day, and this appalling night! — had dissolved. He had been sustained for sixty confident years by the hope of achievement, of something akin to supreme power. Now he was without aid, surrounded by gushing water and lowering darkness, in suspense, and with none but gloomy memories for distraction. Shivering seized his whole body. Suddenly, with no previous experience of that emotion, he was gripped by despair.

PART FIVE

BRIEF ROMANCE

19
After the Storm

The night's hurricane had passed by daybreak; and the morning sky was as innocent as water in a newly filled bath. Florence, hearing the batter of rain upon her bedroom window, had shut the window and gone back to bed, sleeping thereafter without disturbance. Only later did she see that her much-loved flowers were beaten down into the muddy soil as if a cruel giant had stamped his way across the garden.

Having mourned, as was natural, she immediately after breakfast put on a brown woollen jumper and trousers, with rubber boots to protect her feet and pink rubber gloves to do the same for her delicate hands. She then essayed the task of salvage. William, most domestic of all her pets and models, picked a gingerly way by her side over the sodden path and beds, and sat down to watch the proceedings with critical interest. William was a large black and white cat. He kept his eyes open for birds, visiting fieldmice, and his friend Randolph, a big Irish terrier who lived down the lane; but most of all he attached himself to Florence.

The two, Florence and William, were both fully occupied when they heard a voice from outside the garden. It was the voice of Mrs Wardle, a more than middle-aged lady from the cottage two hundred yards away, who had made a quick journey from her own garden.

'You all right? Nothing wrong indoors? You're lucky. We've got tiles down, and a hole in the roof. Rain came right on my face. Pillow soaked. Splash! Right on my face. And old John never felt a drop. Never heard anything, either. He'd have snored through it all if I hadn't of screamed. I thought we should be drowned!'

'How frightening! I'm very sorry.' Florence stood upright.

'I run downstairs to get a pail and towels. And when I got back, there he was, snoring again. I give him a dab with a wet towel. Made him as grumpy as an old sow; but he got up then, and somehow managed to stop the hole with a bit of old tarpaulin. The rain sounded like a flock of birds caught in a hedge. Awful, it was. John was half a mind to come and see if you was all right; but your roof looked sound, so I told him to stay where he was. Made us a pot of tea.'

Mrs Wardle ran home, pleased to have told her story to a good neighbour; and Florence bent down again, thankful to have escaped the greater shock of flooding.

She had live quietly in Slocumbe, making her little drawings, and maintaining cordial relations with Mrs Wardle and others, for just over five years; and she had counted upon continuing in this way for at least another decade of peace. Now the storm became, to her troubled thought, symbolic. The Pattersons, descending upon the Manor, had brought as much discomfort to her heart as deluge had done to the Wardles' home.

Poor Mrs Wardle! Always ready to cheer others with her good-nature, she had really made light of her own midnight fears and discomforts. She and her husband, the 'old John' who always figured in her narratives, were never intrusive, but unlimited in kind feeling.

'I don't want more than that,' thought Florence. She looked approvingly at William, another non-intrusive character. 'That reminds me; I must ring Bertha. I'll just finish this bed.'

The bed was still unfinished when Bertha herself called 'Yoo-hoo' from beyond the low brick wall.

Muddy to the elbows, and with splashes of wet soil upon her face, Florence greeted her friend with pleasure.

'Hello, Bertha. I was going to telephone to ask how you were.'

'I couldn't wait. I knew you'd be busy. You look like a seventeen-year-old!'

'Covered with mud!' retorted Florence. 'And beginning to notice the cold wind. Come indoors, and we'll have some coffee. You look splendid, yourself.'

'My red face. I know it. Not from shame, though. I'm past shame. It's just pleasure. Like a cat purring. A reflex action.' She prepared to walk round to the front gate, still talking in her loud voice. 'I used to think cats only purred when they wanted to. Now I know they can't help it. "Something here inside," as the song says.'

'William purrs all the time, whether he's pleased or not. And wags his tail, too.' Florence opened the gate. 'He's doing both now; so I think he's seen those hungry little birds.'

' "Heedless of their doom, the little victims chirp," ' misquoted Bertha, who was full of apt lines. 'Does he catch them?'

Oh, no; they're on the best of terms.'

'Too well fed. Of course, he's your model.'

'Far from model. He's a very greedy cat.'

'I wish I wasn't greedy. I fight against it — always the loser; and, in an unpleasant sense, the gainer!' Bertha entered the cottage. 'Oh, it's always lovely and warm in here. I shall begin to purr, myself. I'll just slip off my coat. Do you like my new jumper?'

It was a delightful jumper, in pale grey, which made Bertha look younger and slimmer than she had done for years; and it could be praised without insincerity. Florence was not surprised to learn that the choice had been made by an energetic shop assistant who had parried every objection to it.

Seated, and in comfort, Bertha viewed the coffee-pot with almost voluptuous delight. She continued, however, to talk.

'What a storm last night! I thought the house would be blown down. But we're unscathed. Very satisfactory. You've been fortunate, too, apart from the poor flowers. But other people have suffered. The milkman told me there must have been a tornado down the London road. Trees uprooted, the road itself deep in water, hedges flat, brimming ditches, and all the fields like lakes. Terrible! He hadn't seen it himself, he said; but one of their other men hadn't been able to get through. He said it made him think of old Noah. Fortunately we only got the edge of the storm here; the village is protected by Morston Hill; and it had all gone by five o'clock, leaving a trail of havoc.'

The chatter ceased as Bertha sipped her coffee, but for a moment only.

'Lovely! Always a treat.' She looked around the little room, and over to the table in the casement window, where Florence's work was not visible. 'Do you realize I haven't seen you for nearly a week? I simply had to pop in. I've got news!'

'Don't say the Pattersons are leaving already!' scoffed Florence, whose spirits were so much improved by Bertha's company that she could refer to that family almost with flippancy.

'Don't be ridiculous! They're not fly-by-nights; but great people. No. What's happened is that yesterday afternoon, before the storm, I met *her*. Quite a long chat. Very gracious and friendly. She says she's been unwell; but there's no sign of that. Absolutely calm and dignified. But then she's "county," and I suppose she was taught deportment at some posh school for gentlefolk. And she's never had to worry about anything.'

'Lucky woman!' Florence did not forget the anxiety which too often lay behind Bertha's incessant gossip.

'Well, I suppose she is lucky. She's always been waited on hand and foot. It isn't only that she's Lady Patterson. She's naturally the sort that gets waited on. Takes it for granted. That's something you and I never learned to do. We're grateful even to London shop-assistants. But she's very nice and simple, for all her grand manner. I rather expected to be snubbed.'

'Why?' Florence was offering a saucer of warm milk to William, who had been clawing the hearthrug. 'It's only pretentious women who snub.'

'I always think it's a sign they're not sure of themselves.'

'It may be because they're conceited.'

'She's not at all conceited. And

Florence! She's heard of you!'

'Graciousness indeed!' remarked Florence, rather disturbed.

'She asked me a lot about you. I don't mean inquisitively; but as if she was really interested — you know, what sort of person you were, and what you did. She's seen your garden and the cottage: loves them. I told her you were my friend. She said you sounded charming. I think she means to come and see you.'

'See me? Oh, heavens!' Florence's heart sank. She could imagine the glowing picture which had been painted by this true but tactless friend.

Bertha did not hear the exclamation. She had imparted her most significant news. But there was something else to be said in favour of Lady Patterson.

'She was very sorry to hear about Ralph. He's having one of his bad turns, and I told her I was worried about him. She asked if there was anything she could do; did he want books or anything? I said he had all the books he needed; it was just his poor old heart and anaemia, and that he'd be better when warmer weather came and he could sit in the garden. That was how we came to speak of you. She was enthusiastic about your daffs; said she was planning to have some on both sides of her drive next year. Sir Roderick isn't a gardener himself; but she thought it would be a treat for him to come home and see them after a tiring week. He gets very tired. Takes a lot out of himself, poor man. She says he doesn't exercise enough.'

Florence heard very little of this long recital. She picked up one point of it, however.

'I'm sorry Ralph has been poorly,' she said. 'He's very brave; a stoic. Is he better?'

'Well, he's better; but depressed. He doesn't like the look of the world.'

'Who does?'

'I *know*. All those horrible revolutionaries and murderers. It's not like our good old world. I couldn't discover what Sir Roderick feels about it. Lady Patterson smiled — a very sweet smile — when I asked her, and she said: "You'll have to ask him yourself," I said I should be frightened to do that; and she said he'd probably ask what *I* thought. She said he was fond of asking questions, and always listened to the answers, which was more than most politicians do. They think they know them all, and can't bear contradiction. She said they were very stupid men. I told her that was what I thought, too. Oh, I can assure you we got on splendidly. She shook hands at parting. It was very charming. I'm so glad the Pattersons have come to live here.'

'Are you?'

'Yes, I am. They give you such a feeling of confidence, somehow. I've seen the daughter, too, a Mrs Hamburg. Not as friendly as her mother. Rather shy. Looks down her nose. I suppose it's the younger generation. They think one will disapprove of them, and they try to get their blow in first. Isn't it strange how everybody now expects criticism. I know I do. And it's often true. This coffee *is* delicious, Florence. I wish mine ever tasted as good. Your magic touch! I see William has finished his milk. Lucky cat! No troubles; and everything provided. Sometimes I wish I was a cat. Or a Patterson! But I suppose even Pattersons have their black moments. Are you working very hard?'

'Not as well as I should like.'

'They say all artists are creatures of mood, though one wouldn't think it of you. Always the same, as if your life was as perfect as your coffee. Don't you sometimes have bad moments?'

'A few,' admitted Florence. 'Not very interesting ones.'

'You keep them to yourself. I'm not like that. I talk too much about mine. Do I bore you with them?'

'Never.'

'I'm sure you wouldn't show it if I did. You and Lady Patterson are alike — naturally sweet-tempered. I know you'll take to each other instantly. Be like sisters. Oh, yes, you will. She was nice to me, and said we must go on meeting — asked if she could come and see Ralph. But once she sees *you* my poor nose will be quite out of joint. Oh, dear, I wish I was different — had more to give.'

Bertha sighed, reluctant to leave one whom she trusted, yet eager to be again at

Ralph's side, in case he needed her care.

'I must go!' She jumped her feet, and reached for her coat. 'I'll ring you later, to say how Ralph is. Look! There's the sun coming out in a glorious blaze! After the storm, tranquillity! Like *The Pastoral Symphony*. Lovely music! Goodbye, dear. You're like *The Pastoral Symphony* yourself — without the storm. Wonderfully healing!'

She waved from the gate, while Florence, after waving back more soberly, stood thoughtfully in the porch. When at last she moved indoors, and saw the empty coffee-cups, her spirits were low.

'Poor brave woman!' she thought. 'And why does the other one want to see me?'

20
Retrospect

Just over thirty years earlier, when she was twenty, and in uniform as a private in the W.V.S., Florence had met with Syd Patterson. Syd, an ex-fighter pilot, brave and reckless until a mishap, for which he was not responsible, destroyed his flying nerve, was still serving with the Air Force, on the ground. The two had taken an immediate liking to each other, and often met; But Syd was drinking a good deal, and more than once, having arranged to meet her, he failed to keep the appointment.

After such a failure he was always self-condemningly contrite, and told the truth.

'It's just me,' he said. 'I'm like that. You may think it's the old nerves; but it's only occasionally them. There are other reasons. At least, one other reason. The truth is, I've got a brother; an older brother. The most discouraging brother in the world. Treads the path of virtue. Sticks to his book and his word. I don't mean he's pious; not at all. But — well, he came first. He's always been there, if you know what I mean. . . .

'Do you know? The model. The first precious cast. They talk about heredity; and I suppose there is something in that — genes and things; — but there's a lot in atmosphere, too. Whatever I did, I could never catch up. He was my mother's favourite; could do no wrong. Also, he's bigger and solider than I am, physically and mentally. Of course, I've always thought I was the genius of the family — ought to be free, untrammelled . . .

'He never agreed. He thinks a man should keep a steady eye on his own advancement, nurse his gifts, cultivate his advantages. That's his fetish. Look here, I'll introduce you when I get a chance; see what you make of him. I think you'll agree that he's inhuman. Naturally, he's the pet of his C.O. He would be. With his legal training — just started at the Bar when this bloody war began — he's a master of paper work. I'm not so sure about his fighting ability. I don't mean he's afraid. He just wouldn't run the risks I've run. Mind, I'm fond of the old fellow. And I hate his guts, too. See what I mean?'

'About a quarter of it,' was Florence's reply.

'Ah, you're a peach! Any other girl of your quality would have turned me down for standing her up as I've done. You don't. Wouldn't dream of it. That's why you do me good. Or would do, if I hadn't got the bug of unreliability. I shall never settle; and I blame a lot of that on Rod — my brother. You'll understand when you see him. He's a sort of Bayard. Never slips. But I've told you his fault — ambition: "By that sin fell the angels" — Shakespeare. Another is pride. Sensitive to the point of madness. He means to get on, but without breaking a single rule. That's why I have to get off — as far as I can from rule. . . .

'He's so damned high-principled! I've been overshadowed all my life. I really meant to get killed in the air. That's why I chose to be a fighter-pilot. I wasn't thinking of that when I got knocked out; but I had it as a general design. Blasted fools rescued me. Well, I know you must find all this a bore. You don't? That's kind. I appreciate it. You're more likely to find old Rod a bit of a bore. On the other hand, you may break through that crust of nobleness that gives me the willies!'

This, she now saw, had been a crucial conversation. It had made such an impression upon her that she could recall almost every word of it. Syd, always attractive, had respected her too greatly to philander as he did with other young women. He may not have wanted her to fall in love with him; but he did, short of love, want her to know what he believed to be the truth about himself. Probably he had been half in love, and too self-distrustful to plunge deeper. Hence his constant flights from seriousness. Was this the truth? She had believed so, at the time.

Rod, when they met, showed no comparable self-distrust. Nor did she at first perceive the condemned faults of pride and ambition. Where Syd was wiry, ginger, rubber-faced, and full of nervous gesture, Roderick was quiet. He was the taller by quite three inches; his features were firm and regular; his carriage was that of a born soldier. Steel-blue eyes seemed to penetrate sham at sight. A beautiful and resolute mouth confirmed Syd's admission that he was no coward.

What else had she noticed at their encounter? Great courtesy of manner, with reserve and perhaps caution. Syd was disposed, from inner tension, to be over-familiar; Roderick's chivalry would never crack. Yes, a Bayard. Was his indifference to temptation a little repelling?

His voice, very clear and musical, gave the impression that he was used to communicating his thoughts — or giving commands — so unhesitatingly that agreement or obedience followed at once.

With the eyes and lips she had already noticed, this voice assured Florence of his quality. In a comparison, Syd faded. 'I've been overshadowed all my life.' When they stood together he was not so much overshadowed as dwarfed. His body shrank. His voice dwindled to a grizzle. His whimsical face became that of a chilled and shivering monkey. She had never seen such an alteration. Poor Syd! She applied his words, and pitied his sense of inferiority.

Poor Syd! Poor Syd! In company with him, Roderick alone was seen and heard. Florence, young, inexperienced, and needing, above all, signs of masculine strength to counterbalance her own delicacy of spirit, found him a man indeed.

She dreamed of Roderick that night, was eager for their next meeting, and when that came, was enchanted anew. Soon aware that his interest was equally warm, she was in ecstasy. Being away from home, because of her W.V.S. duties, she had escaped from her father's anxious supervision, and felt deliciously free. She went so far as to show some of her little drawings to the new friend, from whom she received ardent praise. It was the first thrilling encouragement she had experienced; and her determination to become an artist, on however miniature a scale, was fixed.

Rod, it appeared, was not by choice a professional soldier. He had always meant to be a barrister. 'You see, it's my life,' he confided. 'I've always wanted to spend my days in Court. Yes, with a wig on. It's not unreasonably hot. I hadn't thought of it as anachronistic. There's something to be said for what you call prehistoric adornments. They add dignity — solemnity — to the proceedings; and separate Judges and Counsel from litigants. No, I can't agree that it's all show. One day I'll take you into Court — when the war's over, of course — and you'll see for yourself.'

When the war was over: he expected their friendship to continue! That was joy! Joy also attended his explanations of legal terms and usages, which often arose as they walked or dined alone together. Her lightness of heart increased; she felt wiser than she had ever been; somebody quite different from the subdued girl who had been kept at home in case harm should befall her; and her laughter was nourished by new tenderness.

One evening Rod took her hand across the table for two at which they were sitting. She did not withdraw the hand. She knew that the moment she had so often dreamed of had really come; and was so happy that she hardly heard the words he was using. Very quiet, confident words came at first; but they grew less coherent as he stumbled into a kind of speech that was strange to him. He was not addressing a Judge, nor pleading a case in which he was only professionally interested. There were the words, the almost abject words, usually heard by maids in fancy alone.

Florence, who was without cruelty, did not play with him. She replied with the greatest simplicity: 'Dear Rod, don't worry. I've loved you from the first moment. With all my heart. Nothing will change me.'

'Nor me,' said Roderick.

There followed days which afterwards assumed an air of trance. She had not walked from her billet; she had been borne by the wind. The car she drove sped along the byways, even at night, when sidelights were the only permissible illumination, by a sort of magic power, escaping every hazard by miracle. And when she and Rod were able to meet they needed no words to express their mutual emotion. He, being given eloquence by nature, could indicate some of his problems; she, never talkative, allowed play to her gift for mockery, which he did not always understand. Otherwise they rejoiced at being together, and in love.

Such days in time of war, could not last; and Roderick was sent overseas, where, although he was safe and fairly comfortable, she pictured him in constant danger. She herself gradually accepted his absence as inevitable. Their correspondence, hasty and unsentimental, and marked by no express promises, was full of the assumption that, once the war was over, they would be together for life. Both had too much pride to risk effusiveness; but both wrote simple truth, and Florence adorned her notes with the little sketches and caricatures which kept Rod perpetually amused.

He told her so. She responded by sending more. Having already resolved to follow her talent, she found pen and pencil at last as fluent as her imagination. She knew her talent to be a small one; but she was rich in it. 'Keep on. Keep on,' wrote Roderick. 'You'll delight multitudes. The last sketches were better than ever. They filled me with pride.'

Could any other praise have been as intoxicating? To be so prized by the man one loves 'was very heaven.' ('Wordsworth,' as Syd would add, with his habit of naming the author of every tag!) She could imagine no greater happiness — no greater, at least, than anything short of being in Rod's arms.

Those, and other adoring thoughts, were a feast to indulge whenever the routine of daily work allowed. Rod was perfect. Rod was her ideal, her inspiration.

21
Rod's Mother

In three months he was back in London — 'very busy,' he told her in the short announcement following his arrival there. 'Meeting all sorts of interesting people. I'll tell you about them when I'm able to get a little leave. Meanwhile, all my love.'

That was enough for comfort. If he was in London, he was not in battle. True, London was a target for air attack; but there was protection there, and he was not fighting. Florence proudly imagined him in company with the interesting people, attracting them all by his charm, but remaining true to her as a Bayard was sure to do. She had no fears; only longing for his company and pride in his triumphs.

Syd alone troubled her confidence by a grumble.

'Old Rod seems to be having a gay time in the Great Metrolops,' he remarked casually. 'Nobs of the finest order. You'd think he'd be able to get away from them for one weekend; but being invited to country houses and made a fuss of, he feels he's a bit too good for the rest of us. You remember what the Seven Deadly Sins are, of course. Gluttony's not one of Rod's. But there's such a thing as not being able to stand corn. And he loves to be made a fuss of. It feeds his ambition. He's always had a taste for grandeur. "My friend, the Duchess." '

This was Syd's lifelong jealously showing itself in a new form. He must have guessed more than Florence knew about the vows she had exchanged with Roderick; but he was not teasing. His tone was full of underlying bitterness. Therefore what he said went straight to her heart, leaving there the disagreeable impression it had been meant to make.

When Roderick, handsome as ever, did at last appear she had the sharp, stabbing thought: 'He's changed!'

The fear was dismissed as soon as they were happily alone together; but when he was gone again it returned. The difference in him was so slight that only abnormal sensitiveness would have detected it; but it was enough to keep Florence wakeful.

For a while she told herself that his more worldly tone was a superficial infection from the grand company he had been keeping. It had led him to be more gracious, and less spontaneously tender, in manner. It would pass. But Syd made another comment, which again went deep into her consciousness.

'Old Rod's got too much damned condescending for my taste. He's come to the conclusion that we're rather small beer — one smaller than ever. Did you notice?'

This shrewdly malicious remark explained Roderick's diminished interest in her own little drawings. After smiling over them rather abstractedly, as if his attention lay elsewhere, he set them aside with a pat of approval.

'Delightful,' he said. 'Charming.'

Next, he left her in haste, looking at his wristwatch with the air of one with an urgent appointment. In an undertone, he explained his haste.

'It's rather important, dearest. There's a chance that I may be put on the short list of candidates for Hever.'

Florence was taken by surprise.

'What, political candidates?'

'What else?' In replying, he had put a finger lightly to her cheek. He might as well have called her a 'pretty little dear,' she afterwards reflected; following this mild resentment with the thought, in consternation: 'Grand people. Politics. They're not in my line at all.'

Still later, Syd had a visit from his mother.

'You'll hate her,' he told Florence. 'I do. She's small. Gimlet eyes. Witch's chin. And, by God, she hates me. I don't know why she troubles to come and see me. She didn't bother when I crocked up. Simply wrote and said the journey would be too much for her. Well, I ask you!'

Florence, by now aware of every danger

to happiness, thought, but did not say: 'She's not coming to see you, my boy. It's me. She's somehow heard of me, and I'm to be subjected to those gimlet eyes.'

Rod's mother, as Syd had remarked, was a small woman, smaller than Florence herself, and she had a decidedly shrewish aspect. Not only did the gimlet eyes look quickly in every direction, as if their owner feared traps and suspected poison, but a sharp nose, rather like a starling's beak, followed the eyes and suggested that she was about to snatch a crumb that slower birds had coveted. Her voice scratched the ear; her hands were like a parrot's claws; her general disapproval was conveyed in shrill exclamations of impatience.

'Don't be stupid, Sydney!' she cried, when Syd, excited by his mother's presence, tried to lighten the conversation with extravagance. 'You know I detest it. And you, Miss Marvell, what do *you* do when you're not in uniform? I suppose your father can afford to keep you idle. He can't? What are you going to do, then, when this wretched war is over? Draw? What an idea!'

'Lovely drawings, Mother,' interjected Syd, in loyalty. 'You must see some of them.'

'I suppose you find them easy to do.' Mrs Patterson showed complete lack of interest in trivialities. She evidently dwelt in thought only upon important matters, such as social position. It was significant that she did not once refer to her son Roderick. He might not have existed; or, if he had a place in the world, it was beyond reach of such groundlings as Syd and Florence.

The visit was quickly over. Having satisfied maternal curiosity, Mrs Patterson left by an early train, brushing aside Syd's suggestion that she should stay longer.

'Quite impossible. I'm dining with Lady Twentyman. Goodbye, Miss Marvell.'

When she had gone, Syd turned to Florence.

'Remember what I said?' he asked.

'I remember.' But Florence spoke apparently carefree words mechanically. She read deeper than Syd had done. With

259

rebellious pride, she was thinking: 'Not approved. Not the sort of girl to sit down with Lady Twentyman. She may be right; but, for all that, she's wrong about me.'

One more communication from Syd came a few days later, when they were walking together by the sea.

'You'll be demobbed before I shall,' he told her. 'I shall be stuck here, doing the chores and taking the kicks, while you'll be settling down with your old pens and brushes. No fun for me. Nobody to talk to. It will be Hell. I've been able to rely on you for company. And jolly good company, too.'

'Very kind of you,' acknowledged Florence.

'Oh, you may scoff; but it's true. You don't realize what a pal you've been, listening to my jabber and sympathizing. By the way, did Mother remind you of a rat in a trap? I caught her eyeing you a lot. She also asked a lot of questions. Had Rod seen much of you? and so on. I was mum. I pretended I didn't know what she meant. So naturally she accused me of being stupid. She always does. Always has done. Doesn't understand that originality is a baffling quality to the unoriginal. I'm original. Did you know?'

'Very original, Syd.' It was smiling. 'And very nice.'

'Good. So are you. Mother wouldn't see that. Just a pretty girl in uniform. You're not related to a baronet, or even a knight. Not an O.B.E. in the family. She's got her sights trained on a girl named Evelyn Something-or-other. Good family. Pots of money —'

'For you, Syd?' But Florence had taken his meaning; and her heart was thudding so loudly that she was afraid Syd would hear and remark upon it.

'As Mother says, "Don't be stupid!" She doesn't care a damn about me. You noticed that, I'm sure. Rod's the man for her money. Don't take me too literally: She hasn't got any money. It's been her trouble all along; too little money, and two lads to bring up. One of them is me — the idle apprentice; no good, let him sink. But Rod — that's a different story. She wants to see him Prime Minister.

Well, well, I just thought I'd give you the tip about Evelyn What's-her-name; and the bait that's being spread for old Rod. Draw your own conclusions, darling. You can still hold on to him, if you like. Most girls would.'

The 'tip' had burned its way through Florence's heart. She did not answer; but her thought was: 'I shall see when he next comes. I'm terribly afraid. *I'm terribly afraid.*'

That night — it was a rare collapse — she cried.

22
The Parting

Roderick's next visit was all-important. Florence's constraint made her less simple, and he may have been affected by the change; but in her hypersensitive state she found everything amiss.

To entertain her — and hitherto no such entertainment had been needed between them — he dwelt upon compliments he had received, the confidential promises of support in his career, and, naturally, his sanguine hope of renown. With every boast (for in fact each was a boast) Florence felt her heart grow heavier. Instead of being impressed by tales of social success, she saw looming ahead a cloud of grandeur for which she felt no inclination; indeed no capacity. It was Rod she loved; not his dream of power.

She had seen his mother. Now she saw that the mother's son was intoxicated by the prospect of becoming — he did not say as much; but this was the picture she formed — one of the highest politicians and lawyers in the country. Syd's hints about Rod's ambition and Mrs Patterson's resolve were confirmed.

At last, unconscious of her own harsh abruptness, she asked:

'I'm wondering what place you see for me in all this, Rod.'

He was taken aback.

'What d'you mean?'

'This grand life you speak of. Secretaries of State, Ambassadors, Lord Justices. I shouldn't know what to say to any of them.'

'Oh, you'll learn.' It was careless, not persuasive. He did not meet her eyes. That, to Florence, was a fact of chilling importance. It meant that he had seen, or been told of, her temperamental unsuitability for greatness. She imagined herself trailing after Rod in an ascent to high places, meeting humiliation after humiliation at the hands of less scrupulous women, and, having failed to 'learn,' being impatiently cast aside as an encumbrance; within two, three, or five years a deserted pensioner, tucked away somewhere while another woman, whether wife or mistress, enjoyed unenviable *réclame*.

His mother, she was sure, had foreseen such probabilities, and was determined that her son not suffer himself to be caught by a suburban miss. His mother did not matter. What mattered was that Rod himself, absorbed in visions of future glory, showed no understanding of the fact that her only personal ambition was to draw and paint unpretentiously but as well as she could.

These were serious points. She loved with all her heart; she would have been ready to sacrifice her own dreams on his account; but she could not accept condescension from a lover. Finally, he had not once, in his descriptions of the company he had been keeping, mentioned the girl, Evelyn, on whom, according to Syd, his mother had 'got her sights trained.'

The silence became unbearable.

'It would break my heart to feel I was hampering you, Rod.'

The response was an impatient frown; the first black frown she had see upon that handsome face.

'But this is something of paramount importance to me, darling. With all these channels opening —'

'Yes, I see that. It's because I see it that I'm full of qualms. It's a terrible responsibility.'

He brushed her honesty aside.

'This is absurd! You'll naturally adapt yourself. I can't see what you're fussing about. . . . You're not usually stupid.'

Stupid! That was a word of ill omen; the worst he could have chosen. It was what his mother called Syd! And Rod's changed manner suggested a doubt indentical with her own. He would not have spoken thus to Evelyn, who, still according to Syd, was of high birth and had 'pots of money.' To herself he had used a term of disparagement heard from his mother; thereby contrasting her incapacity with Evelyn's aristocratic assurance. Not, she was convinced, her pennilessness with Evelyn's wealth.

If Roderick had now, laughing, embraced her, exclaiming exultantly, 'We'll climb together, darling, side by side. It will be the greatest fun. And we'll have delicious times when we've shaken off the solemn formalities and can be alone. . . . Don't forget; I shall be there! I know you'll have a marvellous triumph, with all the Ambassadors whispering state secrets to you!' she would have been his for ever. Instead, he seemed to look at her from a forbidding height; and everything Syd had hinted about his nature rushed into her mind. In this moment of clairvoyance she realized that, for Roderick, love would never be strong enough to absorb criticism or satisfy his heart. For his fulfilment as a man he must aim at, and obtain, power in Politics or the Law, or both. This was his character; and character was Fate.

Still fighting conviction, she said thoughtfully:

'No. I'm not usually stupid. I'm not being stupid now. I'm being wise for both of us. Both, Rod!'

She had seen — or thought she had seen — behind that frown of impatience another expression which suggested a first flying acquiescence in her doubt. Had he glimpsed the possibility of escape from a commitment that he was too honourable to break?

Roderick turned away.

'You're talking like a little fool, Florrie!'

At this, she awakened altogether from a celestial dream of lifelong accords. She had shrunk from the possibility of causing him great pain; but this one speech, showing insensitiveness, and forecasting endless unhappy disagreement was decisive.

The words remembered by Roderick thirty years later were then painfully spoken.

'No, Rod, I'm not a fool. Ignorant, yes; you've always known that. But I've just seen what I think is the truth about us. I'm not cut out for career. You are. I know I'm right. You must marry a girl who shares your ambition for greatness. I'm sure there's such a girl among your grand friends —'

His attention was caught.

'Grand friends?' he interrupted. 'Because I've been telling you . . . Are you wanting to throw me over?'

'Never. I'm thinking of your life. Very calmly.'

'But you're trembling!'

'I know. From head to foot. But I must say this to you. You want great worldly success. It's necessary to you. I want tranquillity. That's the difference. It doesn't mean criticism. I love you. I appreciate you. I think you're . . . that you'll be . . . a great man. *Almost* a great man. You're bound to succeed, unless —'

'Unless what?' It sounded scornful.

Florence's trembling increased so much that she could hardly speak.

'I don't know. It's something instinctive. I don't mean lack of quality, or generosity, or talent. Nothing you can change.'

'Ridiculous!'

'Oh, I'm just irritating you. I don't want to do that. Do forgive me, dear, dear Rod. And don't worry about me. I see what's right — for you. And I'm doing it for both of us. It's all been lovely. Wonderful. But I can't go on.'

Roderick was not used to doubt of his future or questioning of his principles. And he was affected by her conduct. She had accused him of being flawed. Since his temper had also been aroused, he would not plead; but temper invariably made him cold, with a hauteur which destroyed sympathy. Shrugging, he turned on his heel. They parted without a kiss.

PART SIX

THIRTY YEARS LATER

23
Encounter

These doings and sayings were as vivid in Florence's memory as if they had happened overnight. Thirty years of conning had given them the permanence of Holy Writ; and while she had been able to assure Saul that his father was no jilt, her insight into Roderick's dilemma had been confirmed when, six months after their break, he married Evelyn.

The announcement of that fashionable wedding, with its list of distinguished guests, had chilled her heart. She neither wept nor repined; but it took all her natural stoicism to endure the thought: 'I shall never see him again. I shall miss him all my life. But I was right. Horribly, disgustingly right. He's done the best possible thing.'

She had survived. Wretchedness lessened; and gradually she had been able, with pride and irony, to watch Roderick's progress in Politics and the Law. Nor had she envied Evelyn. There were moments in which she giggled over the naughty conviction that she had escaped a deadly fate. 'He must love it. She probably does, too. Great family, pots of money, a splendid position in the public eye; and Success! Wonderful! To me, it would have been Purgatory — plain, simple Purgatory!'

So far, then, she had attained a somewhat rueful contentment with obscurity. But her meeting with Saul had undermined a lifetime's endurance. It had recalled the first joy of love for Roderick, stabbing her with regret that she had never borne children whom she could love and protect from harm and terror. Lucky Evelyn, to have both son and daughter! Unlucky Evelyn, to miss the rewards of loving trust!

'Why on earth should she be curious about me? I don't want to see her. I never did. We belong to different worlds!'

There was alarm, but no pride, in this exclamation. Florence knew that her own world was a small one of amusing occupations and inventions, attractive little watercolours, Jane Austen and Parson Woodforde, the immature notelet of enthusiasm from some child who loved her drawings; her garden, her pets, and for human companionship, Annabel, Bertha, Mr Leadbitter, and the garrulous friendliness of her neighbours. All were undemanding, and a refreshment to her simplicity.

'They're what I need. I should like to go on living quietly here, a middle-aged spinster, until the shadows fall. Then be forgotten.'

Continuing in this vein, she felt sure that there could be no such contrast with Roderick's wife as Bertha prophesied. Great ladies had their own friends. They did not press unwanted familiarity upon obscure female artists. Once curiosity about the oddities of such trifling persons had been satisfied, they turned away. 'Yes, quite charming. Quaint little cottage. Quaint little creature nibbling away inside it, like a guinea-pig. And now back to real life, and the society of really interesting, really important people!' That would be Lady Patterson's conclusion. One encounter, a few exchanged words, and then, thank God, 'no more of thee and me.' All the same, Evelyn's curiosity was both inexplicable and unwelcome.

Saul was a different matter. He, like his father, would ride off to career and masculine preoccupations, entirely forgetful of the elderly dame to whom he had poured out his boyish desperation. He might easily develop shame over an unfortunate loss of nerve, and would then shun her as a witness of it who might presume upon her knowledge.

'I shan't do that,' murmured Florence. 'You needn't be afraid, Saul. Didn't I let your father go? Yes; but that might have broken my heart. Nonsense! "Hearts do not break; they sting and ache," as poor Katisha sings. I wonder if Rod has forgotten how we saw *The Mikado* together? I expect so; but it was lovely. Just he and I, at the back of the Circle. I was so happy that I thought my heart would burst with rapture. But it was the last time. Syd warned me of the poison in Rod's ambitiousness; and his mother decided at once that I "wouldn't do." Some girls — Syd said so — would have hung on; I couldn't. If Rod and his mother were proud-stomached, so was I. And though I despised her more than she despised me, she was right. I shouldn't have "done." So it's all turned out for the best. Rod's achieved what he wanted; and I found I wasn't really necessary to him or to anybody else. Very salutory to a vain young thing! Not palatable, even at this distance . . .'

Having soon afterwards paid one of her regular visits to Ralph and Bertha Pledge, Florence received two other shocks. The first concerned her host; for Ralph had had one of his bad turns. He looked like a corpse. Heavily bearded because his trembling hand could no longer direct a razor, he lay back in an armchair, his face pale, his eyes half-closed, and his poor mouth gaping wide. She was so much troubled by the sight that she did not dare to look at Bertha; but sat down quickly by the invalid's side, taking his cold hand in her warm one, and struggling to think of some words of cheer.

The effect of her clasp was magical.

'Dear Florence!' Ralph's mouth no longer sagged. His dead eyes brightened. He smiled.

'Been pining for you!' cried Bertha. 'Wants all your news!'

'All? That's out of the question. But — ah, yes! I'll tell him the story of Annabel Marvell!' Florence was inspired. 'Once upon a time . . .'

'That's how the fairy tales begin. Is it legend or fact?' Bertha insisted upon knowing.

'Both.'

She then described how her telephone had rung last night and how Annabel, her voice pitched high, announced that she had just landed the part of a talkative old maid in a television serial. The engagement would run for thirteen weeks; and as this was a certainty, and she had never before acted in front of those great lights and giant cameras, Annabel was in an actress's heaven.

'Me fortune's made!' she squealed. 'Something in the kitty at last! A TV star! And the precious infants who run the show think I'm wonderful. They say I shall steal it. I haven't told them I model myself on dear old Bertha; but that's the truth. Don't betray me! She won't recognize herself. After all, I'm an artist, like you, dear. The difference between us is that I'm brazen. I put the idea of me being good into their minds by saying so myself. It pays, you know. "Stir it and stump it, and blow your own trumpet." You must come up and lunch, to celebrate. Bring your boy friend, Michael Angelo! I'd like to dazzle him again. Are you having bread and cheese for supper? I'm not. I've treated myself to a couple of cutlets and a half-bottle of Portuguese *vin rosé*. Shan't sleep a wink tonight.'

This, suitably edited, was the story that gave the Pledges a splendid ten minutes.

The invalid chuckled again and again in the depths of his beard. His eyes shone like a bird's. He rubbed life into his chilly hands.

'He-he-he! Almost as good as seeing Annabel herself! A tonic! What sort of part is it?'

'That you must find out from the show itself. I gather that she has to talk a good deal.'

'She'll do that to the life!' cried Bertha. 'She's a proper chatterbox. But I hope she's not going to use *me* as a model!'

The twilight breeze cooled Florence's cheeks, which had been flushed by the warmth of the Pledges' tiny sitting-room, and settled her mind, which had been stirred by lively chatter. As the High Street was almost deserted, she walked briskly, glad to be alone once more and upon the homeward way. After feeding her pets, who would pretend to be starving, she could relax over one of her favourite books. Lovely!

The first indoor lights were beginning to twinkle here and there, while overhead, in a pale sky, early stars, like fairy lamps, aroused dreams and tender links with youth. Peace filled the air; shadows took fantastic shapes; Annabel's rejoicing at a triumph made her merry; and Ralph's new vitality, although that had its saddening undertones, gave her great delight. So, more remotely, did the thought of Saul's revived courage, for which she took modest credit. She spoke aloud, almost silently, as she walked.

'Old Bertha can't always hide her anxiety. Ralph sees that, and thinks of himself as a burden. I must tell Annabel how they both laughed. I hope she'll remember Bertha's sensitiveness to ridicule. She's sure to. Her brazenness is half the time protection against the megrims, poor girl. It's awful to think how unhappy even cheerful people are! All trying to escape from the hideousness of life!'

These unusually sententious comments upon human nature were interrupted, when she was halfway along the High Street, by an untoward event. She was nearly abreast of the Post Office when a tall man came unexpectedly from the big doorway. By the light shining within, his face was so clearly illuminated that she at once recognized Roderick.

'Oh, golly!' This time the words were not spoken aloud. 'How awkward! Perhaps he won't see me, won't recognize me!' It was horrible to feel so deeply embarrassed.

At first the twilight promised escape, although the supposition that she might have altered too much for recognition was disagreeable. She instinctively lowered her head.

Roderick, however, having reached the pavement, glanced to his right, towards a young woman who seemed to be in a hurry. From casual interest in a stranger, he passed at once to the welcome of a friend.

'Why, Florrie!' Extended hands checked her. She felt her own small fist swallowed and held by two larger ones. 'This is delightful! How are you?'

The old smile was there; the smile that had once lifted her heart to ecstasy. It almost did that today, by its warm spontaneity; but she saw within the smile traces of unmistakable nervous strain. He was tired; more distinguished in appearance than he had been when young; and, as was natural in one long engaged in public life, instinctively gracious. But the informality was for herself alone. He was still, at heart, the man for whom she had been ready to sacrifice happiness, but not independence.

'Hello, Rod.' It was equally simple, and equally endearing. She did not know that Evelyn had never once called him 'Rod.' Evelyn disliked all abridgment of Christian names, as an affectation used by politicians who, for votes' sake, wished to be thought pally. This was why she had called her boy-child Saul, and her girl Sandra. But Roderick, this evening, although he had so lately damned Florence as a self-righteous wiseacre, found the abbreviations of his own name as pleasant as a caress. Time having dissolved in that single instant, he was tempted to kiss at least the cheek of his old love.

24
Heart to Heart

'Look here, we mustn't just meet and part,' he cried. 'Where are you bound? Could I be allowed to join you on your way there?'

Florence was stern.

'I live at the other end of the village — the wrong way for you. You'd better go straight home.'

'That — as I've met you — would be quite impossible.'

He laughed in saying this, shedding every unpleasant preoccupation, and re-establishing their old intimacy. At the same moment he suited his normally long stride to her shorter, quicker step. If

Bertha, at home tending her Ralph, and trying to amuse him a second time with exclamations over Annabel's coming triumph, could by miracle have been simultaneously there and here, she would have been stirred by devil-inspired inquisitiveness. Her eyes and mouth making three round 'o's like a pawnbroker's sign, she would have felt her brain to be on fire with curiosity.

However, Florence was not really the girl she had been thirty years ago; and she escaped from what might have been a too-emotional response to his laughter by saying:

'I met Syd the other day — also by accident.'

'He told me he had seen you. Boasted of it, in fact. He's rather flamboyant still, as I expect you noticed.'

'I suppose you could call him flamboyant. I felt he wasn't happy.'

'No, he's not happy. He blames me for that. Didn't he, to you?'

'I can't remember his doing so. He behaved as if he were dissatisfied with himself.'

'How was that?'

'I can't explain. It was just an impression. I thought he was doing what we all do in moments of depression.'

'I don't believe you have any moments of depression. I've just had one that lasted more than an hour. I was marooned the other night for about that length of time in the storm. My car stalled. All I could see and hear was rushing water. I felt like Noah.'

'You probably felt like Rod Patterson — indignant with the elements.'

'It was most disagreeable. My chauffeur, a man of decision, insisted that I should stay in the car while he got help. So he went off, leaving me alone with what I expect you'd call my conscience.'

'Yes, I should most likely call it that. Were you really alone?'

'Quite alone — with my conscience. I had all the time in the world to realize my own futility, and to remember every person who detests and despises me. A fairly long list; and no friends to counterbalance them. I suppose that was worst of all.'

Florence shivered, picturing the scene and his mood.

'I'm sorry you had such black thoughts, Rod. They're not natural to you.'

'No, not usual; but not to be forgotten. Nothing can be more bitter — and lasting — than the sense of futility. I had what's nowadays called "the moment of truth." An absolute conviction of worthlessness.'

'Well, that's obviously due to physical discomfort.'

'No, my conscience. It was a very long hour. But the time did pass. Blenkinsop came back, with boots, oilskins, and another car. We splashed about a good deal, and managed to get home. A hot bath; some even hotter toddy; and my enemies became pygmy-like. All the same, I'd had a foretaste of Hell. I've never been able to say, as Syd does, "It's not my fault." Nor have you, Florrie!'

'Syd says I've always been a prig.'

'Perhaps more of a devil. A speaker of cruel truth — which I didn't fail to remember in that hour. You've had a good life, haven't you?'

They were now halfway along the High

Street. Darkness was increasing. Almost nobody else was in the street; shops were closed; there were few street lamps; and it was not yet time for the Three Diamonds or the Dragon public house to switch on its lights. A beautiful softness was in the air, as if the countryside had invaded the village and made it magically serene.

These chances had affected their conversation, giving it a close personal turn which neither had intended. Roderick repeated his question as to whether she had had a good life.

'A lucky one, Rod. Perhaps not particularly valuable to others, as yours has been.'

'I wonder. But you've enjoyed it? I'm sure you must have done. That's a rare achievement, you know.'

'I'm afraid it is.'

That was all she could articulate; and her voice was so low that Roderick had to stoop in order to hear the words.

The following silence, which to Florence was full of emotion, lasted an entire minute, during which they walked more slowly. Then, as if his thoughts had been ranging, Roderick spoke again.

'There's another thing I want to say to you, Florrie. My boy, Saul, came home a couple of nights ago. I hadn't see him for a long time — several months, in fact; — and I've had no idea what he was doing. He came to my study at night, after what must have been a crucial talk with a wonderful lady he'd met on his way home. A wonderful lady.'

Florence felt her heart plunge. She had made Saul promise not to mention her name. Had he broken his word?

'Where was this?' she added.

'On the train. They shared a compartment, it seems. I thought she could be nobody but Florrie Marvell. Was I right?'

'I don't recognize myself.'

'But then, of course, I was always more appreciative than you were of Florrie Marvell.'

'Yes.' There was no longer any need to be non-committal. The only possible course was to speak plainly. 'Will you be able to help him?'

Roderick's answer was equally blunt.

'To be quite candid with you, as liars say in the witness box, I don't know what I can do. I'm taking him to see a criminal solicitor. That's to say, a solicitor of the highest probity who knows everything about the London confidence tricksters. He'll advise us what to do.'

This brought some comfort. She answered, with candour:

'I'm glad to hear you say "us." It suggests that you'll give him what he most needs.'

'What would you say that was?'

'Love.'

Roderick was struck by the word.

'Oh? You liked him, did you?'

'More than liked. Much more. I thought him a lovable child.'

'I see. Did he, by any chance, complain that I'd neglected or influenced him to his disadvantage? You know what I mean.'

'He made no complaint of you at all. He was simply distraught — desperate.'

'Desperate, was he? Well, his desperation has gone, for the time being. We've established a *rapport*. But you'd already given him back his courage.'

'I did nothing but tell him to go straight to you. At first, he refused to do that. I think he was afraid of what you'd think of him. I said, if he wouldn't, I would. That was all. I was pretty desperate, myself; afraid he'd throw himself out of the train.'

'As bad as that, was it? Then you saved his life, Florrie. No wonder he extols you. Thank you. The trouble is — I don't try to extenuate — that I've been too busy to look after him. I shall do that in future — get to know him quite well. You think he's worth knowing, do you?'

'Don't be silly, Rod.'

Nobody, for thirty years, had called Roderick silly. Until the talk with Sam, he had been used to ceremonious respect. So he retorted:

'Yes, you always insisted that I should be wise. Always showed extraordinary determination! Some would use another word.' He looked down at her as if she, like Saul, was a lovable child. He was no longer in love with her; but he had never known any human being so easy to talk to. 'In this case, certainly, the wisdom's been on your side. Great wisdom, Florrie. Great understanding.'

Florence brushed away both taunt and compliment.

'Why do you think these men did what they did?'

'My suspicion — only a suspicion, of course — is that they had it in mind to blackmail *me*. "Pay up; or your name will be dragged in the mud." That's always the blackmailer's line.'

Florence was horrified.

'Blackmail? But it would be wanton villainy!'

'What else do you expect in the modern world?'

'I don't know anything about the modern world. Even so, villainy is villainy.'

'A man in the public eye — I'm sorry to be pompous, Florrie; but I want to make myself clear — is always vulnerable. His good name is his lodestone. Usually, like the Russians, they go for sexual peccadilloes. Failing these, something to do with money or his children. Saul, in fact. However, that's only surmise. I'll let you know what Munster — he's the Solicitor — says. Saul and I will both come and tell you, when we've seen him. You'd like that, wouldn't you?'

Florence, still appalled by the word 'Blackmail' and the awful possibilities it opened, made no reply as to the suggested call.

'Will you be safe?' she demanded.

'That we must see,' answered Roderick.

They were nearing the cottage, which she indicated by a slight movement of the hand. Roderick smiled at the prospect.

'That's yours, is it? A lovely place. An exquisite nest for . . .' He teasingly left the description of its occupant unfinished, adding: 'Florrie, I don't want to lose contact with you. You've been a true friend to my boy. He won't forget it. Nor shall I. And there are other things I should like to consult you about.'

She immediately took fright at the suggestion.

'I can't imagine what they are.'

'Not interested?

'Full of interest; but apprehensive.'

'Syd, for example. I'm very worried about him. He gave me a lecture, and marched off in dudgeon. Do you agree I've been a bad brother to him?'

They had reached the cottage gate, and were confronted by Florence's daffodils, ethereal in the darkness.

'I should have said a good brother; but in one sense a reproach. You spoke of his habit of saying "It's not my fault." Do you want to come in?'

'No, you won't want me now. I should like to bring other members of the family to see you — for their good.'

'Oh, I hope not!' She did no more than express sudden panic. 'As you see, the cottage is only big enough for one.'

'We'll camp in the garden,' said Roderick.

'That would scandalize the village. Give you a lasting bad name for unconventionality. Quite as bad in its way as blackmail.'

'Are you thinking that you would suffer?'

'Of course not. I'm not in the public eye.'

'Yes, I was afraid you'd bring that phrase up against me. You have a hard heart, Florrie.'

'I know what villages are.'

'They're only microcosms. But you're quite right. Always right. Your one defect. Forgive me. I'm trying to thank you for what you did to Saul. You understand? Of course you do. Good night, dear girl.'

He was gone, a splendid, gracious figure, erect, and without a backward glance. Florence, turning under her porch, watched him until she felt completely alone in the darkness. A chill wind seemed to have arisen. Shivering, she went indoors.

25
Panic and Recovery

Once within, she gave way to long-suppressed agitation. Already moved by sights of Ralph Pledge on, apparently, the threshold of death, she had received a violent shock from the meeting with Roderick; and his affectionate candour, from which all resentment had been removed by time, following the excitement caused by Saul's astonishing likeness to him, had overstrained her nerves. Old love, together with intervening pains and regrets, swept back into her heart.

Roderick had spoken as he might have done to a dear friend. Bertha's assumptions about his splendid freedom from cares had been shown to be groundless. And Bertha herself, so loyal to a dying husband, and so courageous in endurance, became a golden example to lesser beings. By comparison, her own life was exposed as a long trail of selfishness, a wretched preference of comfort to adventure.

Standing in the tiny living-room of the cottage, she saw the lattice windows for the first time as deliberately protective bars to the world of reality.

'What am I to do? I've thought myself ideally happy, doing work I enjoyed doing; talking to poor old Bertha as if she were a gadabout, whereas she's heroic; taking pride in my little drawings; and feeling secure. Now I'm no longer secure. I'm revealed as a dodger. And I can't adapt myself to any other way of life. I'm too old!'

Years ago it had been different. During the war she had escaped from home and paternal supervision. She had driven cars about the country, in darkness as well as by day, without fear, thinking only of the moment, and, with Rod, experiencing the delicious happiness of loving and being loved by the finest man she had ever known. After their parting she had suffered profoundly; and after her father's death she had assumed responsibility for her own affairs, and to some extent of Annabel's, in a spirit of hope. The acceptance of her first drawings, and the response of children to their successors, had given her wondering satisfaction; and the satisfaction had continued until only the other day. Active from morning to night, never lonely, and never despondent, she had been happy.

All was changed.

'I don't know what on earth to do!'

Normal resoluteness was gone.

Whether she dozed for a few minutes or was simply lost to her surroundings, she could not have decided; but in that lapse of consciousness she must have dreamed of running away from Slocumbe. The Pattersons had run from one home to another; why shouldn't she do the same? But in the Pattersons' case flight was merely an exchange of grandeurs, while in her own it would be an act of cowardice. Besides, she would have to find somewhere else to love; and she had not time to hunt for a new cottage in another county.

Even temporary refuge was impossible; for Annabel, who was poor, lived in London, which would be impossible for the pets. Nor had she a circle of acquaintances, eager to help her. Rod said he had no friends; but there must be scores of people who would be proud to be his hosts for a few weeks. And he had money. She had none. Expecting to remain in her cottage for as long as she lived, she had envisaged no change.

'I'm trapped!'

These were the words which startled her into wakefulness. She looked down at her hands, which had ceased to tremble, and sat erect in the chair. As if he had been waiting for this sign of welcome, William, satisfied with his tea, jumped up, gave her another of his searching glances, and leaned against her breast as he began to wash his white-edged black paws. The tremendous purr which followed his leap died away. Relaxing, as food and warmth spread their comfort, he dropped off to sleep like a contented baby.

Florence, keeping still, and perhaps affected by William's satisfaction, was now able to think less confusedly. Self-confidence returned to a nature which, although hypersensitive, was essentially resolute.

'It was silly of me to think of running away. Of course I won't do that. I've got to stay here. The pets; Rod; Saul; Bertha and Ralph: I can't desert any of them. In some dreadful way — not the pets, because they belong to me and are always here; but the others — all happen at this moment to make demands on me. I want to be let alone; that's very selfish. And just because I dread meeting Rod's wife — I don't know why I should be afraid of her — I've let myself get worked up.'

The reference to Rod's wife set up a feeling of hostility towards Evelyn. What sort of woman could she be, when her son disliked her and when Rod, who should have been strengthened by her love and understanding, confided in another woman? Was she heartless? An egoist? One of those high ladies who thought only of their own superiority to the common herd? Bertha, primed by Charles Dacre, the agent, said she walked about the Manor as very much the *grande dame.* Bertha, poor modest Bertha, was impressed by her condescension. Her voice had been rather 'cultured,' and therefore unpleasing to one who felt distaste for all pretentiousness. . . .

From Evelyn to Roderick. Florence again saw his unguardedly grim expression in that first glimpse on the Post Office steps, and the sudden lightening of it as he caught sight of herself. She repeated, almost verbatim, what they had said to each other while walking along the High Street, well understanding that, so far from making a coward's appeal for pity, he had paid her the greatest compliment of all, reliance upon candid sympathy.

This again reminded her of Saul, who had shown the same confidence. Though frightened by a sense of emergency, and of inadequacy, she had drawn enough strength from within to impress him. She had given him courage to do what she felt to be right. That was quite certain. He had been altogether different after his talk with Rod; and Rod had confirmed her judgment. Rod — dear Rod! — had praised her.

Blessed praise! How it linked Saul with Rod in her heart! Both had a fundamental weakness which she alone perceived and could help them to overcome. This was a wonderful fact!

'After all, I am Florrie Marvell!' she exclaimed, in rare vainglory. 'I was right. I'm always right!' For the first time in her life she experienced the consciousness of power; and it was so sweet that every regret and every variety of self-distrust was lost in new determination: 'I mustn't fail them. They need me. If I hadn't, long ago, been a selfish coward, these things would never have happened!'

This mood of exaltation, like the earlier panic, was quickly followed by more characteristic steadiness. She had been over-excited. William's relaxation suggested the way to composure. Nothing

302

was to be gained by alarm, self-blame, or the grandiose. She was once more little Florrie, the industrious, undistinguished artist, attached to her pets, grateful to Mr Leadbitter for his unvarying kindness, and happy in Annabel's first chance of real success. Viewed soberly, her activities and responsibilities were alike trifling. Father's insistence on modesty as the fundamental virtue had been truly wise.

'Dear William! You've set me a good example!'

She stroked William's black back, gently touched his white, soft, and for the moment clawless, paws, and was rewarded by a faint rumbling of cat's pleasure. He and she were friends. This happy ministration to his comfort indicated her most satisfying role in life. To attempt one more ambitious would be an act of exaggerated self-importance.

Comforted, Florence closed her eyes, breathed deeply as William had done, and followed his example by falling fast asleep.

26
Syd in a New Light

Ten mintues later she was awakened by the shrilling of her telephone bell; and the voice which when then penetrated her drowsiness was like a sharp barking of a small dog. Mr Leadbitter was in his business mood.

'Look here, Miss Marvell, I want to ask your advice. Do you mind? Can you spare time? Good! Get a chair! . . . Well, now, how are you? No harm from your London jaunt? Working? Good! Well, then, do you know a man named Sydney Patterson?'

It was a name Florence did not wish to hear; but she controlled her voice.

'Yes, I do know him.'

'Intimately? I mean, background and everything? He's the brother of Roderick Patterson. I've read in the papers that Roderick has just gone to live in your village.'

'My village, yes.' Florence was able to deride Mr Leadbitter's compliment; but she was seriously troubled by this ominous prelude.

'The world regards it as yours,' barked the voice. 'And right so. Patterson, in village terms, must be an upstart.'

'That is my own opinion, of course.' Florence closed her eyes in speaking, and took a deep breath.

'It should be. But this Sydney, who seems to have knocked about a bit, has written a book. What?'

'I said "Oh, dear!" '

'I thought you did. It's a sort of crazy autobiography. Most of it is about his travels; but there are references to his brother. Schooldays, and so on; War years; differences of outlook and career. Extremely malicious. That's always dangerous for a publisher. We've had the script vetted for libel by our solicitors; and they think there's no gross libel. More innuendo than anything else. Brotherly disrespect. The point I want to put to you is whether Roderick Patterson is the sort of chap to turn nasty — get an injunction. Is he vindictive?'

'Certainly not!' cried Florence, indignantly. 'The reverse. Syd must know that. And Syd should be ashamed of writing unkindly of him.'

'Oh, well, public men are targets, you know. The penalty of fame. Every tin-pot journalist feels entitled to jeer at them.'

'Syd's not "a tin-pot journalist." He's Roderick's brother.'

'No man's a hero to his brother; and I should say this one feels pretty spiteful.'

'That's horrible, Mr Leadbitter!'

'People enjoy seeing the great cut down to size. It makes them feel bigger themselves. You've heard of the inferiority complex.'

'Syd must have it!' cried Florence. She was burning.

'Very likely. We shall probably turn the book down for prudential reasons; but it's got some rather delightful drawings. He's talented, you know.'

'Yes, clever. Cleverer than Roderick.'

'You think that? Most interesting. Also a lot of ingenious little details about their boyhood together; Roderick as the industrious apprentice. Quite a malignant portrait of their mother, who's dead, and can't sue. Nice references to you, as somebody who shared his war.'

'Shared? I was on the ground. He was in the air.'

'He's still there, in his own estimation. But what we're concerned about is the brother. Do you know him as well as you know Sydney?'

'I know him. I was talking to him an hour ago.'

'Oh, really. A friendly chat?'

'Quite friendly.'

'There's a curious story about a young woman who jilted him in his early days. Sydney says he married his present wife to spite the other girl.'

'That's absolutely untrue. He wouldn't do such a thing.'

'It's offered as an illustration of his

egocentric character. You don't agree? Right. There's a sort of claim to responsibility for the jilting; rather obscure; sort of "I took a hand." You know nothing of that? No. Evidently Sydney dislikes Lady Patterson. His picture of her — very amusing indeed — would have to be edited.'

'It sounds to me as if the whole book needs editing out of existence!'

'Well, not the whole book. He calls it *Romance of a Nomad.* Most of it is an account of travels far and wide, with comic sketches of all the odd people he's consorted with.'

'Aren't they all likely to "turn nasty," as you call it?'

'They might. But they're small fry, and can hardly be damaged. Roderick's the big fish. It's the stuff about him that would ensure Press coverage, and sell the book.'

'Disgraceful!'

'All right. You're against it. I was doubtful. After all, it could only be a *success de scandale;* and Mr Gimblett wouldn't like his good name sullied. He's a very "respectable" man. Pure Victorian. Thanks.'

Florence, shuddering in distress, and feeling contempt for Syd's bad behaviour, expected the conversation to end here. She was wrong.

Having reached a decision about the book, Mr Leadbitter switched to another, but related subject; the real purpose of his call. From a bark, his voice dropped to a murmur. If she had been less agitated, Florence would have visualized him with a hand cupped around the mouthpiece of his office telephone.

'Don't go yet. Are you all right? I thought you sounded tired. I don't want —'

'Not tired, Mr Leadbitter. Only vexed.'

'Yes, I'm sorry. Inconsiderate of me. But there's something else I should like to ask — as we're chatting. It's rather more personal. I understand Roderick Patterson has a beautiful blond daughter. Do you know her?'

'Not at all.' It was very sharp. Florence was on the point of putting down the receiver. She felt she could bear to hear no more about the Patterson family.

Mr Leadbitter, however, could not see her expression of disgust; and his voice was like velvet in her ear.

'Oh, that's a pity. A great pity. I thought you'd know everybody in the village. Well, the Pattersons. Not? I'd like to give you just a line on the daughter. She's married to a man called Trevor Hamburg. Ever heard of him? He's got shares in Gimblett's. All sorts of people, nowadays, have such things. They don't interfere; but they like books and dividends — when there are any. In fact Trevor's the reason why Master Sydney's book has come to us. The two of them have been in touch.'

'That doesn't predispose me in his favour,' interrupted Florence.

'Ah, yes, I understand. But I can assure you Trevor's quite a nice fellow, in a saturnine way. Talks slowly; makes me think of blotting paper, or dragging my feet through heavy sand. Can you hear him?'

'I hear you — with impatience!'

'Do try to be patient. I'll be as quick as I can. Now, Trevor . . . His manner's against him. I think his trouble is shyness. Once you're past the manner, you find he's quite simple. In fact I like him very much. Otherwise I shouldn't bother you. Trouble has arisen between him and Patterson's daughter. Serious trouble. A complete break. He blames the mother. Says she's as hard as nails, and a snob. Do you happen to have come across her?'

'No!' It was uncontrollably vehement. Florence was seething with distaste for everything she had heard. She wanted to be done with Mr Leadbitter and his laboured details of an unknown man.

'Not interested in the lady?'

'I don't know her; and I don't know her daughter.'

'And don't want to?'

'No.'

He sounded downcast.

'Well, it was just a chance.' She hoped he was cowed. But the voice persisted. 'I'd hoped you might help me to save a poor devil from going out of his mind.'

'No, Mr Leadbitter. I don't see how I

could help at all.'

'Hm. Hm. I'm afraid I've bothered you insensitively. I didn't mean to do that. Forgive me. Perhaps I ought to have mentioned that Sydney's references to *you* are encomiastic. He calls you "my dearest friend; a Marvell indeed!" '

'Then he's a hypocrite!' cried Florence, warmly.

'Aren't we all?'

'I'm not. You're not. You've always been wonderfully kind; and I appreciate that. Thank you.'

'For nothing!' commented Mr Leadbitter. 'I'm afraid I've spoiled your day.'

'Not spoiled. Made it a nightmare.'

'That's terrible. Now I shan't sleep. No, really. I shall be cursing myself for bad deeds. Could you come up to lunch one day soon? Enable me to make amends?'

'Of course I'll be delighted to come. Thank you. But not to talk about members of that family!'

'Taboo, are they? And yet I should have liked to hear an unbiased opinion of Sydney Patterson. You wouldn't care to see the script, I suppose?'

'From what you've told me, I should be tempted to burn it.'

'He has a duplicate. I think several copies. Authors of his kind do, you know. Very downy.'

'Hitherto I've liked him. Now I think he's a treacherous and hateful creature.'

'I'm more concerned about what you think *me!*'

Florence did not hear the words. She was in no state to do more than receive Mr Leabitter's apologetic farewell.

Above all else, she was infuriated with Syd, and terrified lest his book should be published by somebody less scrupulous than her friend at Gimblett's. Such a publisher would arouse the greatest possible 'Press coverage,' with much injury to a resolute and honourable man.

'Ten times Syd's quality!' she fumed.

The word 'blackmail' rang in her ears. This was worse than blackmail. It was an attempted assassination. She could do nothing to prevent the publication by another firm. And, as to Gimblett's, Mr Leadbitter had spoken in confidence. She therefore could not warn Rod; but even if she warned him it would do no good. Syd must have written in such a way that suppression would be difficult, if not impossible. Knowing that Rod had malignant enemies, he must have planned to assist those enemies. She could hear him laughing at his own cleverness, see him waving his stick in triumph, and prodding it into the ground as he walked. Horrible, horrible character!

A jilted Rod; how gratifying the insinuation must have been to a jealous mind! He had not hesitated to slander even herself. True, perhaps for prudential reasons, he had not named her. She and Rod alone would recognize the travesty. But she was not the person aimed at. Syd had wanted to vent his spleen upon Rod's wife, to wound her by the suggestion that she had been married in pique, whereas the fact was altogether otherwise. The whole story was a lie.

Memory flew back to those days of misgiving and agonized decision. It had been Syd who insisted that Rod was insanely ambitious. It had been Syd who reported Mrs Patterson's insistence that Rod should make a 'good' marriage. It had been Syd who first named Evelyn as the destined bride. Were all these things stages in purposeful mischiefmaking? Had he exploited her anxious questioning, in a determination to break a love affair he disliked?

'No! No! I can't believe I was as gullible as that would make me seem! Was I not?'

Annabel had described to Mr Leadbitter their father's discouragement of any high expectation from life. She had represented her sister as a docile little mouse, humble to the core. That was ridiculous. It was a caricature, to be dismissed with laughter. And yet, the caricature supplied another element in the confused anger she now felt. Emotion akin to hysteria recalled the shaming disclosure of a secret to that suicidal boy in the train: 'I might have been your mother.' Folly! Folly! She had been unnerved by sudden emergency. She was still unnerved; but by accumulated strains. The words, though crazed, had been true; the strains had become demoralizing.

Memories, regrets, speculations. What was the truth about Evelyn Patterson? Bertha, the self-sacrificing old goose, had described her as 'gracious.' That was the reaction of natural humility to condescension from a woman of rank. Saul had shown resentful detestation of his mother. Syd, detesting his own mother joined the daughter's young husband — what was his name? Trevor? — in comparable detestation. Was she a bad woman, selfish and domineering? Wasn't it possible that, like 'any man in the public eye,' she was vulnerable to attack from all quarters? These quarters might well include a terrified son, a malignant brother-in-law, and 'a poor devil who is going out of his mind.' Were they all insane?

She leapt to her feet.

'I'm getting as bad as they are!' she cried. 'I must stop at once!'

She could not stop. Through all these excited considerations ran the dread, created by over-tender conscience, that in some way her own past actions had produced unhappiness for everybody.

27
Sandra

While these events were taking place within a short distance of the Manor, the last Patterson inmate was shunning other members of her family. Sometimes she wandered uneasily about a house which was not yet familiar to her, or along paths in the garden or grounds where solitude was possible; but most of the time she remained in the bedroom, listening to radio programmes on her transistor which bored her because they were irrelevant to her own problems. When irritated, she switched off, only to find exasperation in the following silence.

After the final quarrel with Trevor, in

which she had spoken thoughts long hidden, and denounced his father as an ignorant old miser, Sandra had waited in vain for Trevor's submission. It had not come. She had been left alone with servants in their home, and none of his friends had called or telephoned. At last she had left the house, recklessly visiting people for whom she knew he felt dislike. This was to prove her independence. But Trevor, 'coming the strong man,' as she contemptuously put it, was not brought to his knees. Her behaviour had become even more reckless.

It was because of this recklessness that, to Sandra's astonishment, Trevor instituted his divorce proceedings. Consumed with anger, she at once gathered clothes and personal possessions, ostentatiously leaving behind all the presents he had given her; and journeyed down to Slocumbe, driving her own car at breakneck speed. To her mother she had given the bare news of his suit, not at all considering the situation of the three men whom he had named as co-respondents. Not one of them meant anything to her.

Two of these men, she quickly learned, were prepared for their own sakes to enter denials of the charge; the third was a rake who thought it amusing, and in fact gratifying, to appear in what he expected to be a *cause célèbre*.

Defiance accordingly became, upon Sandra's part, complete. She was determined to be free of a base husband. 'Let him sue!' she exclaimed, with loathing. 'Despicable cad!' Her mother, on first hearing of the break, gave encouragement to this defiance. 'You insisted on marrying him. I was always against it; but you wouldn't listen. Now you see I was right. Get rid of him. He's in a different class from ourselves, as his actions prove.'

Mother, however, having talked to Father, whose notions of female behaviour were Victorian, became less assured. She foresaw social embarrassments, not only for Sandra, but for herself. In such cases, people took sides, and were censorious. Also, to Sandra's sensitive temper, the dumbness of some of her so-called friends implied criticism. A few of them professed sympathy; but none was zealously partizan. She understood for the first time that in any matrimonial trouble the wife is invariably the easier party to blame and to drop.

Now Mother had taken to her bed, pleading *migraine*. Nobody remained who could listen to complaints of Trevor's behaviour, even if pride had allowed Sandra to utter them. Father was interested only in the Law and Public Affairs. He looked serious; and said nothing. Saul, the duffer, fled at sight of her. She did not mind that; but she resented his treatment of her as a leper. At last, feeling entirely deserted, she was seized with doubts of her own charm and brilliance. This was fatal. Bitter unhappiness could not be borne without tears. The tears came. Her beauty suffered; and her mirror, seen through mist, told her that it had disappeared altogether.

On one of her miserable journeys round the garden she had a shock. It was an unexpected encounter with Saul. He, too, was disconcerted; but a meeting between them was inescapable. Moreover Saul appeared alert; and Sandra could not help being struck by the change from his normal dejectedness. There was even a smile upon his pale face, which we saw for the first time to be rather handsome. With a mixture of distaste and involuntary affection, she stopped.

'Hello, where are you going?' she demanded.

'Nowhere,' answered Saul. 'Just killing time.'

'Why don't you pull yourself together, and do a job of work?'

'I'm waiting on Father.'

'But he's not here.'

'I know that. He's had to go to Arlingborough. Politics. But he's going to take me to London. We have an appointment. I don't know when it is.'

'What, a job?'

'No, a Solicitor.'

The word 'Solicitor' was like a stab. It caused Sandra to move rather quickly away.

'I don't envy you, then.' She was going,

when Saul, seized with an impulse, perhaps compassionate, although he knew little of Sandra's affairs, stopped her.

'I say, would you like to meet a most wonderful woman?'

Trevor, in the days of their engagement, had used that description of herself! He would not use it now. Experience led Sandra to assume that Saul's 'wonderful woman' was some girl, or married woman, who had caught his fancy. She was at once a condescending elder sister.

'What do you mean?'

'She lives in this village. She really saved my life. I thought I was done for.' Arm outstretched, and pointing, he seemed ready to lead the way at once to his inamorata.

'Oh, but I couldn't go visiting like this.' Sandra meant that she was wearing no make-up, and that her beauty was gone.

'She won't mind.'

'If she's a girl, she will.'

'She's not a girl. She's more like a mother. An artist.'

'Hm.' Sandra considered! Her curiosity was aroused. 'Wait a few minutes. I'll

322

put something on.'

As she spoke, she hurried away.

While running, Sandra muttered to herself: 'Silly nonsense. But it might be amusing.' She had no expectation of amusement; only of distraction, and she checked herself more than once as the instinct to hide returned. In the end she completed her journey, wondering at Saul's new keenness and at her own shedding of obstinate solitude; and within ten minutes was back again in a different frock and with revived assurance. Saul was walking up and down near the spot at which she had left him. The change in his bearing was still impressive.

'Ridiculous boy! Making a fool of himself! "More like a mother"!' But her interest in the adventure deepened. She was to meet somebody now, somebody outside Trevor's circle, whom she could surprise by her brilliant charm. But what sort of artist could this woman be? What was her name? Why did she live here, instead of in Chelsea or St. John's Wood?

Saul had called her 'wonderful.' All

women were wonderful to callow youth. Still, this one, though probably fat and grey-haired, had affected Saul. It might be diverting to find out the sort of woman he considered 'wonderful.' 'Like a mother'; not a sister. What a funny boy he was!

They had never walked together before. She imagined they must make a good-looking pair, both tall, and both comely. Saul looked creditable, leading the way with a buoyant step unlike his usual indeterminate drag; and he also, which was rare, showed some inclination to converse. He even drew attention to some trees in the drive, which he identified as if a new interest in forestry had arisen in a mind which Sandra had always found listless. Absurd enough, of course, as he was extraordinarily ignorant of most things; but striking to somebody who had been too much absorbed in her own affairs to observe these novel surroundings.

They reached the High Street, where they saw various housewives with baskets, and were themselves, as foreigners always must be, objects of interest. Saul, as if confident of his route, turned sharp right towards what Sandra supposed to be the fag end of the village; and within a few minutes they came in sight of the garden where she remembered having seen lovely immature daffodils.

'Oh, is this where the woman lives?' she demanded. 'Ah! I thought —' Speech was checked. It would be unwise to tell Saul anything about a previous visit to this part of Slocumbe. Indeed, now that they were approaching an encounter Sandra began to think her impulsive consent to it had been a mistake. 'She won't want to see us. She'll think it intrusive.'

'No, she won't!' Saul insisted. 'She's not that sort. You'll see.' He became greatly excited. His dislike of Sandra's manner was in abeyance. Her very presence gave him the encouragment which, if he had been alone, would have been lacking. 'If she's at home, of course!'

'Yes, yes. But for goodness' sake tell me her *name* before we get there. I can't just call her "Daffodil" or — what's the name of the cottage? — "Spring?" — I suppose that means "the water of life."

Rather pretentious!'

'Sh!' commanded Saul.

This was the explanation of yet another threat to Florence's peace of mind. From the table at which she sat, trying to work with forced concentration (although her thoughts were all the time being tossed into confusion by memory and doubt), she saw two figures walking up the brick path leading to her front door. As she had done earlier in the year at sight of Bertha Pledge, she exclaimed aloud: 'Oh, bother! I'm not in the mood!' She meant, 'Not in the mood for visitors,' which was a decided understatement.

Upon recognizing Saul, she felt her mood change abruptly. He, at least, dearest boy, would always warm her heart. But who was his companion? Sight of her caused an uncontrollable flurry of nerves. Nevertheless, she opened the door looking quite calm; and upon a closer view of Sandra received certain intuitions. Translated into words, they were: 'The languid girl who said "some old crone." Good-looking, spoilt, restless, cruel; but desperately unhappy. Swollen eyes; crying. "I'd hoped you might help me to save a poor devil from going out of his mind." Are there two of them in that situation? What on earth am I to say?'

It was Saul who eased her dilemma. He plunged ardently into the room, spied the unfinished watercolour, and blurted out an apology.

'We're bothering you! I'm ashamed. But my sister's not well; and I knew you'd do her good!'

Sandra remained silent. She was astonished, not only at her brother's extraordinary speech, but at sight of their hostess. Having expected to see an untidy, ink-stained creature, absent-minded and running to fat, she was face to face with somebody full of smiling dignity. The hand which took hers was firm; the grey eyes into which she looked down were all-comprehending. Shaken by a quick warmth of envy and attraction, she felt herself to be wholly at a disadvantage.

Defensiveness gave her a condescending air, which was noted by both Saul and

Florence, with different interpretations. She said:

'Don't you find interruptions insufferable? I should send the people away at once.'

The disconcerting reply, made with a smile in the thoughtful eyes, was:

'No visit from Saul could be anything but welcome. I'm glad to see you both.'

This last was only half-true; but while Florence accused herself of hypocrisy Sandra was only aware of the smile. She was further affected by a contrast between this cordial room and the Manor's spacious grandeur; such friendliness momentarily banished misery. Although she had scoffed at Saul's infatuation, she was too intelligent to underrate the reserved yet warm-hearted person whose home it was.

Florence, lacking the detachment to picture herself and her surroundings as others saw them, was equally moved. She dismissed her first impression of Sandra's cruelty, and immediately discounted at least some of Mr Leadbitter's report. Mr Leadbitter had judged with the bias of friendship for the husband; and bias, she had been reminded by the news of Syd's book, arose from conceit or a sense of personal injury. Besides, this girl was Rod's daughter, as Saul was his son. Had she no claim to sympathy? What was the truth?

Saul, meanwhile, had returned to the unfinished sketch, which was of Tom, Smudge, and Peter, the three guinea-pigs, munching full-flowered dandelions. He delightedly called Sandra's attention to it; and, finding her visitors amused, Florence tried to entertain them further by producing watercolours previously made for the same book. Sandra, who had expected something cruder or more sentimental (she did not know which), was enchanted. The drawings, completely simple in design, were made effective by delicate fancy and translucent colouring. Therefore, without echoing Saul's enthusiasm, she made it clear that she greatly admired what she saw. She also asked if they might be shown some of Florence's published books; and for perhaps ten minutes attentively examined them.

'They're beautiful! You really love animals,' she observed, with energy.

'They're the closest friends I have,' explained Florence; 'apart from Mrs Pledge, whom you may have met in the village.'

Sandra's interest led to a brief reference to Bertha and her invalid husband, heard in compassionate silence by the visitors. Then Sandra, obviously animated by relief from her preoccupations, exclaimed:

'I think you must be wonderfully happy, Miss Marvell!'

'It's because she's so kind to everybody!' cried Saul. 'That's the secret. She understands them at once!'

Sandra turned to Florence.

'Do you?'

'No. I stick to my cats and guinea-pigs. But of course I know very few people.'

'She knows Father!' Saul could not restrain the revelation. It was the most exciting fact he could adduce.

Sandra clouded at once.

'Oh, lots of people do that,' she said, snubbingly. 'Or think they do. I doubt if anybody really knows him.' She missed

Florence's glance of warning to her brother; and picked up one of the little books which she had especially liked. This time she noticed the publisher's name at the foot of the title page. 'Oh, Gimblett. It's a good firm.' A thought struck her. 'Do you deal with them direct, or through an agent?'

'Direct. With the Art Editor, at least. I don't know Mr Gimblett himself. He just sends me messages from Olympus.' Florence, who had almost mentioned Mr Leadbitter by name, stopped in time; but her reference to Mr Gimblett was a sign, unremarked, of confusion.

Sandra came unwittingly to her rescue.

'The Art Editor is Tom Leadbitter, isn't he? I know him. At least . . . I've met him.'

Why had she corrected the phrase? Obviously she did not mind speaking of Mr Leadbitter: therefore she had no animus against him. But the correction showed a variation in candour; and this variation suggested a concealment of feeling. Florence ventured to say, both frankly and in tact:

'He's one of my few friends.'

'I don't wonder.' Sandra indicated the book she held. Intense curiosity led her to ask: 'Have you seen him lately?'

'I've spoken to him on the telephone in the last twenty-four hours.' Florence wondered if a desperate impulse to put one more question — 'Did he tell you anything about me?' — had been repressed. But they were still strangers, meeting for the first time. Sandra assumed Florence to be uninformed and altogether detached. Florence was deterred by Saul's presence from putting any question at all. Therefore no confidences passed; and it was not until later that regrets upon both sides arose.

PART SEVEN

RESCUE OPERATIONS

28
The Secretaries

Two people who, because their work kept them in London, had hardly been seen at the Manor were the Private Secretaries — John Dickson and Ellen Dundee. Mr Dickson, aged twenty-seven, noted Roderick's appointments and wrote his letters; Miss Dundee, who concealed her exact age but was somewhere in the forties, kept Evelyn up-to-date on Feminist literature, wrote or telephoned the dinner guests, and fended off importunate Women's Societies. Miss Dundee liked to describe herself as 'Social Secretary.'

Mr Dickson strolled elegantly through

life after taking a good degree at Cambridge, and as a diner-out among his contemporaries was considered witty. Miss Dundee's speciality was blandness. She had not wit; and was large, angular, and full-toothed. She cherished memories, which she slightly embellished, of gaiety in youth, did not dine out, and supported an artful father whom, because he had once been Secretary of a Literary Society, she regarded as an intellectual. The only characteristics shared by Miss Dundee and Mr Dickson was a conviction of innate superiority.

Otherwise they were at variance. Mr Dickson had a deep admiration for Roderick (which he concealed under derisiveness, calling him 'the Old Man' or 'Our Oracle'), coupled with regret that his employer had not taken a University Degree. He also concealed a lesser admiration for Evelyn by referring to her as 'the Dragon.' Miss Dundee, supported by cultivated disdain for the male, thought otherwise. To her, Roderick was an alarming but futile monster, and Evelyn a Queen among pygmies. Neither Mr

Dickson nor Miss Dundee cared much for Sandra, whom Mr Dickson styled 'a pretentious chit,' while Miss Dundee thought her 'a charming gairl who'll grow up one day.' Both found Saul, because of his shyness, entirely negligible.

Today, Miss Dundee and Mr Dickson were journeying together to Slocumbe. Mr Dickson drove his own sports car with *élan;* Miss Dundee shivered beside him, braking with both feet whenever a dog or a pedestrian seemed to be in danger, but in reality enjoying her trip with the sense that she was a child again, tobogganing down steep hills. 'Most stimulating!' she exclaimed, upon safe arrival. 'Glad you liked it,' responded Mr Dickson, who had once or twice deliberately frightened her.

This view of Slocumbe was favourable. It was a fine day; trees in the neighbourhood were leafing; at least two shops in the High Street were sporting flags in honour of the Pattersons. The newly gravelled roadway to the Manor was now complete. A gratifying air of prosperity was all about them. Only a small amount of work was in store. They would eat well, find new books at their bedsides, and be able to relax.

'How I wish my dear old Daddy could be here!' sighed Miss Dundee. 'How he'd relish the peacefulness, and a glimpse of Sir Roderick's wonderful library!'

'Which it will be one of my jobs to arrange on the shelves!' Mr Dickson was less ecstatic. 'The Old Man will shut his mouth and shrug his shoulders. Well, I never know whether he wants them put in sizes, or by authors or subjects.'

'Ask him!' advised Miss Dundee.

'Oh, he just mutters,' answered Mr Dickson. ' "Put them where I can find them." In town, I can produce anything he wants at a moment's notice; but here he'll be left to his own uncertainties.'

'Dear Sir Roderick!' sighed Miss Dundee, feeling thankful that she would never be required to hunt among the books for one that probably wasn't there.

They arrived to an unexpected scene. It was teatime; and in a large, panelled room they found Lady Patterson, pale with illness, sitting by a log fire, with Son and

338

Daughter Patterson close at hand. Never before had Mr Dickson and Miss Dundee seen the three together; and it was astonishing to them to discover that Saul could be animated. Indeed, he was self-assured enough to jump up, come forward, and bring further chairs near the fire. Mr Dickson gave Miss Dundee a quizzical glance, as if he asked 'Which of us is the more astonished?' He looked round the room with new appreciation of its grandeur.

'When I was here last, this room was a shambles,' he said, taking advantage of the fact that he and his fellow-Secretary were being treated as guests. 'Now it's a centre of life! Do you find the house comfortable, Lady Patterson?'

'I find everything extremely uncomfortable,' replied Evelyn, who was very tired. 'But we shall all get used to it in time.'

She was at her coldest, as if meaning to snub Mr Dickson for over-familiarity; and he, with dry respectfulness, made no further attempt at cordiality. Indeed, his manner became formal. After all, he was

Secretary to the lady's husband, not to her, and as one who usually found women distasteful he felt he could safely repay a snub with distant politeness.

Miss Dundee grew more talkative. She spoke of their journey, the beautiful scenes through which they had passed, and at last mentioned that she had brought a number of letters — 'interesting letters' — which she thought her employer would like to see.

'One, in particular, from Lady Grange,' she said, archly, 'telling you that her daughter has had a little son. The image of her own father, she says, which has made everybody laugh.'

Evelyn did not laugh. She was feeling so unwell that she could hardly remember Lady Grange or Lady Grange's daughter.

'A good thing the child's not like its mother,' remarked Sandra.

'Perhaps he is?' suggested Mr Dickson, recovering a little spirit. 'Underneath, you know. It does happen, I believe.'

Evelyn addressed Miss Dundee.

'I think I shall go back to bed. I wish you'd come up in about half-an-hour,

Ellen. You could read to me. Something very light. I badly need sleep.'

In speaking, she rose. Everybody else rose; and the new arrivals were motioned to stay where they were. Then, with faltering steps, and a bow to Mr Dickson, who held the door open for her, she disappeared.

'She's aged a lot,' remarked Mr Dickson, when he and Miss Dundee were able to speak together alone. 'Do you think she's as feeble as she seems? Likely to pass out?'

'Oh, no,' Miss Dundee answered. 'She's very strong. *Migraine* is most debilitating; but it isn't dangerous yet.'

'What shall you read her? James Joyce?'

'I think it will be P. G. Wodehouse. He's a capital dispeller of headache — and memory.'

'Hm. Too exciting for a sick mind, I should have thought.'

'I know Lady Patterson's taste. She needs diversion.'

'What from?'

'Herself, Mr Dickson.'

Mr Dickson rallied.

'It never occurred to me that she had any humour *at all.*'

'She's full of it. Not your kind of humour, of course.'

'My kind's the best there is. Radiant; but not noisy.'

'Still undergraduate, I think.'

Aghast at such impudence from a middle-aged spinster, Mr Dickson changed the subject.

'He's been a bit short on the 'phone. Unusual. Do you think — in view of her *migraine* — that they've had the inevitable, irrevocable row? A general break-up? You and I both back in circulation at a month's notice?'

'You have a sensational mind, Mr Dickson,' replied Miss Dundee, with her most crushing jocosity. 'Nothing whatever is amiss between them. What trouble there is, lies elsewhere.'

'What, the boy? I thought he seemed exceptionally bright today.'

'Not the *boy!*' said Miss Dundee, firmly. 'In any case, he'd be Sir

Roderick's affair.'

Oho! The chit! Well, it doesn't surprise me, with that selfwilled toss of an empty head. The moral, which I learned at school and intend to observe through life, is that if one wants peace one should never marry. Marriage breeds complications.'

'It sometimes breeds more than complications, Mr Dickson.'

Astounded by such coarseness from an ultra-respectable spinster, Mr Dickson, who under his sophistication was entirely inexperienced, responded only with a curled lip. He, however, had the devastating sensation that he had been given a glimpse into that mysterious and cloacal region, the female mind.

29
A Change of Mind

Florence laid down her pencil and looked out, past the garden and the gate, to the tail-end of Slocumbe's main street, where it narrowed before dwindling to a country lane. As she might have said, she was in no 'mood' for work. Instead, with a ruminative habit foreign to such metropolitan types as Mr Dickson and Miss Dundee, she concerned herself speculatively with the characteristics of the Patterson family.

Four members of this family were now known to her, two of them, Roderick and Sydney, intimately, two others, Saul and Sandra, with only the familiarity arising from judgment of a quick brain and a warm heart. Saul was her new love; Sandra the subject of emotional perplexity; and she was beginning to recognize that the fifth Patterson, Evelyn, a complete mystery to her, was at the heart of all her uncertainties. What was the truth about Evelyn?

This particularly curiosity must wait. Unaware that she had reached a decision, Florence turned to the telephone; and in a short time heard a tiny voice remark, with perfect detachment, 'Gimblett's.' The voice strengthened when she had given her name and asked for Mr Leadbitter. 'I'll put you through.' Further slight delay was followed by the familiar bark.

'I wonder whether you could see me if I came up tomorrow?'

'Over lunch? Certainly. Meadows's, one o'clock?'

'I don't think you should lunch me.'

'Why not?'

'Too expensive.'

'All goes down to the slush fund. Favourite author-artist.'

'But it's not about myself that I want to

see you.' Florence, like Frederick in *The Pirates of Penzance,* was scrupulously a slave to duty. 'Unless you'll let me pay.'

'Unthinkable. Is it about the Patterson book?'

'No, the other man.'

'What, Trevor? Want him to come, too?'

'On no account.'

'Quite easy, you know.'

'Just you and me.'

'All right. I'll be waiting at Meadows's.'

Once the appointment was fixed, it became alarming. Only the fear of seeming ridiculous prevented Florence from ringing again, crying off. 'What an idiot!' she exclaimed. 'Always an idiot!' Reaction had come too late: she was committed.

Meadows's was a discreet restaurant in the neighbourhood between Piccadilly and Hanover Square, where *tête-à-têtes* were in order. Thickly carpeted, and lighted only by red-shaded table lamps, it offered hospitality at night to smart little parties and married men with women friends; but in the daytime it held no suggestion of secrecy. There were tables for three or four persons, and tables in alcoves where two might converse together in comfort. Mr Leadbitter, warned that confidences were to be exchanged, had reserved one of these tables. He was at his most debonair.

Begged to choose the meal, he ran an experienced eye over the menu, not forgetting to glance unobtrusively at his companion and to decide that his approach to their reason for meeting must be indirect.

'I suggest *Tournedos à la Reine,* spinach, and *sauté* potatoes. Ice cream to follow. That all right? And a bottle of Meursault. Right. I've seen Sydney Patterson. A roisterer. Not really surprised at refusal, I thought. Funny mixture of brag and defeatism. Shouted that we were missing a world-beater. Others would jump at it, et cetera.'

'Is that true? Half-true?' Florence became anxious. 'I recognize the mixture.'

'Quarter. All publishers funk libel. The big ones won't risk it; the small daren't. For them, one successful action means bankruptcy. Patterson can't understand the difference between what's spoken and what's written. You can cause a roar over drinks at the bar; but in print the same joke brings in the solicitors. I told him that. It didn't register.'

'Nothing does, with Syd. I'm very worried about it.'

'My fault. I'm sorry. What about the other? Feel able to talk to me?'

Their glances met. He was seriously attentive; a trustworthy friend.

'I want you to tell me more than you were able to do on the telephone. You said he was almost insane.'

'That's true. Another mixture. Brusque. No manners. Under that, passionate. Under that again, hard as concrete. At bottom, raw with — the cant word — a sense of inferiority. A big dog's longing for a lapdog's treatment. He's a very difficult creature. Yet I like him.'

'Why do you like him?' Florence had listened with distaste to the description of Sandra's husband, feeling that he must be as unlovable as a gorilla.

'Good heart. Absolutely straight. A

348

woman of quality would penetrate all the layers. Polish him into a Koh-i-noor. This girl's self-infatuated; and a bitch.'

Florence, remembering Sandra's face, could not agree.

'How well do you know her?'

'Only as his wife. One or two dinners. Parties. A looker; but so self-centred that she tries all the time to tantalize him. Some women are like that. Among the rough, they get knocked about. I mean, physically. I don't know what drives them. Sensuality? The craving for power at all costs? You can't understand that. I don't myself. The thing to do would be to drown them both; but she's his woman; the only one he's ever wanted. Unfortunately she's goaded him into taking divorce proceedings.'

'Divorce?' Florence had been horrified by the arraignment of Sandra. Mr Leadbitter's final revelation made her feel that every previous assumption had been an old maid's sentimentality. 'Then I can do nothing.'

'You mean he's burned his boats?'

'With a high-spirited girl, yes.'

'She's been pretty reckless, you know. I should rather call her high-handed. Going her own way. Goading him, as I said.'

'He must have contributed to that.'

'No doubt. Yes, both at fault. She has most to lose. Matrimonially, he's a good catch.'

'She's not the sort to think in those terms.' Florence was ruffled by Mr Leadbitter's cynicism.

'No; but other women might do so. He'll find plenty. They swarm round a disengaged husband. Any suggestions — I mean, as to what I want to see?'

'None at all. They'd be better apart.'

'For good?' Having heard, and accepted, only the husband's story, he had made up his mind with medieval simplicity that the wife's submission offered the only cure for a fatal break. 'Don't forget she's asked for it again and again.' Florence, as a woman of earlier date than Sandra, responded with a look so significant that he added: 'I'm sorry you feel the divorce ought to go through.'

'It's what she must feel. I should, myself.'

'You? Oh, but you're quite different. I wonder —' Mr Leadbitter checked the personal inquiry, and after a pause substituted another. 'You don't think an unexpected encounter, that we could arrange, would produce a surge of the old feeling?'

Florence was scornful.

'As this isn't a Victorian novelette, Mr Leadbitter, I'm sure she'd walk straight out — and detest us both as atrocious busybodies.'

He digested this piece of common sense, frowning, and nodding sharply.

'You know more about your own sex than I do. My wife says I only read the large print.'

'What does your wife think of the business?'

'I haven't discussed it with her. I'm all for peace in the home.' His broad smile indicated that he had at least some comprehension of a beloved mate. 'I applied to you as a detached and sagacious person.'

'Neither male nor female, I suppose. It seems to me that this Trevor reads only his own mind.'

'It's a common habit. But you dash me, Miss Marvell. I give up. He'll go off his head, marry a drab, and pay the price. She'll pay a price, too. A heavy one.'

For a while this was all they could say. Mr Leadbitter looked down at the table, drank carefully from his glass, and gave a slight shrug. He was evidently at the end of discussion. So was Florence, until she was seized with an inspiration.

'Before he ruins himself,' she whispered urgently, 'he must discontinue the divorce proceedings.'

Mr Leadbitter whistled.

'You can't expect him to do that.'

'Then I can do nothing for him,' repeated Florence.

30
Mr Munster

While she had been travelling to London by train, Roderick and Saul had made the journey by car, affected in different ways by the stolidity of Blenkinsop's back. Roderick saw it was as a curtain against which to arrange his many preoccupations, legal and political. Saul felt the menace of a steadiness lacking from his own nature. It threatened, as did the interview to come.

This interview was with that terrifying Solicitor, Munster; and, bereft of Miss Marvell's support, he returned during the journey almost to the state of panic from which she had rescued him. 'No, I can't! I can't!' ran his flurried thought. 'It would be better for everybody, everything, if I were dead!' Emotion mounted; his legs trembled; he bit his lip; he almost screamed the words aloud.

Roderick, who had been far away, addressing the House of Commons in a mood of irony, glanced aside and noted his son's pallor and convulsive movements. Mentally ejaculating: 'Altogether too febrile. What's to be done with him?' He put a reassuring hand upon Saul's knee.

'All right, boy. Keep up your courage. Remember what Florrie Marvell said.'

Saul jumped. 'Florrie Marvell! Father knew! He must have guessed! And "Florrie!" ' A dozen questions which he dared not ask fled through his mind. The coming interview was forgotten. He was liberated from overmastering dread. The relief was so great that he clutched at the kindly hand. For the first time in his life he loved his father.

The interview, as is often the case, proved much less frightening than the anticipation of it had been. Blenkinsop threaded a careful way through dense traffic, and stopped directly before the entrance to a block of offices in Norfolk Street, off the Strand. Here Roderick led the way as one well used to such places; and in a moment they had passed Mr Munster's door.

Here a youth at an unlittered desk took one glance at Roderick, recognized him, and remained seated. Another man, elderly, with a head shaven so close that one might have supposed him just released from prison, jumped to his feet.

'Will you come this way, Sir Roderick?'

Saul had only a glimpse of this man, saw that his eyes were grey and uncommunicative, and followed his father into an inner room. Shelves in both rooms were covered with black tin boxes bearing names in large white letters; but in the confusion of the moment, while his heart plunged and beat fast, the boy's attention was given wholly to the plump, genial Mr Munster himself. This was not a person to cause terror; and his handshake was responsively warm. About sixty years of age, short, plump, and white-haired, he retained the facial chubbiness of infancy. Only his mouth, which could become a straight line, suggested an iron will. And his manner to Roderick, whom he addressed by Christian name, was so suavely, yet affectionately, respectful that Saul was unaware of a quick, all-comprehending glance at himself.

They were immediately in the middle of a narrative which Saul could hardly believe was his own tumblingly related story of chicane. He marvelled at the skill of his father's *précis*. Thus did a man speak who had spent a lifetime in mastering briefs and ordering arguments. No wasted words; allowed no emotional pauses; no lapses of memory. All was concise. Never once did Mr Munster have to interrupt for some elucidation. Having learned that morning to love Roderick, Saul learned to appreciate his extraordinary ability. He listened breathlessly, looking at Mr Munster's carpet, which had come, many years ago, from Persia, and which helped not only to promise secrecy but to make every syllable spoken as clear as candour itself.

The story was finished, Mr Munster remained impassive. Saul, daring only to peep at the round face, was breathless. What would follow? Would it be some condemnation of his own folly? Or a shrugging admission that nothing could be done?

At last the silence was broken. He was being directly addressed in a voice of silken courtesy.

'You never heard any names, I think? Christian names only? Was one of them Danny?'

It was uncanny. He could not have believed such knowledge to exist. Only after great effort could he respond.

'That was . . . what he told me to call him.'

'Yes, I understand. A long, narrow head? An air of incorruptibility? A slight Irish accent? Yes, it sounded like Danny.' To Roderick, Mr Munster added: 'That was Daniels. You remember, you got him shopped for ten years.'

'I remember.' It seemed that Roderick

could not be surprised. The name, and the case, had been drawn from the file of a capacious memory. But Saul, hearing the two men exchanging quite ordinary comments upon one whom he had regarded as a benefactor, was astounded. He watched his father's face. It wore an expression he had never seen before, an expression of concentrated thought. This father was unquestionably a man of stature. By comparison, Daniels became in a flash of startled insight completely spurious. How contemptibly gullible he had been! But what was to follow? He had become a mere spectator, waiting breathlessly for what would next emerge.

It came.

'Danny always had expensive tastes; and a long bitter memory.' Mr Munster spoke almost approvingly. 'A remarkable man. In politics he would have made his mark. Exactly the right temperament for success. He malignantly shopped all his rivals — and his enemies. A very bad man indeed.'

'You have a poor opinion of politicians, James,' said Roderick.

'Present company, of course.' Mr Munster smiled. 'In this case his coadjutors were the merest tools. As far as' — he indicated Saul with the smallest possible nod — 'is concerned, I doubt if we shall have much more than a temporary embarrassment. The Police have complete records of them all; Murzy, Johnny, Perce — those were the names you heard, weren't they?' He looked straight at Saul, who stared in dismayed recognition of the names. 'It's the familiar gang. The trouble with them all is that they can't go straight. You put them away; and when they come out they coalesce, not realizing that all they do is unmistakable. You remember the case, Roderick?'

'Perfectly,' was the cool reply. 'Danny shouted at me from the dock. He said "You'll pay for this! God will punish you!" I thought it melodramatic.'

'He meant that *he* would punish you. That's the basis of the exploit.'

'Directed at me,' agreed Roderick. 'Yes. During the cross-examination he forgot himself only once. That was when he said

"I call on God to prove my innocence." '

'One should never call on God in a Court of Law.' Mr Munster's face wore the same enigmatic smile. 'The cry only reaches as far as Scotland Yard, where belief in Divine intervention is discounted. Well, my dear Roderick, I'll make the necessary inquiries of the Godless.'

As he spoke, he rose to his feet, smiling cordially at an old friend, and extending a cool hand to Saul. In that brief contact Saul was conscious of an implacable personality behind the smile. Humiliated, hardly able to suppress tears, he followed his father from the room; and a moment later they were in the street.

Once on the pavement Roderick looked at his watch.

'I told Blenkinsop to come back in half-an-hour. We've been twenty minutes. He'll be early, so we may as well wait here. Did you find it much of an ordeal?' He was full of kindness; for without seeming to do so he had seen how tense his boy had been throughout the interview. He noticed for the first time how handsome Saul was. Very creditable, in fact. This business must be settled at once. Then progress could be made.

Marvelling at his father's coolness, Saul could only stammer.

'I didn't really understand all Mr Munster said. I felt awfully stupid and ashamed.'

'Quite natural. Don't worry about that.'

'I can't help worrying.' They were speaking in undertones, more intimately than would have been possible before the interview. 'I'd thought Danny —' He grew hot, and then so cold that, as had happened in the railway carriage, his teeth chattered. 'Well, I've told you.'

'Yes, Danny's a plausible rogue. I don't wonder he made himself so attractive.'

'But Mr Munster seemed to think the whole thing was directed at you — in revenge.'

'Very likely. You hear what his reputation is. A long and vindictive memory. But put that aspect out of your mind. The man's under arrest. I see Blenkinsop coming. Are you faint?'

'Dithery.'

'Yes. I suspect you'd like some lunch. Now, wait a minute. I don't want to lunch at one of my Clubs. We should see two or three inquisitive people there. Inquisitive, not about you, but about something else that is causing talk.' He did not mention that the 'something else' was the Prime Minister's health. 'We'd better go to a quiet restaurant. Then I shall be able to explain what Munster meant.' He considered, as Blenkinsop steered the car to the kerbside. 'Where would be best? I know; we'll go to Meadows's.'

To Saul, the name was unknown; but Saul, full of what had just passed, was in a state to accept any suggestion his father made. He therefore made no reply. Roderick gave the choice a moment's further thought, motioning to the boy that he should enter the car.

'To Meadows's, Blenkinsop. You've been there before, haven't you?' And, to Saul, as the journey began, 'It's rather an interesting place. It will make you think of coronets and Cabinet secrets. All very discreet. Very impersonal. But the food and service are both good; and we shan't be interrupted.'

That, indeed, was his aim. Nevertheless the decision led to unforeseen consequences.

31
In the Restaurant

As they entered the restaurant, Saul was made to think of other hushed places he had visited, from Westminster Abbey to the British Museum Reading Room; but here there were no startling echoes. All noise was reduced to such a murmur that he instinctively tiptoed after Roderick in the wake of the Major-Domo. But as he did this his downcast eyes were attracted by a sudden movement to his right. There, almost hidden by an ingenious hanging cascade of flowers, a startled luncher who had recognized his father was apparently trying to escape attention.

He went close to Roderick, speaking

under his breath.

'Trevor's here, Father. Do you see him?'

Roderick looked, without seeming to look. He was seldom surprised; rarely at a loss. Making an instant judgment, therefore, he answered almost inaudibly:

'Go on to the table. I'll join you in a moment.'

So it happened that, upon reaching the table he had designed for his celebrated visitor, the Major-Domo found only Saul at his heels. Nevertheless he flourished a large menu into the boy's hand, bowed, and waited, while Saul, holding the menu, remained unseated, and watched what followed.

Roderick had turned to the almost hidden figure; and as he did so Trevor Hamburg, swarthy, flushed, and as suspicious as a wild cat, jumped to his feet. He was so much embarrassed by this unexpected encounter that, at first blind to his father-in-law's extended hand, he made a sudden grab at it.

Used to every kind of greeting, from the hostile to the abject, Roderick did not abandon his grave cordiality. He had wanted to see Trevor, with the object of rescuing a marriage; but he had not been sure what approach could be made without jeopardizing a daughter's legal position. Also, other matters had pressed urgently for attention. Here was an opportunity for at least some contact. Whether any good followed would depend upon his own bearing and Trevor's response to it. He was greatly aided, of course, by wide experience. Evelyn would at once have penetrated his mind and irritably recognized his manner. Trevor was in no state to do so.

Trevor, in fact, taken by surprise, was so much moved by consciousness of Roderick's superior finesse that he continued to flush. His eyes glowed. He could hardly speak. A young man's egotistical flamboyance, which would have carried him through any conversation with his coevals, fled. He had never been able to accuse Roderick of condescending to him. The sense of inferiority came from within. But now? How much did the old man know? Had Sandra told him all, or nothing, or merely allowed him to think there was a domestic squabble? He was not prepared, he told himself, to let Patterson, for all his fame and dignity, take a high line; but the old fellow's greeting held so much friendliness, as if nothing whatever had happened, that he was confounded.

'How are you, Trevor? You see that Saul's with me. Father and son getting to know each other. Would you care to join us for coffee?'

Silky old man! Trevor's lips twitched. He trusted nobody; and yet he felt Roderick was straight. Not a bit like that supercilious old tartar, her mother. You could talk to him. Yes; but he'd support that little bitch, because he was her father. Would he? A man of the world. But oh God! The whole situation was Hell! He'd be more likely to understand than anybody else. Would he? Would he?

These were all emotional reactions, passing in a second of time. Spoken truth was blurted out in a rush of words.

'I'm . . . I ought to say . . . I'm alone you see; but — in fact — my friend

Leadbitter's here. . . . He's with a woman friend — somewhere down there. I'm . . . I'm supposed to be waiting for them —'

'Oh, I see. I'm sorry. You won't be able to join us.' Roderick was at his most conciliatory. 'I wish you'd been able to. However, perhaps another time —'

Trevor interrupted, still in desperate pursuit of candour.

'I'd like that, too, sir. Nothing er . . . It's just that Leadbitter . . . Well, he suggested that I should be here, in case . . . I can't explain. He thought she might be able . . . I think she may be a friend — of yours. The fact is, I don't want to miss them, if she's —'

'I understand.' Roderick did not remember to have met this Mr Leadbitter; and he could not at once imagine what this woman — his friend? — was expected to do. Nevertheless it was clear that some kind of encounter had been planned between the friends. 'A sort of rendezvous?'

'Yes . . . not exactly a rendezvous. She doesn't know me. May not want to. It was just an idea Leadbitter had —' Trevor could not proceed. Red and embarrassed, he made a mute appeal for understanding; and some quality in his distress went straight to Roderick's heart. Having dealt with many stumbling witnesses, he knew the art of reassuring most of them — including Trevor. Sandra must be involved in this curious affair. Who could the woman be? Very singular! He must if possible set the poor fellow at ease.

'All right. If, later on, you find yourself free, do join us. Saul's waiting over there. You can see him standing up.'

With a smiling nod towards Saul, and a direct, significant glance of kindness at Trevor, he deliberately made no gesture of farewell, but moved slowly to the appointed table. He was unaware of the fact that his poise and magnificent carriage had drawn the attention of all who were lunching that day at Meadows's; and he had no idea that among those who watched his progress were both Mr Leadbitter and his unidentified friend Florrie Marvell.

This pair had reached the moment of ultimatum. Silence followed. Nothing more could have been said that day if Roderick had not appeared. Sight of him, and the flushed young man at the corner table, completely changed the position. Florence, already warm with emotion, was stricken with horror at her own bitterness; Mr Leadbitter, at first disconcerted by a further blow to what he had considered to be a masterly stratagem, could not check admiration of the dignified figure he saw. The contrast between such courtesy and the gawkiness of his friend could not be denied. He held his breath as he watched.

'Calamitous!' he muttered. 'Can't do anything now.' He was curtly addressing himself. 'Oh, well.' It was an admission of defeat.

He had not reckoned upon his companion's reaction; but Florence was assessing everything anew. After a flurry of spirits, in which confused thoughts such as 'I can't do anything.' 'I'm too old.' 'I want to be left alone,' and I'm a coward,' darted through her head, she had received light, as if in answer to prayer. With experience as her guide, she saw that at all costs a marriage must be saved. If so, action must be immediate. No protracted quarrel could ever be healed without impossible concession. She focussed Sandra as a girl who needed to be pursued, even after marriage. Power was essential to her vanity. Because of it, she could be cruel, shameless. But, behind that vanity, whatever the appearance, lay a nature uncertain of itself. Sandra was a female Syd. More than that, she was Rod's daughter.

This was the final point. Rod's daughter. Because of it, tragic imaginings pressed close upon a tender heart. They were very frightening indeed; unbearably so. Once again slave to her sense of duty, Florence forgot everything else.

'Wait!' she exclaimed. 'That man in the corner. He's your friend, isn't he?'

'Told him to be here,' grumbled Mr Leadbitter.

'Why?'

'In case you'd help. Introduce you.'

'Idiotic!'

'Seems so now, I admit. What has Patterson said to him, do you suppose?'

'Knowing Rod, I should say he's exercising his charm.'

'Has he got any?'

'Immense, in private life.'

'Not his public reputation. Trevor's always found him cagey.'

'I should say Trevor was afraid of him. Poor boy!'

There was no disguise in either. They had become fellow conspirators. Mr Leadbitter took another line.

'Stupid oaf, you mean?'

'No; just obtuse about his wife. Having married her, he assumed that she'd be quiet. When she wasn't, he tried the strong arm. That was extraordinarily unimaginative.'

'What about *her?* What about *her?*'

'Equally unimaginative, I expect, and more conceited. But she has quality. I don't know what influence Rod has with her. If you'll do as I suggested, I'll speak to him. Together, he and I might do something; but only if your friend co-operates. Having see him just now, I think he will.'

'This is frightful,' muttered Mr Leadbitter. 'You terrify me!'

'Your friend is the one who has become terrified. It's a fatal defect in a man to become terrified of losing his wife. She'll instinctively play on his fear.'

'Not playing now.' It was a grunt. Mr Leadbitter did not like Sandra. High principled, loving his wife with protective indulgence, and unstintedly admiring such women of talent as Florence herself, he yet, as a man, believed that errant wives should be brought to heel.

'No,' agreed Florence. 'She's not playing now. She's only gone further than she meant to do; and he's made it impossible for her to go back with any self-respect. Her pride's involved.'

'Do you mean he's to crawl? I can't see him doing it.'

'Not crawl. Make the essential gesture. I think she's desperately in love with him.'

'As the cat's in love with the mouse.'

Florence did not answer. She had seen the two men she loved — father and son — and compassion for two other lovers, who in relation to each other were fools, had become overwhelming. She was resolved that, Rod or no Rod, she would see and talk to Sandra. But, first, some understanding must be quickened in Sandra's duffer of a husband by Mr Leadbitter, who was not the most serviceable instrument for the job.

32
'Leave It to Florrie'

They were again at odds, the one intelligent and apt to rely upon his judgment in matters of art, literature, and business affairs; the other stubbornly judging by intuition alone. Wanting no more for herself than the modest success she enjoyed, she had become a Mother to those children who were in trouble — whether Rod, Saul, or Sandra.

'I don't want to be bothered. But I've got to do it. I can't help myself,' she decided, with self-scorn. 'I'm feeble-minded. Idiotic!'

Mr Leadbitter, who could not read the thoughts of others, was impressed by what he saw as cool determination. A person whom he had previously seen as endearingly *naïve* had become baffling, almost a Sybil. She had not spoken (as he might have supposed) as a Feminist, defensive of her sex; she had revealed, instead, a capacity to see as deeply interesting the inevitable conflict between two characters of considerable arrogance but exceptional sensitiveness. He pondered. What should he do about Trevor? What could he do but follow the Sybil's instruction?

Absorbed in their problem, neither he nor Florence noticed that Saul, sitting with his back to the wall on the other side of the restaurant, and stealing timid glances in all directions, had recognized Florence. He started, half rose, and turned to his father.

'Miss Marvell,' he whispered. 'She's over there? Do you think I might go over and speak to her?'

'Hm. They probably won't want to be interrupted.' Roderick saw Florence with great interest. He was almost tenderly amused by her aspect of intense seriousness. It reminded him of the past, when she had been more than usually exasperating. 'Do you know the man? I don't. I expect she's advising him for his own good.'

'That's what she always does.' Saul was enthusiastic.

Roderick, less enthusiastic, answered rather drily.

'For somebody who hates busybodies, it's a curious habit.'

Saul flushed with loyalty.

'It's only when she's asked,' he declared, beginning to tremble. 'I want to tell her about this morning — Mr Munster.'

'No,' answered Roderick. 'You should never say anything confidential before a third party. It's dangerous. In any case, you can give her no definite news.'

'But I want to tell her *now*. I owe it to her.'

'I don't think she'd thank you. I quite understand your feeling. But I should wait until they're going. Then you could run over. Meanwhile, eat your lunch — if you can!' He was consciously the goodhumoured Father, softening discouragment with a smile; but he contemplated Florence anew. Why had she changed so little? Was it from that appalling sense of always being in the right? He had never known anybody so pig-headed. Her present companion, his head so close to hers as they conferred, could not appreciate the fact. He was evidently much younger than she; and was no doubt receiving oracular advice in a spirit of reverence!

Perception came. Young Trevor had spoken of a friend, and a woman, for whom he was waiting. The friend was a Mr Leadbitter; Florrie was the woman. Something to do with Trevor's affairs; therefore with Sandra's. But Florrie had never met Sandra. Where did she come in? This was very remarkable. He became so deeply curious that he unobtrusively watched the pair at the other table.

As he did this, his orderly mind was separating the impressions he had formed of Munster's quiet remarks on the unvirtuous Danny. There was no doubt that Danny had schemed some repayment to the Counsel who had ensured him a prison sentence; but whether the implication of Saul had arisen by chance or design was not clear. Probably chance. Then there was Trevor. He wished he liked Trevor better. And there was always Florrie. It was amusing that she should be drawn into Patterson affairs now when, thirty years ago, she had been so eager to evade them. How pretty she still was! Pretty enough to stir young Saul's emotions. Too straight to exploit an advantage there, he believed. But she had somehow escaped the wear and tear that had aged Evelyn.

He had hardly eaten what had been laid before him, although the first mouthful had been delicious; and he believed the same might be said of Saul, whose dreaming silence was disturbed every moment by glances across the restaurant. This simple-minded youth was on what used to be called tenterhooks — his nerves at full stretch — as he waited for the movement which would allow him to approach his benefactress. What was he thinking? What would he blurt out before Mr Leadbitter?

'I never had such excitability,' thought Roderick. 'Is he dangerously unstable? Or is it genius? He gets neither from me. I should have said, neither from Evelyn, though her father must have been an impulsive old boy to marry again in haste. There's always Syd. Ah, Florrie's handling her gloves. What happens now with Trevor?'

Saul was already half out of his seat, and looking imploringly at his father for permission to run across the restaurant. Roderick delayed him with a slightly raised hand. Would not the intervention affect Mr Leadbitter's plan? Clearly Trevor was to be spotted as they were going out, and to be presented to Florrie as somebody needing help. From her? Why? She couldn't be at all involved. What nonsense it was! And here was this boy, wriggling like some youngster with his eye on the Christmas tree! No, she was shaking her head, decisively, as if she were saying to Mr Leadbitter: 'No, I don't think I should be the right wife for you,

Mr Leadbitter. You need somebody as ambitious as yourself!'

'Good heavens! Was she really saying that? Where had the words come from? They were quite staggering.' And as he thus exclaimed, Roderick found himself alone. Three people, one of whom was Saul, were standing at the other table. Only one thing was to be done. Roderick also rose and crossed the restaurant.

He saw Florrie's colour rise. She was not as calm as he had supposed, and she gave him her hand almost inattentively while listening to stammered words from Saul. Roderick could not hear those words; but they were evidently both intelligible and welcome. Then she turned to himself.

'Mr Leadbitter has a friend here, Rod.'

'I know. I've seen him. I've asked him to join Saul and me. That was before I saw you.'

Florence glanced inquiringly at Mr Leadbitter, whose further plans had now been frustrated.

'I was going to take him away, sir. With

a message from Miss Marvell.'

'A message? Is that what you want, Florrie? Or would you like him to come here?'

'I don't know. In a place like this —' She instinctively yielded to Roderick. They all did; but Saul, being unaware of any difficulty but his own, hovered, wishing only to be with his benefactress for as long as possible. He, too, looked at his father.

'Bit awkward,' muttered Mr Leadbitter. Then, to Roderick: 'You know what the trouble is, don't you?'

'I guess. And I gather that we all have the same objective.'

'Have we? I hadn't counted on you.'

'I declare an interest. A family interest.'

Silence followed. At last Mr Leadbitter, at his most abrupt, asked:

'What do you advise?'

'That we should leave it to Florrie.'

It had never occurred to Mr Leadbitter to think of Florence as 'Florrie.' He was a punctilious man, who disliked the modern habit of using Christian names with his authors and artists, and he had always thought of her, with respect, as 'Miss Marvell.' Nevertheless, he was shrewd enough to realize that his 'Miss Marvell' was on terms of closer acquaintance with this formidable lawyer than he had assumed. Her resentment of Sydney Patterson's lampoon was explained. But she had denied all knowledge of Trevor's wife. He was puzzled. Being puzzled, he sought help from his friend Miss Marvell.

'Go, or stay?' he demanded.

'Would he come?'

'Doubtful, with this —' The word 'conclave' was suppressed.

However, he consulted Roderick with a measuring glance; and, following the impression he gained, he nodded sharply, and left them.

Standing them with Florence and Saul, Roderick showed his reliance upon the spoken word by asking a question.

'How do you come into this, Florrie?'

'Mr Leadbitter is my publisher,' she answered.

'Publisher?'

'I live by my pen. You used to find my

sketches amusing, Rod.'

'Much more than amusing, of course. I'm afraid I haven't kept up —'

'Why should you do so?'

'At least, it would have been courteous.'

Their eyes, filled with understanding, were bright; while Saul, hearing the allusion to his father's old regard for Florence's work, and suddenly recalling the confession she had made to him in the train, became tremendously excited. Here, together, were the two people who had rescued him from despair. Two vital people; and in accord!

'Father! They're wonderful. Sandra calls them "delicious." And that's the very word —'

'I'm sure it is, Saul.' And, to Florence: 'You know Sandra, then?'

'No. Saul brought her to see me the other day. That's why I've become involved — as a sort of mediator. Quite hopeless in such a part.'

'I see. Do you think Trevor will come to us? I don't know what message you sent him.'

'To stop the proceedings at once. Really,

to show magnanimity.'

'And surrender?'

'You could call it that.'

'She's in a very high state of mind.'

'Outwardly. As one knowing herself to be in the wrong. Can't you influence her at all?'

'I have no influence with her, Florrie. A hardening effect.'

'Your wife?'

'She's ill. In any case —' He shrugged. 'No, if anything is to be done, it will be done by you.'

'The last person.' Florence was back in the depths.

'I think you can pull it off.'

There was no time for more, since at this moment Mr Leadbitter returned, holding by the arm, and almost dragging, a man who was so greatly embarrassed that, after a sour greeting to Saul, whom he despised, he stared fixedly at the floor. When, at Roderick's signal to the Major-Domo, chairs were brought, he sat upon the edge of the one placed for him, ready to spring up and depart in fury. He was sure that he would receive humiliating lectures from both Florence and Roderick.

Florence, who proposed, not a lecture, but an appeal, had been distracted by the coming of Roderick. She saw no trace in Trevor of the outraged but domineering husband she had expected to meet. On the contrary, he was the picture of adolescent sulkiness. He might be muscular, courageous, capable of leading shattered troops to desperate effort; but in Roderick's presence he shrank to smallness. He was probably a dolt where capricious women were concerned. Confronted by a tantalizing wife, his only answer, so far, had been obduracy. Therefore he was going to be a difficult problem. Hopeless? Time would show.

And what of Sandra? Was she physically cold, needing a kind of brutality in her lover to rouse sexual emotion, but too artless to encourage a clumsy husband who was afraid of hurting her? There must be many such relationships. Wasn't it possible that Roderick, long ago, had needed comparable wooing from herself? What had seemed to be hauteur could have been pride alone, the inability to plead. This was a new and very painful doubt, born of those very guesses about two undeveloped natures bedevilled by misunderstanding.

A further flying speculation arose. Had Syd, from inveterate mischief, precipitated the quarrel between Sandra and Trevor? Syd had lately presented himself in an altogether new light, not as a reckless scapegrace, but as a malicious, over-malignant, force for evil. His book apparently expressed jealous hatred. Could he have been, deliberately, a wrecker? She shuddered. Flashes of Syd's talk, for thirty years forgotten, returned with such added meaning that she seemed to be aware, as never before, of Roderick's character. He was not the coldly ambitious man portrayed by Syd; but one who suffered intensely from self-distrust. A weak man, perhaps, over-sensitive, incapable of the brazen assurance needed for leadership, but essentially noble; somebody who would not stoop to defend himself against slander or injustice. Was this the truth?

And was it the truth, also, about Sandra? What did Rod think of Sandra? She sought to read his expression, thereby experiencing a further shock. It was still quizzical; but behind the smiling eyes she read, in this mood of clairvoyance, anxiety, pain, and, most affectingly of all, the old sweet kindness for herself. The effect was to rob her of all capacity for thought.

There followed, as was inevitable, an awkward silence. Trevor was at bay; Saul stupefied by the sense of his nearness to Florence; Mr Leadbitter cursing all fools, Roman fathers, and well-meant efforts to do his friend a service; Florence lost in speculation. It was left to Roderick, the most socially experienced of the party, to make a first approach to general ease. Putting his hand lightly upon Trevor's arm, he addressed him in an undertone.

'I should really have preferred to see you alone; but Miss Marvell is a very old friend of mine. Not of my wife, whom she's never met. If she offers you any advice, consider it carefully. There has been no discussion of it. You understand? Miss Marvell is my friend. If, after you've talked to her, you want to see me, telephone. I shan't be in the House this evening; I shall be at Slocumbe. That's all I want to say. That, and to assure you of my goodwill.'

The words were so unexpected that Trevor crimsoned in relief. He regarded himself as a stoic, knew himself for a blunderer, and saw Roderick as, after all, human. He could not speak; could do no more than nod; but the suspense of the last hour was lifted.

Having thus, as he believed, made the way clear for more important matters, Roderick turned again to Florence.

'Florrie, I have to go to my Chambers for what's called a Conference. That means I shall listen for half-an-hour to an angry man who wants to ruin his neighbour. He may ruin himself, instead. I shall tell him so in five minutes. Saul will come with me and sit with my Devil. I wonder whether he and I could afterwards take you back, by road, to Slocumbe?'

'Oh, yes! Oh, yes!' cried Saul, in delight.

'It would be splendid! We could talk all the way!' He meant, 'as we did in the train.'

Roderick was dry.

'Not, perhaps, as bright a prospect to Miss Marvell as to you.' He proceeded, addressing Florence; 'The car is here; Blenkinsop will drive you anywhere you wish — to Mr Leadbitter's office or elsewhere; and bring you to my Chambers. I shan't keep you waiting long. You'll be saved the inconvenience of the railway journey; Saul won't chatter, as he threatens; and I shall be quite silent, as usual. Would that be agreeable to you?'

The tone was perfect. Courtesy, without condescension, to them all, and abstention from further interference in a serious discussion were implied with kingly graciousness. He did not say 'I want you to tell me, in your own words,' as Evelyn always feared he would do to herself; but the persuasiveness which encouraged witnesses was there. Florence, Trevor, and Mr Leadbitter responded as he wished. Much relieved, they watched the great man's departure, with Saul as a humble satellite at his heels; and all breathed unheard sighs.

33
Homeward Journey

Blenkinsop did not know quite what to make of his unfamiliar passenger. Being a good and well-paid servant, he obeyed any direction of Sir Roderick's without demur; but he was naturally inquisitive, with peculiar methods of judging individuals. This person was evidently unused to giving orders or to occupying the whole of a large car. She tucked herself into a corner of it, as a housemaid might do. As a woman she was not florid enough for his own taste. On the other hand Sir Roderick treated her with respect, and the boy, as he always (to himself) called Master Saul, seemed to regard her as a princess. She was coming home with them. What as? Companion to her Ladyship? Better than that, it seemed; but very unassuming. Singular enough. He would have to find out who she was.

Florence, hypersensitive that day, observed Blenkinsop's puddinglike cheeks and blackcurrant eyes with some uneasiness. She knew he was taking stock of her, both when face to face and by way of his driving mirror; but as no expression ever softened Blenkinsop's features she could not guess what his conclusions were. She took it for granted, as all must have done, that he was a reliable chauffeur. Privately, however, she summed him up as a snob and a dull companion.

'Probably he improves on acquaintance,' she reflected. 'I wonder if he romps in the kitchen. No; he would think romps unbecoming.'

Having sat behind Blenkinsop while they waited outside Roderick's Chambers, she was glad when they were no longer closeted together, and when, sandwiched between the two men she knew, she saw Blenkinsop giving his whole attention to the road.

There was plenty of room for three in the back of the car; but the journey to Slocumbe had hardly begun when Florence felt her arm brushed and her gloved hand taken by Saul. Understanding that for him, after the morning's interview with Mr Munster, some physical contact with a friend was necessary, she suffered the clasp in kindness; but for the present her mind was elsewhere. Poor boy!

Almost simultaneously Roderick, at her other side, spoke so as not to be overheard by Saul.

'Any tangible result?'

'No.' She was equally discreet, her lips no more than an inch from his ear. 'At first, point-blank refusal. I was afraid he'd go. Fortunately, Mr Leadbitter went.'

'Very wise. He's intelligent. And then?'

'Better. He listened. Finally, he agreed to think things over and telephone. I'm terribly doubtful.'

'At any rate, you've done your best.'

'I wonder. I feel awful, Rod.'

'Your tender conscience?'

'Hatred of interference. Responsibility.

I know it's cowardice.'

'You took that responsibility with —' He indicated Saul with the slightest movement of the head.

'That was bad enough. Single-handed rescue. This, being complex and double-charged, is worse.'

Florence saw him smile; and felt a pressure upon her fingers as Saul dumbly protested against his exclusion from their talk. Full of his own affair, he wanted to go on talking about it, giving his impressions of Mr Munster, and telling Florence how magnificently Roderick had behaved. He could not imagine what their murmurs were about. Something to do with Trevor, apparently; but he was not interested in Trevor. Why should his beloved Miss Marvell be?

As the car proceeded upon its way, the big West End shops gave place to a long succession of houses, and, by degrees, to twinkling street lamps. Only Blenkinsop's back remained constant; and when clouds brought early dusk upon the London suburbs even that lost definition. He let his chin rest against Florence's shoulder, and was lost in thankfulness for her blessed presence.

They were now away from houses and street lighting, with the beams from Blenkinsop's headlamps distorting the grass verges into strange shapes, when Roderick spoke aloud.

'Do you know anything about the local doctor, Florrie?'

'Doctor Whitelaw? He's very popular. A strange tall man, who does all his visiting on foot. He attends a friend of mine; and he evidently understands the case, though he can't cure it.'

'What, heart trouble?'

'A general collapse. He's kept my friend alive. It's been like a miracle.'

'I was wondering about Evelyn — my wife. She's been to specialists: no good. I thought a good local man, who could attend quickly, might be better. The trouble is *migraine*. You don't suffer from that, I assume.'

'No; thank goodness. I'm sorry to hear about your wife.'

'Yes.' Roderick said no more about wife

or doctor; merely: 'I suppose you live very simply.'

'I vegetate.'

'Except when you're acting as medicine woman to the Pattersons.'

Florence, now appalled by her responsibilities, could not appreciate this example of his teasing. It was Saul who took the opportunity to fling himself into the conversation.

'She ought to be a Consultant, Father.'

'She is that, Saul. You see that I'm consulting her.'

'Better than any doctor!' It was fervent. Florence felt her hand pressed.

Darkness was all about them. The three were so much alone in the world that they were almost thinking aloud. Roderick said:

'Florrie, it would be very kind of you to see my wife.'

Florence, lulled by the car's easy movement and these quiet exchanges, was suddenly aghast at an insensitiveness. Stupid creature! Nothing could be farther from her wish or capacity. If speech had not been choked by feeling she could have shouted 'I can't! I can't!' Why can't you *see* it's impossible?' But as swift as her terror came the revulsion. His very insensitiveness was a tribute to the girl who had loved him so long ago.

Roderick continued:

'Evelyn's a desperately lonely woman.'

How preposterous!

'But surely she has many friends?'

'Not one. In our kind of life we have society, full of good manners, insincerity, highly sophisticated talk; but only superficial friendships. "Is so-and-so dead? Ruined? No more invitations to dinner, then." Perhaps you don't understand that? Your friendships are for life.'

'Apart from this dying man and his wife, the only close friend I have is Annable. You remember her? My sister.'

'I do indeed. A very outspoken young woman.'

'She's still that. Very dear to me; and full of spirit.'

'I remember.'

'At the moment particularly full. She's been given a good part in a television serial.'

'Oh, does she act?' Roderick exposed the politician's ignornace of all but politics.

'Mr Leadbitter has admired her acting since boyhood.'

Having been snubbed by this acid retort, Roderick became courteously penitent.

'And I never knew? First your work, and now Annabel's acting! Very bad. Very bad indeed. You see how public life destroys one's outlook! Evelyn's better informed. She's by way of being a Patron of the Arts.'

He was back to Evelyn. Damn the woman!

This, for a time, was the end of their duologue. The road ahead became a brilliant green wall which receded as the car advanced; and the three passengers were lost in their own preoccupations.

Florence repeated to herself the conversation with Trevor. He had at first been truculent; but it was the truculence of suspicion. Once he grasped the fact that his sense of injury was understood, he responded with greater candour, pouring out the story so long dwelt upon in solitary anguish. To Florence it was plain that he was afraid to yield a single point less his whole cause collapse. How could she possibly force him into some understanding? 'I haven't done it; and I can't do it! I'm too stupid!'

To her left, Saul was recalling all that had passed in Mr Munster's office, from his early agonies to the disclosure of Danny's career and probable motives. At the thought that these had involved a scheme to injure his father, he quivered. At remembrance of his own folly his legs stiffened. Then ardent thankfulness at what he hoped would be salvation led him to relax into a stupor of content. He was with the two to whom he owed everything. Both were to be trusted without limit.

Roderick's thoughts were presently revealed in simple confession to Florence.

'I have to make a speech in the House tomorrow night; and the following night I'm speaking in my Constituency. Fifty people at most; but all of them critical, with some hecklers armed with ridiculous questions. Two Committee Meetings beforehand — you know that Committees take up a lot of time; and one of them is on a matter of Privilege, where I'm the only legal member. Very taxing. I'm afraid my speeches will be like ditchwater. I'm out of humour with such engagements; but they're necessary, and I shall have to work hard this evening and tomorrow. An M.P. doesn't lead the idle life he's supposed to do. Fortunately, my Secretary is at the Manor. I shall dictate notes to him. An estimable young man, with perfect manners. I sometimes speculate on his nonentity; but I like him, and he's very conscientious. That's something you'd approve, Florrie.'

'It's not common, today,' said Florence. 'If one's to believe the newspapers, which it's hard to do.'

'What a cynical remark! As to both Press and Secretaries. Mine impresses me as somebody who'll be content to be an underling all his life. Do you understand that?'

'I do. It's not everybody who can suit himself to his Fate.'

'Hm. No. But he took a good degree.

He's simply not ambitious. D'you think it's a form of moral cowardice?'

'I don't know.'

'You admire him for it?'

'I sympathize with it. I've always been a coward, myself.'

'Yes, you have, haven't you!'

Both were back in the past; and Roderick's thoughts were kinder than his companion's. But Roderick had not just emerged from desperate cajolery of an obstinate young man, trying to make him see that a sacrifice of pride was the only way to save his marriage with an even more obstinate girl who was prepared to run them both on the rocks for vanity's sake.

Already sore at her probable failure with Trevor, she anticipated almost with terror the even more difficult job of making Sandra see reason. Roderick was leaving everything, in the grandest manner, to her. It should have been his responsibility, and his wife's responsibility, to preserve a daughter's happiness; but these people — she really did, in her exasperation, call them 'these people' —

were jockeying and inadequate, characterless nobody — 'nonentity' had been Roderick's word — into the position of a general busybody.

'I'm not cut out for the job. Poor duffer that I am, I'm bound to make a mess of it and be disliked ever afterwards by the whole family. Why can't they see that?'

She longed for the journey, and the day, to end. She longed for her own little home, and her pets, and her solitude. Completely wretched, she withdrew her hand from Saul's clasp, and shrank farther away from Roderick, closing her eyes and clenching her teeth. Only when the first lights from cottages on the outskirts of Slocumbe indicated their whereabouts did she stir again into life.

Lights shone from her own windows, left there, she knew, by faithful Mrs Worth, her daily help, who must also have kindled a fire in the sitting-room grate and fed the indoor pets. Mrs Worth had more imagination than grand folk; and the place would be as bright and tidy as any of the cottages they had passed. Another 'nonentity' who was content to work at what she knew she could do well! No dreams of wealth or splendour troubled her mind; she came and went, sometimes with news of illnesses in the village, but generally as quiet as a mouse and as cheerful as a morning blackbird.

Blenkinsop's black shapelessness disappeared as he left his seat in order to open the car door; but as his movements were ponderous Saul was first out on the path, waiting for Florence to step down. He had not again tried to take her hand, and he did not do so now. Nor could she clearly see his face, except as a whiteness above the level of her eyes.

'Thank you, Saul. I shall be thinking of you, and hoping everything goes well.' She offered her hand in gratitude for his silence.

They were not alone, however. Roderick also had left the car. He stooped to speak very quietly into her ear.

'Florrie, you mustn't go before I tell you what a blessing you've been this day. I haven't pestered you for details of your talk with Trevor. I know it must have been an ordeal. Let me know if the outcome gave any promise. I rely on you completely. You know that, I'm sure. You thought me inconsiderate in speaking of Evelyn. I was stupid to do that: but I do entreat you, in the same spirit of reliance, to consider it. You're a healer. The evidence is beside you. This boy's a different being. I think you'll be successful with Trevor. If there is anything I can do, now or later, tell me.'

To her astonishment, he kissed her cheek.

34
Afterwards

Once indoors, Florence felt anger rising.

'Ridiculous!' she fumed. ' "Healer"! Does he think I'm to be carneyed by flattery? And a kiss, after all these years! I'm just an old spinster, agitated by a kiss, as if I were a schoolgirl!'

But her room was warm. It was home. And before her, stretching at full length in the armchair, ready to be petted, and unreproachful for a whole day's neglect, was William, bright-eyed, and, as ever, consoling. 'The more I see of men, the more I prefer cats!' In such affectionate company Florence could no longer be angry.

She began to smile at Roderick's clumsiness, and after smiling she thought with more complaisance of his fatuous remark about her imaginary healing powers. It had been silly, but genuine and pathetic; not the condescension of a great man, but an appeal for kindness. Why had he told her, in the car, of the work he had to do that evening and on the next two days? Was it an awkward apology for the neglect of his children? Was it not, rather, a cry for help?

'But I'm not of the helping sort!' she declared to William, whom she often addressed in candour. 'I'm like you, comfort-loving. Living alone for all these years, I've become self-centred; proud of my own self-sufficiency. And now I've been pitchforked into affairs I don't understand, and don't want to understand. I'm cold. Base. A detestable character.'

She dwelt in contrition upon her detestable character. Suddenly she jumped to her feet.

'I'm not at all hungry, after that wonderful lunch; but I need sustenance.

So I'll get you a little early supper, my William, and make myself a cup of tea. Then I'll sit by the fire and try to recover my calm. I wonder what that poor bristling young man is doing now? Torturing himself? Hating me as an interfering fool? If he persists, I'm finished. My reputation for healing will be exploded. I shall be an object of contempt.'

Continuing to look down upon William, who was listening with a lazy smile, she added:

'I'm afraid he'll persist. In a month or two he'll find another woman to look after him. Men do. Women don't so easily find another man. And Sandra will suffer for the rest of her life, thinking of all the things she ought to have done. I know that, from experience.'

Completely disheartened, she reconsidered her appeals to Trevor, Mr Leadbitter's brisk words of inquiry when they met again in the Gimblett office, her solitary drive in charge of that monstrous creature with the pudding face and inquisitive eyes, and the journey back to

Slocumbe, reproaching herself for the unintentional harshness to Saul. Poor boy! He had needed comfort; and because her mind was in a state of dishevelment she had robbed him of it.

The truth was, she had never before experienced a day so crowded with various strains and embarrassments. And the culmination of it, as far as she could see, was old Rod's kiss. It expressed so much stored sweetness that she gulped her tea, and in choking felt tears rush to her eyes.

At the end of an hour, when she was in the kitchen, the telephone bell rang. At first she could not bring herself to lift the receiver; but a guess that the caller might be Bertha caused her to stumble back into the sitting-room and answer in a strangled voice which she did not recognize as her own.

A bark, obviously that of Mr Leadbitter, stabbed her ear.

'Hello, that Miss Marvell? Just a minute. I've got Trevor here.'

There was some murmuring, apparently between the two men; and when Florence heard, or believed she heard, the sharp instruction 'Stick it out! Stick it out, you fool!' she was filled with despair. Plainly, she was to get a refusal. Another voice vibrated in her ear. It was harsh, as if the speaker's throat was dry with determination.

'Miss Marvell? Trevor Hamburg. Um . . . I've thought it all out. Told Horace, here, what you said. Um . . . I'll do that.'

'You will?' She was incredulous. She thought her anxious heart had stopped beating. 'Oh, but this is splendid! You're really being —' The word eluded her. At last it came. 'Noble! Very brave indeed, Mr Hamburg!'

'And you'll see what . . . *the other side* says?'

That was daunting; but she could not withdraw.

'If "the other side" is equally brave —'

'Oh, God!' groaned the voice. 'You think she will be?'

'I'll do my best.'

'How soon?'

'At once. Roderick will help.'

'I'd rather trust you.'

No reply to this was possible, and the voice died. Another voice became audible. It was that of Mr Leadbitter.

'Thanks, Miss Marvell. No need for me to say more. Sleep well!'

Silence. Florence pictured the two men in Mr Leadbitter's office, with Trevor already regretting his decision. 'Too late, my boy; you've burned your boats!' Her heart seemed to swell with thankfulness.

'I may not be a healer!' she exclaimed, to William. 'But, as you well know, my dear cat, I have my moments!'

PART EIGHT

SENSATIONAL EVENTS

35
The Stranger

Syd Patterson leaned back in a corner of the saloon bar of a Chelsea pub known to its frequenters as The Ladder. He was alone, which was a state he disliked; an in his breast pocket, with other papers, was a letter from Messrs Gimblett, the publishers, declining his book of selective autobiography.

This book, written spasmodically at intervals during three or four years, had been hastily finished in the past few weeks. He thought it an extremely brilliant account, not only of his own pilgrimage in search of entertainment, but of the age he lived in; mordant, witty, engaging, and profound, but especially mordant. His plan, in writing it, was to establish a reputation and to earn money enough for all future needs. Behind the deliberate plan lay a wish to repay all scores and put Roderick in his place as the mediocre brother of a genius.

Gimblett's letter therefore burned like fire against his breast. It was tactfully cordial, praising the book's style and variety, but saying that it was not quite suited to their list. Blast them! Of course it was not suited to a timidly conventional list. That had been the whole point of letting them have it — to rouse a moribund firm from torpor. And what was the result? Cold feet? Being respectable fools, they couldn't appreciate originality. Plenty of other publishers would jump at the chance of getting such a book. Plenty! Oho, plenty! Gimblett's would rue the day they let a masterpiece slip!

In spite of these and similar brave thoughts, Syd was depressed; and when depressed he always drank greedily. Tonight the glass at his elbow had already been filled several times, with the consequence that his depression had reached stupefying monomania. He remembered all the wrongs he had suffered in fifty-five years of life. They had been many. They had begun in the cradle. Another man, he was sure, would have sunk under them. He had not allowed himself to sink. He had survived!

For all that, they weighed malignantly upon him. The night was rainy. His lodgings were cheerless — a mere floor and ceiling, bed, and chair with broken springs. He lacked a proper home; his friends were overseas; only in the saloon bar of a pub could he find the warmth he needed. And in his cold lodgings lay a brown-paper parcel containing a rejected *chef d'oeuvre*. That was what rankled most of all. Because young Trevor claimed to have some pull at Gimblett's, he had sent his book to them, really as a favour. The favour had been spurned.

Damn young Trevor! And damn that affected wench who had ensorceled Trevor! She was the proper offspring of two arrogant fools. Two arrogant fools, remember, who had a magnificent home, were waited on hand and foot by sycophants, ate in luxury, and believed themselves to be the salt of the earth. Salt! Good God! Parasites! Both despised him because he stood alone. Rod, the arch snob, was outdone by that bitch, his wife. Wrinkling her nose at sight of a brother-in-law who would not truckle, she flounced like a suburban dowager. Flounced! Flounced! Flounced!

Depression gave way to anger. How he would enjoy rubbing that supercilious nose in the dirt! A grand satisfaction! He had pictured her, in his book, as she was. Of course, that was the trouble. Pusillanimous publishers, like the Gimbletts, would always reject the biting truth — from fear of Rod. Rod! Invariably Rod stood in his way, interposing his own self-righteous ambition between genius and its rewards. What, with all his virtue, had Rod ever done? Grinding away at his briefs, stupefying the House of Commons with solemn platitudes, he'd got on, proud of a nullity surpassing all other nullities!

Observing that his glass was again

empty, Syd rose a little unsteadily from his seat and approached the counter. As he reached it, a movement behind, and a gust of cold air upon his cheek, caused him to look fiercely round. Another man had entered the bar; a man well-covered with flesh, with rings glittering on a fat hand in the bright lights. Prosperous! Slick! Cold, fishy eyes full of disdain for somebody whom he took to be nobody at all. It was insufferable impudence! Syd Patterson had always been a brilliant fellow with talent enough for half a dozen. True, he'd been thwarted by Fortune; but soon he would be on top of the world, acclaimed everywhere — when his book was published!

Yes, yes, yes, that was all right; but meanwhile there was a damned brown-paper parcel in the cold digs, and in his breast pocket lay Gimblett's letter. The contrast between what would be and what was struck like a bitter douche. Syd returned the newcomer's unpleasant stare with a scowl.

On the way back to his seat he noticed a

slight unsteadiness in his knees. And at the same moment he spilled an appreciable amount of drink over his fingers. Being fastidious in the matter of clean hands, he swore quickly with rising choler, while, in re-seating himself, he spilled a little more of the drink, thereby increasing his disgust. He would not admit to himself that he was half-drunk; but added one more to the list of his misfortunes.

'Sickening!' he muttered. 'Everything's against me!'

Carefully wiping his fingers with a handkerchief, he raised the glass carefully to his lips, disgusted anew by knowledge that the fingers were not cleansed.

'Ugh! Perfumes of Araby!' was his inevitable comment.

Frowning, brooding, he stared into nothingness, warmth creeping through his head until confusion reigned there. And in the midst of this confusion he found that the stranger had come so near that they were sitting within a yard of each other. Much too near! It was a piece of damned impertinence. The frown darkened. This fellow, of about his own age, with short neck, double chin, full complexion, and protruding eyes, was somebody unholy, the sort that are instinctively avoided. He was clean shaven; his hat was Quakerish; his lips the sort to speak unctuous platitudes from a dais in the local Sunday School. Detestable type! Also, he was fresh from the barber, a picture of cleanliness, the odour of hair spray clinging to his head and obnoxious to the nostrils.

'Good evening,' remarked the stranger.

'Good evening,' growled Syd, like a watchdog. He would have liked to add: 'And now, go away'; but, instead, he indicated his unwillingness to talk by drinking again.

'Not a very pleasant one,' said the stranger, conversationally.

This reminded Syd that if he left the bar he would have to endure the rain and go back to his cold rooms and the brown-paper parcel. He suddenly wished to tell somebody about the parcel, remembering just in time that although this would be a relief to his feelings it would also be a further humiliation. Such a well-fed swine would not sympathize; he would be confirmed in his own self-satisfaction. The best course would be to say nothing. He said nothing.

The stranger, sipping at an innocuous drink, appeared not to notice any grimness. He was, in fact, in the mood for talk, having no occupation for the evening, and having come straight from his Club barber, who had retailed an important piece of gossip. This barber, as is usual with barbers, learned many secrets from his clients, and spread them generously for the good of all. And, naturally, his clients came away enriched by curious facts about other individuals. This was what had happened to the stranger.

'Depressing,' he observed to Syd. 'One's depressed.'

'One's depressed,' agreed Syd, surprised at the man's perceptiveness.

'Not only by the rain. By public events, too.'

'By everything,' was Syd's harsh retort. 'Human Nature.'

'All over the world. You've travelled, I think?'

'All over the world.'

'You look bronzed — as if you were a traveller. How do other countries — their Governments — compare with ours?'

Syd wanted to say: 'I'm not prepared to discuss anything with you, or anybody else'; but he felt bound to make a reply, so he substituted the words: 'Equally futile. Some more corrupt than others.'

The stranger leapt upon ·the word 'corrupt.'

'That's the fact that distresses every thoughtful observer: the steadily increasing corruption of Governments. It's due to the upsurge of adventurers, don't you agree?'

'I don't know,' muttered Syd, impatiently.

'As the world grows smaller and the masses more greedy, corruption is bound to increase. I'm afraid the whole System will fall into disrepute. What then? Anarchy?' As no reply came, the speaker added: 'I'm not too happy about this country, you know.'

'Mediocrities,' growled Syd, drinking deep. 'All mediocrities.' He thought of Roderick. His head appeared to be swelling softly, like a child's inflatable balloon. His lips were so swollen that they pronounced the words with difficulty. His companion's face had become a grotesque mask, representing to a restless mind the final stupidity of platitudinousness.

The stranger lowered his voice.

'Very odd things are happening here. You don't see or hear of them through the Media. They're suppressed. Some people talk melodramatically about "a conspiracy of silence"; but it's not a conspiracy. It's a general fear of saying openly what the nation ought to know. That leads to an increase in political intrigue. The least scrupulous engage in it all the time. Consequently, without our being aware of it, they pull strings and deceive us. This man is to be cried up, and pushed; the other one, because he won't stoop to intrigue, is to be played down.'

Syd's attention was caught. This was what was happening to himself. Intrigue was at the bottom of the rejection of his book.

'The honest man doesn't "make the grade," as they call it,' he cried, striking the table.

'Exactly!' replied the stranger. 'Exactly!'

He looked very mysterious indeed, as if to show that he was master of a thousand secrets. Having heard one of them this evening, as a true Englishman he longed to impart it. Not quite at this moment, perhaps; but before him was a handsome fellow, obviously intelligent if a little cross-grained (for the scowl could not be overlooked), who could be coaxed into pleasant discussion for half-an-hour or so. And, being a man of miscellaneous knowledge, and an ardent Tory politician, with time to fill before his next engagement, he proposed to deploy his secret.

Syd was too much confused by what he had drunk, and too much obsessed by bitter reflections, to follow what was being said. He saw a sleek, very prosperous man, of a kind he most detested, whose gills were red and whose manner was smugly obtrusive; and he listened with distaste to what the creature was mouthing. 'Mah! Mah! Mah!' Loathsome! So much dislike for this man was beginning to seethe within that he was ready to quarrel without warning.

The stranger bent a little nearer.

'I see that we understand each other. We both have the good of our country at heart. It is the good of the country I'm thinking of. And I heard today — on very good authority — that *behind the scenes* something has happened of extraordinary moment. This must go no farther, of course; but I understand that the *Prime Minister* is seriously ill, and that his illness is being *deliberately* hushed up! Of course, he's getting on in years — we all are; — and like other elderly men . . . you understand? . . . he's naturally been feeling the strain. . . . '

Syd wanted to say 'I couldn't care less!' but he repressed all speech, because his lips were dry and he could not be sure of forming the words clearly. This fact increased his anger; but the stranger evidently took silence to indicate agreement. He proceeded, with an even greater air of discreetness.

'You see what happens? A vacuum

forms. Perhaps a little panic. That's where the danger lies. What we — I mean the country, not merely the Party — what we need is sober judgment. Leadership that's above suspicion. There are several men of the greatest probity. I won't mention names; but the first that comes to my mind is disqualified by the fact that he's in the Lords. You follow?'

Syd had ceased to listen. He drained his glass, and again wiped his fingers upon his handkerchief, which was exasperatingly damp. Satisfied that he was being heard with sympathy, the stranger whispered:

'What's to be done? I'll tell you. There are several other men of the highest class in the Commons. One, in particular. A man of tremendous ability; honest, eloquent, a gentleman in every sense of the word. Indeed, his name will spring to your mind. I mean Sir Roderick Patterson.'

Syd jumped. Fury swept through him.

'Oh, he's no good!' he cried, loudly.

It was like a discharge of cannon. It astounded the stranger, who became unexpectedly warm.

'What! Why do you say that?'

'I say it because I *know.*'

'This is extraordinary!' Syd was confronted with a deeply flushed face. 'I should like to hear your reasons.'

'Well, for one, the bloody fellow's my brother!'

For an instant incredulous, the stranger perceived that the assertion was genuine. Some resemblance to Roderick Patterson in the distorted face before him must have been convincing. Still flushed, but with changed manner, he almost obsequiously bent his head.

'I'm greatly honoured by your company,' he said. 'You have a brotherly love for him, I'm sure.'

'I have no brotherly love for him, I tell you!' bawled Syd, in a paroxysm of savagery. 'I detest him. I know him for what he is. You speak of intrigue. He's a man of it! My God, when you talk like that you show your bloody ignorance. You crawl! You fester!'

'My dear sir!' The stranger drew back, intimidated by the display.

'Yes!' shouted Syd, leaping to his feet

and sweeping the glass from the table in a wild gesture of dismissal. 'And I'll tell you something more. He'll never be what you pretend he is. He hasn't got the ability! Nor the guts!'

Both were now standing, the two faces very close. Attempting to placate by a smile, the stranger destroyed what remained of Syd's self-control.

'Oh, my dear sir! My dear sir! You've been drinking! You're not yourself!'

'My God!' Syd's hands flew up. They gripped a flabby neck. They shook a heavy head from side to side. And with a great effort they threw the stout body several feet away. It fell, struck another table, and collapsed. A dreadful gush of blood from a gaping mouth stained the floor.

Syd was filled with horror, while the barmaid, who had been watching two men talking, as she had supposed, quietly, gave a shriek.

'Dad! Dad! Here! Quick! Murder!'

There was a sound of trampling feet. Several men crowded into the bar. Syd, completely dazed, stood looking down at his enemy, who was dead.

36
Roderick's Day

With a busy day ahead, Roderick did no more than skim the headlines of the half-dozen newspapers upon his desk. Bank robberies, the death of a famous film actress, an earthquake at the other side of the world and a charge of negligence against some Public Authority were dismissed in a series of rapid glances. But we all, however inattentive to other things, recognize our own names in a page of print; and his eye could not miss a headline near the foot of the *Post's* opening spread.

SIR R. PATTERSON'S BROTHER
IN TAVERN AFFRAY

430

'Oh, God! What's this?' His heart jumped.

The paragraph was short: 'Mr Sydney Patterson (55), Sir Roderick Patterson's brother, was involved yesterday evening in an altercation, the cause unknown, with an elderly companion. The scene was a Chelsea public house, and the elderly man, whose identity is not yet established, died instantly. The police were called, and Mr Patterson will appear in Court this morning.'

That was all; but to the reader it was petrifying.

'Good heavens! Good heavens! What on earth happened? Altercation? Affray? He must have been drunk. Crazy fellow! Still the fighter-pilot; and everybody a Hun. But this is serious. I must see him at once. Yes; but I shouldn't arrive in time for the hearing. I must get hold of Munster. He won't be at his office yet. Probably at breakfast. Well, he'll have to be interrupted!'

It was simple to dial the right number; and there was no delay.

'Munster, I'm sorry to disturb you like this; but my brother's in dangerous trouble. Oh, you've already seen that, have you? Yes, very bad. Could you possibly get your Clerk to go along to the Court — to represent me? Since his crash in the war my brother has always been erratic; but he's never done anything like this. I can't let him down. He'll probably refuse help. False pride. They won't allow him bail; but charge him at once with manslaughter. If your Clerk could see him, and ring my Chambers, I shall be there in a couple of hours, and can arrange for a proper defence. Is that possible? Thank you. I'm very grateful. Yes, I agree; the paragraph's alarming. Right.'

Mr Munster, apart from his two interjections, made no comment. His breakfast, no doubt, was philosophically resumed. For the moment, nothing further could be done.

Roderick had seen Evelyn's face, distorted with pain, as she went to bed. She must not be roused from such sleep as she had managed to obtain by her sedatives. If possible, knowledge of Syd's violence must be kept from her for the present. He must warn Miss Dundee to omit the paragraph from her survey of the morning's news.

Syd. He re-read what was reported of the 'Affray.' It was of no help. Such incidents were common enough in the big cities, and this one would not have been headlines if Syd had borne a less distinguished name. Because of that name, his misdemeanour was 'news.' How had the 'affray' come about? Were both men drunk? Had the other struck first? Who was he? A boon companion? A stranger? Manslaughter was an ugly charge. Syd's unbalanced nature had always been a menace. It had now gone beyond menace. Coming at this moment, when so much else was amiss, it was frightening.

Roderick put the newspaper aside. He was speaking that night in the House. The speech was prepared; but he must refresh his mind upon the subject, which involved a defence of Sam's conduct of some obscure African trouble. Whatever he said must be very guarded indeed; but he must be in his place. It was a point of loyalty to an old political friend. But Syd's voice, Syd's departure from the Manor without farewell, Syd's present danger were all present in his thoughts, destroying concentration.

Roderick hardly noticed an ominous pain which ran across his body, somewhere below the heart. The pain was acute; but it passed as quickly as it came, and he was aware only of perspiration upon his brow and cheeks as an unwelcome sign of agitation.

'Damn Syd! I didn't want this!'

He bent over his desk. The pain had ceased. The weight upon mind and heart could be ignored by an effort of will. That was his normal course.

Blenkinsop had read the paragraph. He had quelled excitement in the kitchen by munching stolidly through an ample dish of bacon and egg; and when pressed to speak he merely shook his head.

'Don't chatter,' he acted. 'It does no good.'

'But what will Sir Roderick do?' he was asked.

'Say nothing,' was all that he would answer. 'Like me.'

Although he drove toward London with customary assurance, he kept an eye on Roderick in his mirror during the whole journey, justified in his own taciturnity by his master's air of composure. His thought was: 'Never shows what he's thinking. Never tells me anything. He knows I understand him.' His admiration for Roderick ran side by side with his own self-esteem as personified discretion. All the same, he was burning with curiosity.

They drove straight to Roderick's Chambers, where comparable curiosity was indicated by silence and fleeting looks which did nothing to soothe the man they served. Roderick's clerk, Thompson, however, had news for him.

'Munster's Clerk has been on the 'phone, Sir Roderick. He had a word with Mr Patterson. Mr Patterson doesn't want to see you. In fact he refused to plead; and told Munster's Clerk to mind his own business. Remanded in custody.'

'Of course, that's ridiculous,' was Roderick's sole comment.

'It seems everybody's his enemy, sir. He glared at the beak. Munster's Clerk thought he might be shamming insanity.'

'No sham, I'm afraid. What was the evidence?'

'The barmaid saw him jump up and fly at the other man's throat. She hadn't heard what they were saying. Just saw the attack in her mirror.'

'You say "attack": did she see any provocation?'

'No, sir. They'd been talking quietly. The other man was quite a gentleman. Rather stout. Spoke quietly. She said he seemed very friendly; but of course a man can say very enraging things with a smile.'

'Was any arrangement made for defence?'

'No. He refused. Told Munster's Clerk to "get to hell out of here." Just remanded for the post mortem.'

'Which will be?'

'Seven days at most.'

'I'll wait three. Then I'll try again. Thank you, Thompson."

Roderick saw the man's back with relief. Thompson was middle-aged, and very grey. He had begun to stoop a little, and he wasted no words. But his presence in this mood of agitation was intolerable.

'Fool! Fool!' muttered Roderick. It was not of Thompson that he spoke. It was of a much-loved brother.

In common with many other people in the British Isles, Bertha Pledge had read the paragraph. She jumped up from the breakfast table and ran to the telephone.

'Florence! Have you seen the news? What, not what's in the paper? It's terrible! Why, Sir Roderick's brother! Yes, he's killed somebody! They've arrested him!'

It was a moment before this sensational announcement, so breathlessly made, reached Florence's understanding. She had been busy with her own thoughts, which were of Sandra and a coming ordeal; and this fresh calamity was at first incredible.

'What do you mean, Bertha?'

The news was repeated, with equal breathlessness. It was terrible, as another declaration of war would have been. Syd? Impossible! She knew his wildness; she had recently been so indignant at the attack on Roderick in his book that she thought her heart was closed to him for ever; but this was quite impossible. Impossible!

Bertha, having dashed back to the breakfast table, read the paragraph aloud in a tone which seemed almost one of gloatery. She had never met Syd. She had not known of his existence. She immediately assumed the report to be accurate. Its whole point, for her, lay in his relationship to Roderick and the effect of his action upon the occupants of the Manor.

'Isn't it terrible for them! One doesn't know what to do! Poor Lady Patterson! She'll be frightfully upset. Of course, I don't know her well enough to go barging up there to offer sympathy! That was my first impulse. What do you think I ought to do?'

'Do nothing, Bertha; nothing! It would be indecent!' Florence was choking. She was shocked at the mere possibility of such impertinence.

'But don't you think it would be a consolation? To feel that somebody felt sympathy?'

'She wouldn't see it like that. Oh, Bertha, dear; don't on any account add to her distress!'

The response was one of disappointment.

'Do you really think that?'

'It's not as though Syd himself was dead! That would be different!'

'No. No. I do see. But of course the disgrace!'

'She won't be thinking of disgrace. She'll be thinking of him as Roderick's brother; as himself; somebody she knows and loves.'

Bertha delivered one of her lightning guesses.

'Do you know him?'

'Long ago, when he was an airman.'

'Ooh! How interesting! Did you know him well?'

'I thought I did.'

The very ambiguosity of this answer fed Bertha's natural zest for gossip.

'What did you think of him?'

Even if she had been less shocked by the tragic news, Florence could not have distinguished between her old thoughts and her more recent displeasure, her new suspicions of Syd's malice. He had been dear to her, as a friend, as Rod's brother, and as the ebullient man who came striding through the copse early the other day. She tried to answer.

'He was very attractive. Boisterous. Very brave.'

'Really! How interesting! Were you in love with him?'

'Never.' This, at least, Florence could say with sincerity. 'But when one's known somebody —'

'Yes, it must be very distressing. I hope I haven't hurt you, darling. You know my way. I just felt I must tell you. I wanted to ask what you thought I should do. I quite see that it would be tactless to do anything about Lady Patterson. She'd think me an interfering old fool. It would be different if she was you, dear. Well, thank you very much. Of course, if she says anything to me I shall say how sorry I am. I'm sorry for Sir Roderick, too. I mean, the family. I'm thankful Ralph has no relations. I used to wish he had a brother; but brothers can be a trouble, can't they!'

'Yes, a trouble.' It was drearily spoken. Florence had passed from shock to deeper realization of what had happened. She was trembling from head to foot. Her teeth had begun to chatter. When Bertha suddenly ceased to fill her ears with words which had become unintelligible she replaced the receiver and was alone with horror.

Roderick spoke that night to a thin House. Not more than fifty, all told, were in the Chamber, and of that number perhaps a dozen had entered when it was known that he was on his feet. He had listened to his honourable friend opposite, whose clever, spiteful little speech contained snaps at 'Colonialism' (that modern substitute, invented by those whose territories expanded by conquest overland, for the old word 'Imperialism') and at Sam Wrekin as the representative of a discredited system of enslavement. He had not missed a sneer at himself; nor the phrases which would look well in tomorrow's print. But he had not retorted.

With resolute moderation he had justified Sam's actions or inactions, and although he was heard with interest he knew when he sat down that the interest had been resigned, not ardent. 'Not one of my best efforts. Too tame. Too tame.' This he knew to be his defect as a debater. While, like other barristers in the House, he had an advantage denied to would-be orators, which was that of speaking conversationally, as he would have done in Court, he could not stir his hearers to excitement. So it was tonight. Well, he had done his best, for truth and for Sam. It was not good enough; but it was enough for credit. Now he must go home. He was tired, too tired to stay and hear the verbosity that would follow.

As always, there was a little rustling, a little coughing; and then he was out of the Chamber, through the corridors, and behind Blenkinsop once more. Weariness seized him. Syd had been obstinately invisible. Everything there was blank.

Blank and black. The more he considered that situation the more threatening it became.

The car was in motion among the grey solemnities of Whitehall, which were like the ghosts of history, all of them disapproving what they considered to be the busy trivialities of modern life. Their own triviality had not been less; but their monuments remained, whereas today there were no monuments, but only functional tediums. Uniformity was the vogue: reproached by the beauties of such ephemera as the flowers, stupid men laboured for monotony in all things. Tonight the ghosts transcended the gravediggers.

Now Blenkinsop steered his way through the echoing solitudes of Mayfair and on to the north-western roads. At this time, in the early morning hours, good citizens were abed, and lorries or vehicles erratically driven by those whose eyes were strained or bleary were minor dangers with which Blenkinsop would deal. Roderick left everything to Blenkinsop. He was unspeakably tired. It was necessary to relax. But that alarming dart of pain through his body came back, this time for a longer stay, so that for a few minutes he was full of a sense of nausea.

'This won't do! It suggests angina, which would be very inconvenient indeed!'

'Inconvenient': that was the word. He needed all the bodily health he could command. Being used to every kind of inconvenience in the pursuit of his two trades of Law and Politics, he had hitherto relied upon a sound physique and reasonable diet. He hoped these good fortunes were not intending to forsake him. If they did, what was to happen to his work? . . .

Other things besides his work were at risk. He must give attention to Evelyn's distressing malaise, to Sandra's ridiculous quarrel with that unhappy boor Trevor, to Saul, who would be looked after, one hoped, by Munster. And, of course, to Syd . . .

Thoughts, mastering pain, travelled back to days of boyhood, to Syd's early instabilities, and one or two occasions when Syd had tried to mock him into anger. Being stronger and more self-controlled than Syd, he had endured the mockery; but it had driven arrows into his self-confidence. Syd was one of those people with sharp insight who knew how to wound. One's only armour against him was assumed calm. Probably that armour had served later as protection against bitter public criticism. . . .

From Syd to Mother. Mother's comparable insight into what she considered to be Florrie's weaknesses. 'Take her out of uniform, and she's nothing but a suburban miss, in place behind any counter, but incapable of experience in any true sense of the word.' What a characteristic phrase! How revealing, now, of a small judgment. Mother had been too crude, too possessive, too besottedly determined that he should exalt the family's fortunes by resounding success. He could not blame her. She had experienced poverty, and she had made innumerable sacrifices for her determination. And, of course, finding Syd recalcitrant, she had created one-sided animosity between the brothers.

Syd again; a good, generous fellow at heart, with capacity for brilliance. Why had he failed? Was it only through preference for the road of least resistance? He was disappointed enough now, and too apt to translate resentment for failure into contempt for others. The war had totally harmed him. It had roused the latent savagery. But this exhibition of it was appalling. What was to be done? Would it be of any use to ask Peake to defend? Peake wasn't a criminal lawyer; but he was a man who saw, and took advantage of, every loophole. One of the cleverest men at the Bar. One must ask Munster's opinion. But what could one do with a brother who defied every attempt at help?

Damn this pain! It was making him sweat. At times he could hardly prevent himself from giving an animal groan. Mustn't open his mouth. He had learned at school that it was an Enlgishman's duty to set his teeth and endure. They called it, in the old days, 'Keeping a stiff upper lip.' It was really vanity of the most egregious kind. Old Blenkinsop, quite outside the tradition, was just as determined as stoic. There he was, as unshakable as granite, a large mass of flesh, entirely free from nervous attacks. One mustn't be inferior to Blenkinsop.

Think of something pleasant, as distraction. Florrie, for example. She couldn't help with Syd. Or could she? Fond of Syd. Syd had been sweet on her. Syd said 'She wouldn't look at me. I'm not noble enough.' That meant he had tried to attract her, and been rebuffed. Syd wouldn't try again. Vanity was his sin. His tragedy. And Florrie, who might have rescued him, wasn't inclined towards unsteadiness. She's as simple as a dove; obstinate as a cat; but — oh, God! this agony! — she was a healer. If she were here, she'd . . . Didn't like my kissing her — too 'proper' for such goings-on; — but she was always nice to kiss, and still is. Why hasn't she married?

He continued to think of Florrie, although the sweat was running down to his cheeks. By setting his teeth, and remembering that innocent little face, with its constant change of expression, he bore

447

another bout of pain without crying aloud. The pain had left his heart and travelled up to his shoulder, his neck, his head. It was intense. He must not give way to it. If he could hold out until they reached home his self-respect would have won a battle — a war. What was this trouble? A thrombosis? That might be. That might be. Terribly inconvenient, though.

It was pretty dark in this road. He could not recognize the surroundings; which were absolutely black outside the range of the headlights. Fortunately Blenkinsop knew every road. Fortunately Blenkinsop was in charge. How long had Blenkinsop been in charge? Years. Years.

Oh, God! His heart thudded and flurried; his breathing became full of effort. The pain increased with each moment. It was spreading, growing so severe that he was rigid with the effort to breathe and to restrain absurd bellowing. It was all up the back of his head, over his ears, and down the neck to his shoulders, no longer in spasms, but with cruel assaults upon every part of the torso. This was like the rack! Exactly what victims of the Inquisition must have felt. He understood why they screamed. How much longer could he endure?

An amusing thought fluttered through the sense of torture. What if, when their journey ended, Blenkinsop opened the car door and found, sprawled along the back seat, an insensible body? Would he, for just that instant, cease to be the immovable Blenkinsop one knew? At first it would be: 'Wake up, sir; we're home. Wake up! Wake, up, I say!' And then, as alarm seized him 'Oh, Gawd! He's dead!'

Smiling at the picture of that white face turning suddenly red, Roderick fainted.

37
The Day After

The morning broke clear and chill, with long orange streaks across the eastern sky. Apart from early milkmen and postal sorters, Slocumbe was in no hurry to show signs of life. Most of the cottage windows were dark; cocks prepared to crow, but did not choose, as yet, to make the effort. Doctor Whitelaw, the seven-foot skeleton, having been up at the Manor three hours earlier, tending a great man to whom he had been summoned from bed, lay in heavy sleep. Silence was everywhere.

And then the cocks, having noticed the arrival of dawn, challenged each other. Their cries roused other birds, human beings, and animals. In no time at all vehicles were on the road and kettles were boiling. The orange streaks spread right across the southern sky, and weather prophets drew different conclusions from them. Bertha Pledge hopped out of bed, eager to bring Ralph his morning tea, to draw the curtains, and to begin another day of gossiping with her neighbours.

These neighbours had conferred about the Patterson trouble; but most of Slocumbe's natives missed the paragraph, and did not bother their heads about events so far from home. Bertha was different. She was really concerned for the happiness of others. Therefore her earliest waking thoughts were of Florence and Sir Roderick and his wretched brother. What a terrible thing to happen to that splendid carefree family. And how wise Florence had been to check her impulse to pay a visit of condolence. Of course it wouldn't have done at all. She could just imagine Lady Patterson's chilling stare. It would have frozen her. Florence was always wise — and, in a way, mysterious. Just think! She had known Sir Roderick's murderous brother. She had never boasted of her acquaintance. She was an oyster; a charming oyster, who went quietly on with her work as if she had never known anybody at all. Bertha couldn't help wondering. . . . Had there been a little romance? She must try, of course very tactfully, to find out. Because it really was very interesting indeed. . . .

'I'm afraid, if I'd known him, I should have blurted it out. I can't keep anything to myself.'

She took pleasure in her own candour.

Florence also thought of Syd in the early morning. But then she had thought of him many times during the night, in long wakeful periods of anxiety. William, having been out for a stroll, now crept upstairs and curled up close to her breast, purring and giving comfort by his affectionateness. He was a thoughtful cat, who knew and respected his mistress's moods.

Alas! The morning mood was worst of all; for it was the mood of realism. There was nothing she could do to rescue Syd from the consequences of his own violent action. These were in other hands. Could Rod, with his power and reputation, be more helpful? In some other countries it might have been so; in England the Law was still outside the range of powerful men's influence. It might be an ass; but it was a sacred ass, tended by High Priests. Like a King, it could in its own eyes do no wrong. And any appeal against its decisions must be made in legal terms. A woman's argument, which really would amount only to a claim that Syd was completely irresponsible, had no chane of acceptance.

How would Rod behave? With dignity, she was sure.

'Poor Rod! His dignity is his touchstone!'

It was the harshest comment she had ever made upon Roderick. She did not know that at this moment he was without dignity, almost without life. No news of his last night's collapse had reached the world. Even members of his own household, whispering among themselves as a result of Blenkinsop's brief communication in the early hours, knew only that the doctor had been summoned, and that nurses from the nearst town had arrived almost magically before those members had made arrangements for them to be fed and bedded within reach of the invalid. Bertha could not hear the whisper; she was blithe with memory of yesterday's events. There was but one source of information — Roderick's family.

This was why, when Florence had fed her pets, she was surprised to find Saul at her door. He had come in trouble almost as great as that she had seen upon their first meeting. There was the same pallor in his face, the same nervous movement in his arms, the same incoherence in his speech; and at first she could not understand what he was trying to say.

'Oh, Miss Marvell; the worst possible news! It's really —'

Was he speaking of Syd? She ventured a question.

'Is it your uncle?'

'No, no, no! Father!'

Still Florence could not grasp the fact. When she did so, it was with less of a shock than the one she had felt over Syd. The capacity for shock had been numbed; and she had such confidence in Roderick's strength that she could not associate him with physical collapse. Only by degrees, when she heard that Doctor Whitelaw was back at the Manor, and taking a very serious view of what might happen to his patient, did the extent of this latest calamity become clear.

'Of course he'll get better,' she insisted. 'Don't worry, Saul. He's a very resolute man. It's just that he's been living under strain.'

'But I've seen him!' cried Saul. 'He didn't know me. Couldn't speak. Just his eyes moved a little; and then closed again. The nurses. Of course, they're wonderful; and this doctor . . . But you see how much depends on Father. I relied on him almost as much as I rely on you. He's been so kind!' The boy, in trying to express his feelings, was caught by a great sob, which he checked so vehemently that he broke into a fit of coughing.

'Saul! Saul! You mustn't let yourself —' Florence was not calm; she was strong only in her determination to strengthen an over-emotional creature who might have been her son. She knew that hysteria would rob him of sense, and that he was again in danger of nervous breakdown. 'Listen, dear; your father will get better. You must stand by him until he's well again. Show your love and confidence in him —'

'But if you *saw* him!' The boy shuddered.

'I can guess. When you get home again — he has extraordinary resilience — you'll find he knows you. You mustn't let him see that you've been afraid. Remember, you're his son. His only son. And you can be as brave as he's been all his life.'

The resoluteness of her speech, which was not only wholly assumed, must have influenced Saul; for he ceased to shudder. Perhaps he even pictured himself as courageous? Quietness between them lasted for several minutes.

During those minutes Florence understood that he was struggling with his old fear of absolute aloneness. He had felt that his father's support was withdrawn; but as her assurance restored calm the developing hysteria was checked. He could then tell her, with only occasional lapses into incoherence, what he had learned from Blenkinsop, whose nerve had never failed.

It was not very much. Blenkinsop's gift of narrative was as small as his vocabulary. 'I see in my mirror as he wasn't sitting up. I stopped the car and went round. "Are you feeling all right, sir?" I said. He was all crunched up; quite gone. I shook him a bit; and he opened his eyes. "Not very well," he said. So I straightened him out, and drove hell for leather. Then I routed out Mr Dickson, the private secretary; and we got him indoors and up to his bedroom. Mr Dickson phoned the doctor; and doctor come at once. By that time we'd got him undressed. Then Miss Sandra come along the passage — she'd heard us, you see. . . .'

The rest was in Saul's own words. Sandra had called him, which neither of the others had thought to do; and together, hand in hand, they had watched the doctor's methodical examination, seeing with relief that Roderick was able to smile at them as he tried in vain to say something which they could understand.

'It was awful,' concluded Saul. 'Almost worse than his dumbness. I can't tell you how painful. I wished you were there. You'd have known what he was struggling to tell us. You'd have soothed him. His doctor just says "Mhm. Mhm." And Father looks ghastly.' He broke off. 'Miss Marvell, couldn't you come — now — and work your magic on him? You know he called you a healer. That's what you are, you know.'

Roderick's preposterous word filled Florence with shame. Though she might long to be at his side, she imagined Evelyn's resentment of a stranger's intrusion. It would seem to her to be wanton. Therefore she shook her head; and Saul misread the movement. To him, such reluctance, at such a moment, was a cruelty. He had really supposed that she would at once accompany him back to the Manor.

It was a revelation of character which

hardened Florence's heart towards him. She was face to face with the fundamental egotism of those who count on being helped through life. They are legion. Assuming that the job of a healer is to heal at all times, they ignore every problem but their own. Saul, having been rescued from impulsive suicide and put upon the road to safety, expected her sympathy to embrace not only himself but all belonging to him.

'He thinks me selfish,' was her reaction. 'I am. But he can't *imagine* what's in my mind; and how much I don't know. None of the Pattersons can do that. Only one in a thousand can. Thousand? Million!'

Distressed as she was, this brief colloquy with herself brought a smile to her eyes. Saul, immediately appeased, responded with characteristic jubilance.

'You're marvellous!' he cried. 'Always marvellous.'

Being unacquainted with his legal and political chagrins, and the consequence of that hour of despair in the flood, Florence supposed Roderick's illness to have been

459

caused solely by his domestic concerns. She was wrong. These had played their part; but the fundamental cause lay elsewhere. Intense overwork, and disappointment, had affected his bodily strength. Roderick was as fundamentally sensitive as his brother; and while through determination, he had endured so far, a breakdown was due, and a breakdown had occurred.

Now, only half-conscious, but still perceptive, he almost amusedly watched those who tended him, admiring the doctor's detachment and the nurses' efficiency. The sensation of being able to leave responsibility to others was exquisite.

'Poor Evelyn! She forgets *migraine*. That shows character. She and Florrie are a pair. By the way, where *is* Florrie? She ought to be here.' In this mood of self-indulgence, he felt it to be his right to expect her participation in the general servitude.

The nurses saw that he had become impatient with them. It was a favorable sign; but they spoke of it in undertones to Doctor Whitelaw, who turned lambent eyes under enormous moustache-like eyebrows upon his patient, muttering his eternal 'Umphm.' He then listened attentively to a mumble from Roderick, afterwards, also in an undertone, making an inquiry of Evelyn.

'He's asking for somebody named Florrie.'

'I don't know anybody of that name.'

'It would be a help. Would your daughter know her?'

'I'll ask.'

Evelyn found Sandra and Saul in the adjoining room, where both were restless with subdued excitement. Sandra, in particular, gave the impression that she was deeply affected by what was passing so near at hand. It was to Sandra that Evelyn put the question, but it was Saul who answered it.

'Miss Marvell, Mother. The lady who —'

'Oh, the artist?' Evelyn was alert. 'At the little cottage?'

'Yes, yes, Mother.' This was Sandra, at last. 'At the little cottage. Her name's Florence.'

All was clear to Evelyn. She saw the cottage, the daffodils, the youthful woman from whom Saul had reluctantly parted, and the snapshot she had found among Roderick's papers. Roderick's thought of this woman at the height of his illness was very unwelcome indeed. It was deplorable. But the doctor —.

'Your father wants to see her. Doctor Whitelaw thinks —'

'I'll run down at once!' volunteered Saul.

'No!' Sandra almost shouted. 'I'll go. I want to see her.'

'You?' Evelyn was astounded. 'Whatever for?'

'It's most important, Mother. Most important.'

Evelyn had never known Sandra to look so brilliant. Her eyes shone; her cheeks glowed; all bitterness had vanished from her manner.

'Very well. I'll write a note. You can take it.'

'Oh, thank you, Mother! Thank you!' The response was so fervent that Evelyn was astonished. Making no further comment, however, she sat down at Roderick's desk, fumbled with some pens which lay there, and ignored the whispers passing between her son and daughter.

38
Sandra's Friend

Florence's heart sank when, trying hard to concentrate upon a difficult drawing (two previous efforts upon the same subject had already been destroyed), she saw another member of the Patterson family arrive at her gate; this time the member whom she had been nerving herself to seek.

'If Rod's worse, I shall be entirely wrecked; but the girl —'

She threw down her pencil, and rose. Before she could reach the door it was imperiously rapped by her visitor; and the summons was so sharp that her mood, already dark, became almost unbearable.

Death seemed to hover in the air, and the fear of it to make her movements leaden.

Suspense, however, was brief; for Sandra plunged at once into the subject of her errand.

'Miss Marvell? Excuse me; but you're wanted at the Manor. At once! I've brought you a letter from Mother!' She held it out. 'You'll see what she says. Terribly urgent!'

'Wanted at the Manor?' Florence wonderingly took the letter: this was terrible!

'She explains. Father keeps mumbling your name; demanding to know why you're not at his bedside!'

Still confused, Florence took the brief note.

Dear Miss Marvell, I am sorry to say that my husband has had a stroke of some kind. He is very ill, and we are very anxious indeed. He seems to be asking to see you, and Doctor Whitelaw thinks it might do good if you would grant his wish. Will you please come at once? I apologize for this unceremoniousness; but I hope you will come. It is *very urgent*.

Yours, Evelyn Patterson.

The letter was that of a great lady who expected any request she made to be granted; but the writing showed agitation, and Florence could not hesitate. From cowardice, she had all along dreaded an encounter with Rod's wife, anticipating the inevitable snubs to which she would have no answer. Nevertheless, Rod's need made duty inexorable.

There was no time to change her dress, a fact which would put her at a further disadvantage, since great ladies could always cow the inexperienced by the merest glance at costume less distinguished than their own. Costume and bearing. Why was she so much more afraid of women than of men? Wasn't it because they were, at bottom, more ruthless? She had never been so keenly aware of her slightness and lack of 'manner.' What had made Rod demand to see her? Was he conscious? Was this his way of bringing about the meeting he had proposed? A kind of vengefulness? Was he not inflicting upon her ordeal after ordeal?

Within three minutes she was ready; and she and Sandra were on their way.

At first they were speechless, from a common embarrassement; until Florence thought to mention Saul's visit.

'Your brother told me . . .' Breathlessness was half-caused by the fact that Sandra's pace was as impetuous as Saul's; but not more than half. This wild girl affected her nerves as the brother could not have done. 'I saw . . . Sir Roderick . . . Was it the day before yesterday? I forget. I'm really . . . unused . . . to excitement. . . . I thought he . . . seemed quite well. We met by chance in London —'

'And he brought you home. Saul told me. It was at a restaurant.'

'I remember . . . now. I was lunching with my Publisher.'

'I know that, too.' Sandra's speech, though not at all breathless, was so abrupt as to suggest hostility. 'Your publishers are Gimblett's, aren't they? Miss Marvell,

I understand you've been interfering in my personal affairs.'

They were hurrying along the main street of Slocumbe, and had reached the very spot where Bertha Pledge first announced Roderick's purchase of the Manor. How long ago that was! How tumultuously and overwhelmingly disagreeable events had followed! This was a black spot indeed!

'Yes, I have,' Florence admitted. 'I can't hope you'll forgive my impertinence.'

'Of course I shall never forgive it.' Sandra was momentarily at her haughtiest, the daughter of a celebrated man and a great lady. Her tone shocked Florence into coldness. No protest that she had become involved against her will would answer. She was brought sharply into conflict with an unmanageable young creature.

And then, suddenly, she understood that only in this way could Sandra bring herself to speak at all. The hauteur was not assumed; it was defensive. There was no hostility; there was an almost frantic effort to achieve candour between them, as a prelude to something far more important. The discovery showed how different her own approach must be.

'No, don't forgive me,' she said. 'There's nothing to forgive. There's only a problem to solve. If I can help you, I'll do whatever I usefully can. If I can't, you must ignore me. If you decide to do that, we'll continue on our way without talking. Obviously you must tell me much more than I already know.'

'What do you know?' demanded Sandra.

'I know my own limitations.' Florence could be as abrupt as her companion.

'I wonder if you do.'

'Mine is a very small life; but I've lived for fifty-one years.'

'As long as that? You don't look it.'

At least they were continuing to talk! The very worst must be over.

'I don't look it, because I've deliberately played a small part in life. It suits me. And I'm not naturally a meddler in other people's affairs. You dislike officousness. So do I. I hate it. Believe that, and you'll see me as I am.'

There was indeed silence between them

at this point. It was pregnant. Sandra employed the silence in considering her own reactions. At last she said:

'I don't think you officious.'

'No. As you've seen, my pets all go their own way until they're hungry. Then they come to me for food. When they're fed, they go their own way again.'

'You think of me as a small animal?'

'As somebody used to going her own way.'

'Well, that's true. I've always been allowed to go my own way — except by one person. You know the person I mean. Tell me what else you know about me.'

'Nothing more. I suspect that, like everybody else, you're very lonely. It's the universal sickness. Recognition of that is the basis of religion.'

'Of religion? I'm not religious.'

'You sometimes wish to God there was somebody you could confide in.'

'Don't you?'

'Very rarely. Don't take that for an invitation to confide. It's not. If you did, you'd dislike me ever after.'

'Did you say that to Trevor?'

'We didn't speak of general truths. I simply told him to leave off being a consummate fool.'

'You did that?' Sandra was back for a moment into hauteur; but with a sudden change of mood she made an admission. 'I'm beginning to feel I like you very much.'

'Not too much, please. But, now, yes, if you can. By the way, we ought to hurry to your father.'

'Yes, I'd forgotten. Too busy with myself. We must run. He's waiting. They're all waiting.' The journey was resumed, both stumbling in their haste, and Sandra laughing slightly as Florence's breathlessness. She then asked: 'Do you know what's happened? I had a letter this morning from Trevor.'

'I didn't know. I don't want to know. You must decide everything for yourself.'

'Yes, I know I must do that. But there's something I must "confide," as you call it. He's asked me — in abject terms — to forgive him, forget my injuries, and join him again. Was that your doing?'

'No. He must have done it of his own accord.'

'It's not like him, you know. He's a "take it or leave it" character.'

'I made no suggestion at all.'

Sandra was once again silent. They were in the broad drive to the Manor, and gravel crunched under their quickly moving feet. The great steps to the front door were in sight. For Sandra, time was frighteningly short. It was she who became breathless.

'Of course,' she panted, 'you're simply afraid to take any responsibility.'

'I've been dodging it for half a century,' admitted Florence.

'In fact, you're a coward.'

'Yes, a coward.'

Even then, there was barely time. The admission came almost wildly.

'Yes, I can see you're a coward. A peculiar coward. Just now, so am I. There's a complication. I've started a baby. Though it is, he won't believe the baby's his.'

Florence did not stop. She was on the point of running. She shouted:

'Tell him at once. Instantly. He's in the mood to believe all you say.'

They were within doors, and in the hall they were so near together that Sandra put a protective arm around a new and convincing friend.

'You're a darling!' she whispered. 'I love you.'

Nobody saw the kiss they exchanged. An instant later they were mounting the stairs, Sandra's arm still encircling Florence's waist.

39
The Healer

They were in Roderick's study, book-lined and intimidatingly neat. Florence breathed quickly, in a kind of awe at its cathedral-like loftiness. Through a doorway straight ahead she caught a glimpse of one of the nurses, and then, with relief at the sight of a familiar figure, the exceptional height of Doctor Whitelaw. It was Sandra who moved forward.

'Yes, yes; come in.' It was Doctor Whitelaw's penetrating whisper. He left the bedside; and, bending down to speak directly into Florence's ear, added: 'Ye'll just tak' the chair beside him, Miss Marvell. Let him see you're there. He's restless, poor chap. Keeps muttering "Florrie." It's good of ye to come.'

The bedclothes were drawn high; and beyond the white sheet was Roderick's face, not calm, as she had always seen it, but strangely drawn, as if in agony. His eyes were open; the head kept turning restlessly from side to side. Otherwise only the doctor and a nurse were in the room; and the nurse, a fresh-coloured young woman with calm eyes of experience, moved away at Florence's approach. Shrinking, Florence took the bedside chair, bent over the patient.

'Hullo, Rod!' she whispered.

There was a change in his expression. The roaming glance was steadied. Roderick had recognized her voice. Some movement under the sheet indicated that he was trying to move an arm. Instinctively she moved the sheet in order that the arm could escape; and, when his burning hand was free, she put her own fingers about it. At the same time, with closed eyes, she tried to transmit to him all the tranquility of a loving heart. The others, including Sandra, watched the two hands meet and clasp; and they saw, not only Roderick's firm grip, but also, as seconds passed, the diminished strain arising from this contact.

'Very good,' said Doctor Whitelaw, almost inaudibly. 'Stay where you are. Stay. Stay. Be still. I hoped for this.'

Roderick's eyes opened wide. They smiled. A drowsy murmur followed.

'Hullo, Florrie. I knew you'd come.'

That was all. Her mission had been successful. Though horrified by the tortured face, and deeply moved by the change she saw in it, Florence was able to restrain what would have been a sob if it had passed her lips. She bent lower, to hide from others the brimming tears.

'Keep so. Keep so,' whispered Doctor Whitelaw. 'He'll sleep. But you must continue your work.' It was the command of an enthusiast, who cared little for the cramped arms and body of his curative agent.

So they remained for an endless time, during which Florence gradually became so numb that she felt nothing but exhaustion. She had never before made such an effort; and afterwards understood why mediums, emerging from trance, felt so exhausted. All humour was gone; the artist who drew little animals with delight had no place in this intensity; she had become the human equivalent of a machine for restoring life; and it was terrible to experience such loss of identity.

But at last the burning hand grew less hot. The grip upon her fingers relaxed, leaving them bloodless. She was able to sink against the back of her chair.

'Well done,' said Doctor Whitelaw, with professional inhumanity. 'You'll quickly feel strong again. You can go now. Sit quietly awhile in the next room. I'll call you if necessary.'

It was not he, but the nurse, who seemed to understand her inability to rise; and it was Sandra who eventually guided her unsteady steps back into the study.

'Slowly,' she instructed, in the tone she might have used to a child making its first attempt to walk. 'Take your time. Lean on me, if you want to.'

'I just want not to fall on my face,' said

Florence, with reviving sturdiness. 'I should like to sit down quietly, and have a glass of water.'

'Why not brandy? We're sure to have some in the house.'

'Water,' insisted Florence. 'And that big armchair.'

She sank, guessing nothing of its previous occupant, into the chair which Saul had so uncomfortably used during the interview with his father; but as she relaxed she was forced again to stand very unsteadily. Somebody else had entered the room by the opposite door. The moment she had long dreaded had come. She was face to face with Roderick's wife.

Evelyn had every physical advantage. She was tall, handsome, and used to the obedience of others. She was also in her own home. Florence was weary and made to feel smaller and slighter than usual by her unfamiliar surroundings. Both, however, shared a common fear, for the life of a beloved man. They exchanged bows without speech. It was Sandra who, with new spirit, made the unceremonious introduction.

'It's worked, Mother! He's asleep. And I'm getting Miss Marvell a glass of water. She's tired out.'

Evelyn noticed Florence's pallor.

'I'm sorry, Miss Marvell. It was good of you to come. Do sit down.'

'She's been marvellous!' Sandra paused long enough to fling this additional challenge to her mother. 'Mesmerism at its best! You should have seen the effect!'

She then, disregarding her mother's glance of reproof at such flippancy, ran from the room.

Evelyn, struck by the girl's high spirits, imagined that they were due to the change in Roderick's condition. But her thoughts were concentrated upon their visitor. This was unquestionably the unknown girl whose photograph had been among Roderick's treasures. Why had he kept it? Sentiment? A stronger emotion? Why had he called for her now? Why had she been able to cure his unease? She was as avidly curious as a great lady could be. A dozen questions straggled in her mind. What was this stranger doing in the neighbourhood?

Apparently she had been there for some time. How had the children come to be acquainted with her? Courtesy must be shown. Indifference must be pretended. The only course was graciousness, which would in any case have been shown.

'As I told you in my note, we've been very anxious about my husband,' she explained. 'It's not like him to be ill; and his illness is really alarming. Sandra said you had done something to soothe him, to cure him. What was that?'

'I don't know,' admitted Florence. 'I just sat holding his hand. It quieted his nerves.'

If astounded by this simple statement, Evelyn gave no sign of astonishment. She said, ruefully: 'That's something I've been unable to do. I'm not a soothing person, it seems. I suffer with my own nerves. It has made me quite ineffective. We must be very grateful to you if, as Sandra says, you've saved his life.'

'Not his life. Not his life, of course.' Florence was urgent. 'That needs other skills.'

Evelyn ignored the interruption.

'It's been horrible to see him almost convulsed. Tossing. Muttering. And I couldn't understand what he was trying to say. It was just a meaningless mumble. That was worst of all. We've been married, you know, for twenty-seven years. To have one's husband a stranger is quite excruciating. And this doctor is so very non-committal; as if his knowledges were Masonic secrets or as sacred as the Confessional.'

Florence could only say:

'He's a very good doctor. The whole village loves him.'

'No doubt; but even a good and generally loved doctor can speak. This one might almost be dumb. Nothing but ''Umhm. Umhm.'' When it's one's husband who is concerned, that's surely rather whimsical?'

Resentment was very strong. Evelyn, having been provoked by Doctor Whitelaw, was now considering him only superficially. Her real interest was in the relationship between Roderick and this delicate little woman who in a drawing-room full of distinguished people would be insignificant, yet whose power over him had just been demonstrated. Clearly (if one could trust the air of candour, which if it had been wide-eyed would instantly have been suspect) she was no schemer; and as far as one could judge she felt no triumph in her performance. What, then, was she?

These curiosities passed quickly behind Evelyn's unruffled brow. They were heightened when Sandra, still at a run, brought the tumbler of water; for Sandra's manner had such charming solicitude that she appeared to be a different person from the rude, listless creature who had recently stalked through the house. Like Saul, she was apparently infatuated with Miss Marvell. She had never shown any interest in her mother's illness, which she had treated as a bore or a *maladie imaginaire*. It was neither. To the sufferer, it was indescribable agony.

True, it had been stocially borne. One's pride ensured that. But a warm heart would have responded to one's stoicism. Why should mere faintness in another be so affecting? And why, as her light step proved, was Sandra elated? She glowed with happiness, like a child with expectations of a birthday party. Very odd indeed. Extraordinary!

In spite of her perplexities, Evelyn experienced relief as colour began to return to the pale cheeks of their visitor. She exclaimed, almost accusingly:

'You should have brought sherry, child!'

Sandra's response was gay, teasing.

'She demanded water, Mother. Insisted. She's a very obstinate woman, you know. Compact of will. For once, Mother *doesn't* know best!'

'Sandra! Sandra!'

That retort had been like a stab. It accused Evelyn of parental tyranny. She was seriously offended, not only by the mockery but by the show of disrespect before a stranger. And in the midst of indignation she felt a loss of self-confidence. Was this the way her daughter regarded her?

No sooner had the glass been emptied than Sandra took it into her own hand.

'I'll leave you two together. I must go and telephone.' And, to Florence: 'Do you approve?'

Florence replied only with a smile, which to Evelyn was so enigmatic that it produced further discomfort. What was the secret understanding between these two? Sandra had always been difficult; but the difficulty had been lack of communication. She had given the impression of complete hardness. Why? 'She could always have come to me. There was no reason why she shouldn't have done so.'

Was there not? asked a voice within. 'Have I failed with her, too?' Continuing to stand, Evelyn observed Florence very closely indeed, saw her eyes close as if in weariness, saw her shudder a little and open the eyes again, to smile with what might have been compassion.

'I'm very sorry to have given trouble,' said Florence. 'I don't really know why Rod should have wanted me to come. But of course I'm thankful he dropped off to sleep. I hope he'll have a good rest, and be better. I think I'll go home now, unless

Doctor Whitelaw. . . .' Her voice faded; she was very tired.

'Rod.' It was a name Evelyn had never used. It struck her unpleasantly. But she had recovered from displeasure.

'You must stay until you're quite strong again,' she said, firmly. 'Don't forget that although you've done so much good, you've had an ordeal.'

'Thank you.' Florence was overcome with breathlessness. She lost all fear of Evelyn, for she realized with the pronunciation of that word that her own ordeal could have been no greater than Evelyn's. And indeed the onset of *migraine* had caused Evelyn to become as white as marble. This was no *grande dame;* but one whose heart was overburdened.

Doctor Whitelaw found them as two sisters. He gave his searching glance to both, and advanced into the room.

'I'll be back in an hour,' he said, addressing Evelyn. 'The nurse will do what is necessary. She'll keep Sir Roderick quiet, which is the essential thing.' To

Florence he added: 'You should have a rest; but I may have to send for you again.'

'She could stay here, Doctor. Stay and rest.'

'No; she'll want to feed her menagerie. She has a whole lot of little animals at home. Nurse and mother to them all.'

'That's an immense task.' Evelyn was politely unsympathetic. She did not love animals.

'It's her way,' answered the doctor; 'Like it or not. Well, I've other patients to see.' He made them a fine bow, and was gone.

After this, the rapport was less complete; but Evelyn's curiosity increased.

'You must lead an extraordinary life,' she exclaimed.

'A very quiet one, as a rule,' was Florence's reply. 'And now I must really go home.'

'Don't go! Don't go!' It was an entreaty. 'I wish you could cure *me*. I suffer from appalling headaches. I call them *migraine*. I have one of them now. I can hardly support it.' She closed her eyes in pain.

'You've been in great distress.' In face of the appeal, Florence could not at once leave.

Suddenly Evelyn was moved to speak her true concern.

'Miss Marvell, you seem to be happy in your life. I'm not, in mine. I wonder if you'd think me very *gauche* if I asked why my husband should have been — as I understand he was — muttering your name; why he should have wanted you to be here in this hour; and why you were able to ease his mind so effectively.'

Florence felt her heart beating very fast.

'I think I told you I didn't know. That was true.' Evelyn could not mistake the candour. 'I met your husband by chance when he took Saul to London —'

'Yes; but why did he take Saul? You don't know? You hadn't arranged to meet, had you?'

'No; it was quite an accident. We happened to lunch at the same restaurant with people who knew each other. But he told me afterwards — it was something I'd never dreamed of — that I was a healer. I'm not. I thought he was joking. But when they're very ill indeed, as he must have been, people have strange impulses. I can only suppose that he persuaded himself —'

'I understand. You think it was a sick man's fancy?'

'Just that.'

'But this chance meeting wasn't your first, was it? You spoke of him — forgive me — as "Rod." ' The snapshot was vividly before her. Here, at least, was an opportunity for explanation of that. 'It made me wonder if you had known him long ago.'

Florence knew nothing of the snapshot. Her answer, therefore, although direct, was an evasion.

'During the war, when he was a soldier, and I was in the W.V.S., we sometimes met.'

'Did you know him well?'

'Only for a very short time.' Florence could not bring herself to mention Syd. Any reference to him would have been painful to both. But her ambiguity produced its effect upon Evelyn, who was not easily deceived.

'You probably knew him before I did?'

'Yes, I think I must have done.'

'Were you in love with him?'

'Very much.'

Evelyn drew a deep breath. She had ascertained a vital fact.

Both women, however quiet their speech, were in a state of high emotion. They were not at odds. Neither felt any jealously of the other. Two minds were adjusting themselves to a relationship which only two hours earlier would have seemed impossible. It was Evelyn who first spoke.

'So was I,' she said. 'So I still am. Extraordinary, isn't it?'

Perhaps not quite extraordinary,' observed Florence, drily. 'He's an exceptional man.'

Evelyn was too preoccupied to appreciate the irony.

'I was always very ambitious for him. Not for myself. I wanted him to become Prime Minister. I thought he was the sort of man to be idolized by the multitude. He had brains, courtesy, high principles.'

'All these,' agreed Florence.

'And yet I've failed, as you must have seen I've done with Sandra. Looking back, I don't see what more help I could have given. I've worked very hard — for him. I've made great sacrifices. The hours I've been forced to keep have ruined my health. Sometimes, when he was in the House, and some tedious debate that he was involved in went on and on, I've sat in the Gallery quite stupefied. And then, of course, his legal work has kept him at full stretch during the day. More than the day. If he had an important case, he would stick at it all night. At weekends, even if we had important visitors — important for his career I mean — he's deserted us all, leaving me to entertain them. It's not at all an easy life when one's married to a notable man. One's at full stretch all the time. But what I've told you about were only vexations. They weren't the real problems. The real problems lay in his character.'

'Yes, in his character.' Florence, deeply excited by confirmation of former intuitive judgment, was back in the past. 'It was never a single character.'

'Never,' agreed Evelyn, thinking aloud in response to perceptions as keen as her own. 'Full of contradictions. Unable to decide whether he wanted to be a Saint or a Lord Chancellor.'

Though serious, Florence found these particular contradictions very odd.

'Could he not have been both?'

Evelyn saw no ridiculousness in the contradictions. Having begun what was in fact a self-exculpation, she continued, her voice growing hoarse with feeling:

'Quite impossible in this age. A Saint thinks only of the infinite. Roderick spends a great deal of his time in that region. Or some other unwordly region. At times he's a pure dreamer. I've never pretended to know where he was. A Lord Chancellor, however good a man, deals professionally in Precedents. The Law. The Law. Always the Law. But that's not all. In Politics you must be aggressive and ruthless — a bully, like that horrible creature Plowman, who's a bully incarnate. For Plowman nothing matters but his own advancement. He'll be the next Prime Minister. And his unscrupulous wife, who would commit perjury to help him, will have a triumph. Hateful! I couldn't do what she does: I'm too proud. And Roderick is so morbidly scrupulous that he won't kick any of the curs at his heels. He has what he calls "principles" against retaliation. I always think of him as being like Burke in Goldsmith's poem, "Too fond of the *right* to pursue the *expedient.*" He's refused many briefs; sometimes because the client has wanted the cases conducted in a way he disapproved, more often because of some ridiculous scruple. That sort of thing is all right on the Bench, where one's above fray; but in an advocate or a Party politician . . .'

'He should become a Judge,' said Florence. "All his gifts fit him for it.'

'Do they? I wonder!' Evelyn could not accept this verdict. Her own vision of the future had been very different. 'Why do you say that?'

'Because, with all his noble qualities, he's not cut out for war. He's never been a natural leader of men. It's fatal to greatness. Just as dogs recognize when somebody's afraid of them, so men instinctively estimate a man's capacity for great design. That was drilled out of him in childhood. His mother was determined that he should *make his way;* work, work, work; and by insisting on that, she killed his impulse to freedom.'

'I can't agree. In any case, freedom's an illusion. But his mother! You knew her, did you?'

'I met her only once.'

'You make up your mind quickly, then. Or did she tell you this?'

'He once told me himself — not as grievance, but in passing.'

'She was always a little effusive to me. Did you dislike her?'

'Only when I realized the sort of woman she was: small-minded and materialistic. She made him grind at school, take prizes, force his brain; and he went on grinding because he was trying to do what she had taught him was right; so he ground and ground at his work as she'd determined he should do, until just now, when, as we've seen, something happened, and instinct told him he couldn't bear the strain another moment.'

'What do you think happened?'

'I don't know. A feather might have turned the scale.'

Evelyn, fascinated by this assured explanation from the fragile-seeming little creature before her, who spoke with such light serenity, said:

'I don't know how you've arrived at all this. It has a dreadful ring of truth to me. I've always thought of Roderick as a man of moods, who had to be urged forward. Not, as you suggest his mother did, tyrannized over. I've never preached or scolded. I've simply tried to advance his interests. Do you think something I've done has in any way brought about this breakdown? It would be an unbearable thought.'

'I'm sure nothing, you've done, or left undone, has had the smallest effect on it. It must have been something external; something arising out of Rod's extraordinary sensitiveness. It might be that he was so much affected over Syd —'

Evelyn interrupted.

'Oh Syd, as you call him, is a clown.'

Florence's mind darted upon that word as proof that Evelyn knew nothing of Syd's final wickednesses. She began to tremble at the risk she had just run of great indiscretion; and could say no more.

As she and Evelyn sat looking at each other in an extremity of emotion, Sandra, who had used the telephone, returned. She was brimming with excitement, having spoken with Trevor for the first time since their quarrel; and the conversation between her mother and her friend was abruptly ended. It was never to be resumed.

40
Telephone Calls

Ten days later, Doctor Whitelaw and the two nurses were still in attendance at the Manor; but the tension was less. Sandra had departed; Saul, with his mother's permission, was cultivating a garden of his own in the grounds; and Blenkinsop, having no work to do, was reading a long book called *The Decline and Fall of the Roman Empire.*

Roderick remained in bed. Mr Dickson opened and read all his letters and was in telephonic communication with Clerks and Agents in London, so that if any question arose he could immediately answer it. The one change was that an extension of the study telephone to Roderick's bedside had been contrived. This was not meant for immediate use: the work had been done because Doctor Whitelaw had noticed some fretfulness in his patient over a matter concerning Mr Munster, the Solicitor.

'I want to hear from Munster.' Roderick's speech was still indistinct; but it was clearer than it had been. He no longer asked for Florrie; and for this reason Florence came no more to the Manor. Munster, however, was a name which had become familiar to the nurses, since Mr Dickson had talked to its owner for a few minutes every day.

One morning, around lunchtime, Mr Munster himself rang up. He wished, if possible, to speak to Sir Roderick personally. The subject was very urgent. He would not reveal it to Mr Dickson, who, however, overheard the ensuing conversation, and jotted down the details in case he should afterwards be called upon to refresh his employer's memory. Fortunately, Roderick's part consisted solely of two questions. Mr Munster did all the rest of the talking.

'Roderick? Are you better? Alone? No auditors? We'll assume none. Meanwhile, as to that inquest. You remember? The dead man was a heart case. A long history of trouble. His doctor certified that he was likely to go in any moment of excitement. So the verdict was "Misadventure." Our friend not responsible; goes free. But he's suffered. My clerk says his hair's white. Very subdued. Apparently he has friends overseas, and is willing to go to them. I've ventured to provide money for the air journey. He'll be gone by the weekend. Did I do right?'

How much of this news was immediately intelligible to Roderick, Mr Dickson, listening and scribbling, did not know. He thought he heard the sound 'Yes,' and wrote it down. Still listening, he interpreted another stammered noise as 'Saul'; and Mr Munster's reply, less cautiously phrased than the first announcement, was:

'He'll have to be in Court. They don't expect to call him. No money actually

497

passed. I've persuaded the other gentlemen that it will be better, in their own interests, to make no claim. Otherwise, I said, there would be awkward investigations. They saw the point. I don't think you need worry. The main thing, for you, is to get better, as I gather you mean to do. I'll keep in touch with Dickson. Goodbye.'

The Nurse, taking the receiver from Roderick's hand, saw that he had been much tired by Mr Munster's chat. She checked his temperature, which had risen sharply; and visited Mr Dickson, saying 'If that man rings again, don't put him through.' Having done this, she was pleased to find that her patient was sound asleep, as if, for all the excitement, his mind had been eased.

No more personal calls were made that afternoon. The Nurse went off duty, and was replaced by her colleague. Doctor Whitelaw was with Roderick in the early evening for under ten minutes. Mr Dickson tidied his desk and knocked off work for the night. It therefore happened that, of the Patterson inner circle, only Evelyn could attend to the telephone when it rang after supper. She was alone, rather depressed, but lighter-hearted than she had been of late. Doctor Whitelaw's brief speech with her had been encouraging. He had gone so far as to touch her elbow with a reassuring hand.

'Doing fine,' had been his words. The hums she detested were absent. She seemed to read on the lean face to which even she, a tall woman, was forced to look up, something like a grin.

For this reason her voice, when she answered the telephone, was not forbidding. It was evidently recognized as her own; for the caller at once addressed her by name.

'Hullo, Evelyn. How are you? More hopeful, I gather. This is Sam Wrekin. Oh, yes, I'm always well. How is Roderick? What are the real prospects there?'

'I can't tell you.' Evelyn was at once filled with pessimism at the direct question. 'The Doctor is an oyster. But he did say, as he went this evening, "Doing fine." I can't tell you what that meant; whether Roderick will be up and about in a week, or in a bathchair for the rest of his life. The uncertainty is very trying.'

'Yes, of course. I'm sorry. Look here, Evelyn, I rang up because I have a little good news. You'll have to judge whether it would rouse the lion in dear Roderick if he hears it. You may or may not know that Charles — the Prime Minister — had a stroke —'

'Roderick told me. He thought it meant the finish for himself.'

'I thought so, too. I've continued to think so. But what does the wonderful old man do? After frightening us all, as Roderick has done, he flings off the bedclothes, rises to his feet, and sends for Plowman, who's been very active —'

'Disgusting man!' interrupted Evelyn.

'A little crude,' glossed Sam Wrekin. 'Too energetic. But not more energetic than our revived Prime Minister, who set about him. Not physically, of course; but with a very Shakespearean tongue. "Dost thou so hunger for mine empty chair? . . ." Something about "before thine hour be ripe.'' I always wonder how any actor can make the words sound plausible. At any rate, Plowman received what's called a dressing-down for his presumption. He blustered; but he was shouted into silence. I hear this, by the way, from Charles himself, punctuated with crowing laughter. So, for the moment, Plowman is in eclipse.'

'Good!' Evelyn was warm with gratified hatred. 'For how long?'

'Ah, that I can't say. What I wanted to tell Roderick is that Plowman no longer controls the Party's destiny. And I know Charles has long wanted to show his respect for Roderick. He's several times considered him for — well, let's say Attorney General. The question arises, how soon will Roderick be fit for such a job?'

Evelyn, seeing the prospect of glory, was in terror lest it should be lost.

'I can't say! I can't say!' she cried, passionately.

'Hm. Too bad. I'd hoped for some positive news.'

'I'd give it if I could. It's shockingly

difficult. Something we've — I've — always hoped for. Oh, dear me, how awful it is! I've been afraid he'd have to give up Politics altogether. His strength —'

'Yes, it sounds rather as though the Commons might be too strenuous for him. D'you think he'd consider going to the Lords?'

'I don't know. What would he be able to do there?'

Sam, who disliked Evelyn as a managing woman, laughed noiselessly. He added, in mischief:

'I suppose there's always the Lord Chancellorship.'

This malicious mockery, which she was too serious to penetrate, moved Evelyn to an intensity of delight which checked further speech. She did not hear what Sam Wrekin added, which was 'don't count on that, dear friend'; but left the telephone with her arms characteristically outstretched.

'He *must* get better! He *must* get better!' she exclaimed, striding about the room. 'This is what I've lived for!'

Her mind seethed with plans. She saw Plowman and his abominable wife reduced to helplessness, and herself in a state almost of pity for them. Thus were the tactics of atrocious careerists brought to nothing! Hope and voluptuous confidence surged anew. It did not matter that her head ached as never before. Pain could not quell a reawakened spirit. Roderick *must* recover. He would be at the head of his Profession. Every doubt and recent disappointment was brushed aside. Wonderful! Wonderful!

As vehemence gave way to more sober consideration of Sam's message, she had other thoughts. First among them was a memory of her talk with Florence.

'What a pity I was so indiscreet! I said more than I ought to have done. I was overwrought. My courage was really at a low ebb. She's not the sort to forget. She's probably already amused. But at the time she seemed sympathetic. Oh, yes, I think she was sympathetic. Was she? Of course she's not likely to spread what I said about the village. Even if she's a natural busybody, there's a kind of simplicity that's rather charming. Is it genuine? I never can tell what people are really thinking. She might become a menace, hinting at superior knowledge. "You remember what you said!" My God! That would be intolerable! . . .

'No, no, it will be only a passing embarrassment, when I meet her again. I wonder when that will be? If Sam's right, we shan't see much of her. She'll stay down here in that potty cottage, with her flowers and animals. It's her proper environment. She'd be out of place in London. Just an occasional encounter here. "How are you? Oh, yes, I'm terribly busy. So glad!" And we could have her up at the Manor for tea when a lot of people are here. Sitting like a mouse! Nothing to worry about. After all, in spite of her simplicity, she's not crude! . . .'

'Miss Marvell was cast aside as a nice little nonentity. There were more important people to consider; the Prime Minister, Ambassadors, the *ton;* all sorts of challenging men and women with experience of the world. And Roderick, fully restored to health and strength, the finest among the few!

' "Now is the Winter of our discontent made glorious Summer!" '

How tired she felt! Tired, but triumphant!

Slocumbe telephones were not yet done with news. At the very moment when Evelyn was savouring the brief joy of illusion, Florence Marvell, having supped, sat reading *Persuasion,* with William curled on her lap. William was heavy, and she began to feel very cramped; but the ringing of her phone bell was the most unwelcome sound in the world.

Her first imagining was that the call must be from the Manor. Fear that Roderick was again in danger caused her heart to sink.

'Oh, dear!' she groaned. "It must be that — at this time of day! If it is, I don't know how I can bear it. I'm in no state to work another miracle!'

William would have preferred that she should ignore the bell; but in Florence the sense of duty was so powerful that he was gently transferred to the warm chair and left to continue his sleep. She, meanwhile, answered her caller, expecting to hear an urgent summons.

The voice, altogether familiar, did not come from the Manor. It was the bark, almost quite as unwelcome, of Mr Leadbitter.

'Hullo, Miss Marvell. Sorry to disturb. Something I thought you should hear at once.'

His tone was so sharp that her fears took a new turn. Sandra? Trevor? Had they quarrelled afresh? That would be a calamity.

'All news is bad news. For me.'

'This isn't,' answered Mr Leadbitter, bluntly. 'If it had been, I should have kept it until daylight. No good ensuring you a night of gloom. No; the truth is that your book, *Cat in a Thousand,* has won the Spencer Prize for the best juvenile of the year.'

'What!' Florence could not suppose Mr Leadbitter to be guilty of a joke at her expense. But there must be some mistake.

'Quite true. And well deserved. It's five hundred pounds. A nice little sum. You

506

could go round the world on it. I doubt if you'll do that.'

'Good heavens! I can't believe it.'

'Did you ever know me to deceive?'

'I never associated you with deception. Except about Trevor. No, of course I shouldn't think of going round the world.' Florence was quite flattered. The table below her eyes grew misty.

'And, what's more, you're nominated as one of the Women of the Year.'

Paralysed with alarm, Florence no longer saw the table at all.

'Oh, Mr Leadbitter, you must stop that! At once!'

'Not in my hands.' Mr Leadbitter gave a short, gruff laugh. 'You'll just have to face it.'

'I couldn't. I'd rather go round the world! Send an offensive telegram from Madagascar or the Andaman Islands.'

'No telegram. Begin at once to compose a nice little speech. "William has asked me to thank you on his behalf" —'

'Oh, dear me, don't, Mr Leadbitter. This is no time for badinage! I'm already at death's door! I mean, in despair!'

'Well, well; when I'd hoped to give you happy dreams.'

'As if I could sleep!'

'Start counting your golden goblins. You'll find them more effective than sheep. Sheep are dull creatures; goblins give golden slumbers. I don't know that they do, really; or misers would sleep like Rip van Winkle; but they have a pleasant ring. Oh, I forgot; my wife has just reminded me that I ought to give you our very affectionate congratulations on your power to amuse children. She says it's not to be sneezed at.'

'Thank you. And please thank you wife. She's an understanding woman.'

'So I've always suspected. Well, that's that. I've done my best, including the very affectionate congrats. And I hope, once the shock's absorbed, you'll recover your usual serenity. Good night, Miss Marvell. Sleep well. This is very good news indeed, you know.'

'Good night, Mr Leadbitter. And good night, Mrs Leadbitter. I know, at least, how lucky I am to have such kind and generous friends.'

'Not at all! Not at all!'

He was gone, leaving Florence to count, not sheep, not goblins, nor even the rewards of talent, but her blessings, which were so many that the first of them, contentment with her own lot, would leave an immense store for computation hereafter.

The publishers hope that this Large Print Book has brought you pleasurable reading. Each title is designed to make the text as easy to see as possible. If you wish a complete list of the Large Print Books we have published, ask at your local library or write directly to:

G. K. Hall & Co.
70 Lincoln St.
Boston, Mass. 02111